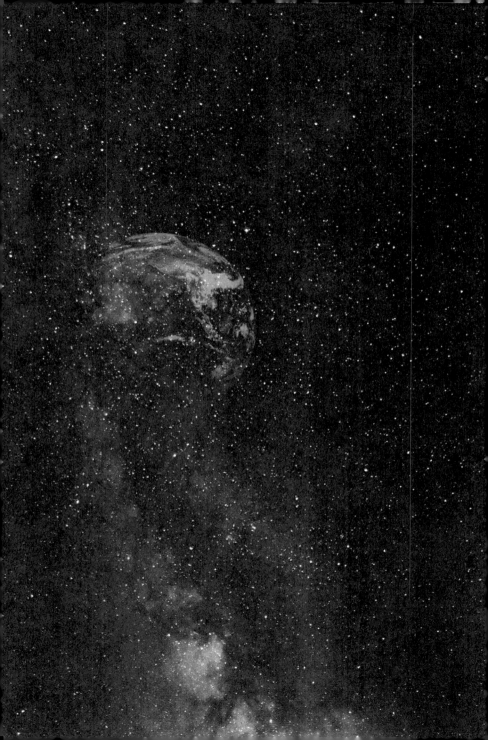

UNbreathABLE

HAFSAH LAZIAF

HYBRID HF FICTION

HYBRID FICTION

UNBREATHABLE. Copyright © 2013 by Hafsah Laziaf
Cover and Interior Design by Hafsah Laziaf

www.hafsahlaziaf.com

This book is a work of fiction. Any references to historical
events, real people, or real places are used fictitiously. Other names,
characters, places, and events are products of the author's imagination,
and any resemblance to actual events or places or persons,
living or dead, is entirely coincidental.

Unbreathable / Hafsah Laziaf. —First Edition.
Library of Congress Control Number: 2013918857

ISBN-10: 0990013812
ISBN-13: 978-0-9900138-1-5 (paperback)
ISBN-13: 978-0-9900138-0-8 (ebook)

For
MY PARENTS,
FOR BELIEVING IN ME
EVEN WHEN I DIDN'T

1

THE LAST TIME I STOOD HERE ON THIS hill, Father was alive, Earth was thought to be destroyed, and I was human.

I ignore the pang in my chest, because tonight isn't for grieving. Tonight is for redemption, for proving to the hopeless human race that Earth is real. Because until three nights ago, Earth was nothing more than a beautiful impossible dream.

With a deep breath, I take off down the hill. Every pounding step sends a billow of sand puffing into the wheezing, dry wind. The planet Jutaire is nothing more than a sea of red, rolling for as far as the eye can see, dotted with boulders and buildings raised to life by man and Jute. If anyone were to glance at the hill now, they would see me, a dark smudge against leagues of red beneath the silky moonlight.

But everyone is tucked in bed, breathing the oxygen inside their sealed homes. They live because there is nothing else for them to do. For them, this night is another and tomorrow will bring a day like any other. That's the despicable way I was for seventeen years. Existing without living.

It was only after losing everything I had—after death stole my father—that I realized there's a purpose to my life.

I have to finish what he started.

I adjust the mask suffocating my skin. Manufactured oxygen tries to soothe the fear drumming in my bloodstream. The clear mask is only half a sphere, much like the masks Father said they wore in hospitals back on Earth, only these are sleeker, fitting tight around our noses and mouths.

Because it only takes one breath of Jutaire's toxic air for a human to die in mere heartbeats.

As I near the Chamber, where the metal and glass are tucked away, the worry gnawing at my insides increases. I'm fully aware of the many ways this could go wrong, and that every way will end the same.

With me hanging limp from a noose.

I clench my jaw and stare ahead. Nothing can stop me, not even the whisper of death.

The Chamber is protected by sweeping lights and a high metal fence. The walls are of faded, deep blue metal, with a barely visible ten-pointed white star emblazoned in its center. I've seen the star countless times from a distance, but never up close. The building is unsuspecting on the outside—like pretty much all of Jutaire—but it houses the most precious elements on our planet.

My palms are slick with sweat when I crouch behind a boulder as a scope of white light sweeps past, illuminating the brittle ground. I count the heartbeats beneath my ragged breath before it swings back.

Forty. I have forty beats to cross roughly five feet and scale the six-foot fence.

Breathe, I remind myself, as worry and fear threatens to overwhelm me.

The light passes. I dash out from behind the boulder and thread my sweaty fingers in the fence, struggling to find footing and climb. I move quietly, though the fence is keen on exposing my existence. I listen to the *thud, thud, thud* of my heart, counting away the time before I am caught.

One. Five. Eleven. Fifteen. Twenty-three. Thirty-five. I drop to the other side with a muted thud. A fine layer of dust coats my mask and stings my eyes.

I scramble to my feet and press against the smooth wall, flinching at the chill of my sweat-soaked shirt.

The positions of the lights and the locations of all three entrances have been ingrained in my mind, flashing behind my eyelids with every blink. It's supposed to be simple, from the plans I had scribbled on scraps of old paper. Yet the voice of my conscience stokes my fear without fail. *This is how Father died. He stole from the Chamber.*

But did he die for what he stole, or for what he saw?

I ignore the nagging question and smooth down the loose strands from my braid with one hand, digging into my pocket with the other. I won't let myself dwell on the thought of Father murdered because he saw Earth. Despite all the hangings the Chancellors order, they wouldn't hang him for such an innocent discovery that could save us all.

Would they?

I pass two more lights as I slide along the wall. And finally, finally, I make it to the back of the building. Relief flickers through me as I rush to the metal door and slip the stolen keycard into the slot.

"Hurry," I whisper, wiping my sweaty palms across my pants. It's almost impossible to see anything beyond the bright beams. Anyone can see me and I won't see them. Before the dangerous thought can fully register, a tiny green light flashes and the door clicks open.

All this worrying and planning, and it's over within moments. I run my tongue along my salty lips as I step inside, allowing myself the slightest bit of triumph.

But I have to be in and out in heartbeats, for it won't be long before my break-in alerts them in the Tower, even if I'm careful enough not to trigger the inside alarms.

I have to grab the metal, grab the glass—Jutaire's most valuable elements. I need them to make a scope, to show the other humans there is something to hope for, something to fight for.

And I will get them.

But the moment I exhale, it hits me: *something is wrong*. The walls around me seem to be holding their breath in anticipation. The air is tight, though the room is large. My breath catches.

Something is wrong.

Panic makes. My chest. Tight.

I freeze, barely noticing the flicker of movement to my right as a screeching alarm crashes the silence. Red lights pulse in the darkness. I press myself against the door in a vain attempt to rewind time.

I force air through my lips.

Then I see him: a man—no, a boy. Every pulse brings him closer, clearer. Long. Lithe. His hair is a jagged mess of darkness atop his head. From his simple clothes, as dark as his hair, I can tell he isn't a soldier, one of the men who protect us from the Jute and enforce the Chancellors' orders. But he has to be the one who set off the alarm, because I've been so careful.

The alarm.

Panic closes off the oxygen to my lungs and presses into my vision. I felt this same way three days ago, when the pale-eyed soldier grabbed the scope from Father's hands and threw it to the floor with quiet fury. When all I could do was stand and watch, horrified, meek, weak. Nothing more than a shadow in a dark house.

The door is behind me. All it takes is one twist of the handle and I could disappear again. And isn't that what I'm best at—disappearing? Running?

But when I think of Father, my resolve hardens again. I can't leave. I can't let Father's death go in vain. He spent his life searching for Earth, *died* because of it.

I take a step forward and take in the Chamber. It stretches wide and long, empty, aside from two piles, glass beside metal, as high as the ceiling—nearly triple my height.

I clutch my pouch close to my chest and take another step forward, my breathing heavy as another thought registers: the metal and glass aren't scarce at all. They're abundant, hidden. Shrouded by lies in four metal walls where no one will see and no one will question.

The Chancellors, the soldiers—they're all liars. Even *Father*, who broke in here days ago, never said a word to me.

The alarm cuts off. The lights stop pulsing, illuminating everything in a bloody hue. My time is running out. I step toward the metal first, reaching for a flat sheet amidst the mess of scraps and nails.

I gasp. I'm falling.

Someone crashes into me, knocking the air from my lungs and the thoughts from my mind. The ground rushes up and the impact of cool concrete racks my body. I hear an *oof* that reminds me of the boy. *The boy.*

I sit up before struggling to my feet. He stands, too, a sharp inhale shattering the heavy silence. I stiffen.

My mask is on the floor.

Time seems to stop when I realize what this means. I hold my breath for barely a beat before that overwhelming desire forces me to inhale the deadly air.

Sweet, musty, delectable. The toxic air of Jutaire slithers through my nostrils and fills my lungs in layers and layers of richness. Shivers tremor up and down the length of my body. A relieved sigh slips from my lips. One breath is all it takes, and I can't stop. I can't think. I can't do anything but breathe.

The air of Jutaire is as dangerous for me as it is for any human. It kills them. It makes me drunk with its sweetness.

This is what I discovered three days ago that Father never told me for seventeen years of my life that no one else should know.

I can't be human.

"Who are you?" An unforgiving silence follows the words. My breath catches.

The boy takes a tentative step toward me—I have to get out of here—then another. *Thud, thud, thud* goes my heart. He stops. I look up, and my heart skips a beat. His eyes shimmer a brilliant blue: the color of the ocean as Father described it to me, countless times on countless nights. Surprise flits across them when he looks closer— and something else. Recognition? His face is chiseled, skin a light bronze. His hair is deep, dark ebony.

Every color on him is profound. Like Earth.

"What are you doing here?" His voice is soft and demanding. I open my mouth, but words don't come. Now that the thrill of the air has subsided, all I can think of is my mask on the floor.

I run my tongue along my suddenly dry lips, but he continues to watch me intently. He doesn't seem to have noticed my mask. Or maybe he did. I can't think.

"I came for this." The words slip out in a whisper. It sounds harsh in the quiet of the room. I sweep my hand out toward the mounds. It's obvious, isn't it? There is nothing else but metal and glass.

He narrows his eyes. "You've ruined everything."

I blink in surprise. Those are *my* words, spilling from his lips. *He* ruined everything, not me. *He* signaled the alarm. *He* was reckless, careless. Our eyes lock.

I open my mouth to say something, anything, when footsteps shatter the silence. The boy looks past me, deathly still. Alarm strikes his face and hardens his jaw. And I can't help it. I memorize him. I don't think I'll ever see him again once I leave this place. *If* I leave this place.

His eyes flash when they dart to the empty sack in my hand, reminding me of someone. But before my mind snatches the hazy memory, he murmurs one word.

"Run."

But I can't. There are soldiers spilling in from the doors on either side, their long shadows filling the room. Whispering voices roar in my ears. In heartbeats, I'll be frozen in panic and I won't know what to do.

The boy grabs my wrist. I flinch, but his grip tightens before I can pull away.

A blast of blue, the size of my closed fist, flies past my right cheek. *Shock blasts*, I think. I grab my mask off the floor and find the courage to meet the boy's unreadable eyes for barely a heartbeat before we're running—and I have no choice but to trust him.

I'm half-dragged between the piles of metal and glass, stumbling over razor-sharp scraps of steel and crystal. Another ball of current whizzes past my arm, skinning my sleeve with a blazing hiss.

One blast is a shock, two is darkness, three is death.

"Faster," I cry. I stumble over my own feet and twist my ankle. Pain zips up my leg. But I grit my teeth against the throbbing pain and push forward.

When he drops my hand, I falter. But the door is only a short distance away, and it's all I need to keep me going. I run beside him. The dark night will save me. Us.

A blast slams onto the door and I flinch back. Sizzling currents die soon after, leaving no mark. Another lands a foot ahead of me and I leap over it, feeling the heat rising from the floor.

"Almost there." I nearly stumble at the unnerving calm of the boy's voice. But it gives me courage.

"Stop!" The soldiers' shouts echo again from behind us. I reach the door and fling it open. Then I notice—

The boy isn't behind me.

The cool, dry wind and smothering darkness beckon me from outside. But I turn back. My breath chokes my lungs. *No.*

The boy has been shot.

2

HE WRITHES ON THE COLORLESS FLOOR.

His features are contorted in pain. His body jerks against the currents of the shock blast pinning him down. I hear the snaps of electricity when his mouth opens in a soundless cry.

The soldiers run closer. I scan their faces, one by one, relieved they're focused on the boy—until one of them looks up. I step back, fear closing my throat when I lock gazes with the soldier who shattered Father's scope. Those pale eyes flicker in recognition. He doesn't expect to see me, not so soon after Father's death. Not ever.

The panic comes crashing. Now, when freedom is one step away, it takes over. It's because of him, the pale-eyed soldier.

He killed the only family I had.

I look back at the boy as his body stills, and find him looking at me, his eyes a roaring rush of deep blue. Beautiful, I realize with a jolt. Determination sets into his face and hardens his features. But he won't move with the soldiers surrounding him.

I trace his lips as he mouths a single word.

Run.

I stare at him. The memories come rushing back, and even as I suddenly remember him, I'm certain he doesn't remember me. His face blurs in my vision. A sob racks my body.

I run.

Footsteps echo my own. I don't have to look back to know it's the soldier who broke Father's scope.

He doesn't want to catch me because I was in the Chamber. No, he wants to rectify the mistake he made in letting me live longer than my father.

I'll end up where that boy will be tomorrow at noon. Crime is punished on Jutaire in one way only: with a noose. And if there's one credit we can offer Chancellor Kole, it's uniformity. Hangings only ever happen at noon, in the Gathering for all of Jutaire to see and know.

Fear edges into my vision, making the dark night even darker. I run faster, until the world is no more than a blur around me, giving me the illusion of safety, because what you can't see can't hurt you. My empty pouch flutters against my thigh, reminding me of my failed mission with every step. A searing pain slices through my lungs, and I can't think straight. My muscles clench, and when I stumble once, twice, down the hill, I'm certain I won't make it.

The soldier shouts again and I hear a few words out of the slew—*wait, come back*—words that confuse me. I don't bother to slow my pace as I take off down the hill and I tumble down half way before picking myself up. Rocks scratch my face and hands. I want to freeze in the middle of our empty planet and disappear into the endless darkness above me, into the stars forever staring at me. Because what reason is there? I've lived a life of nothing for so long.

But when I close my eyes, I see Earth, and beside it, that boy.

Run. The single word echoes in my mind. Every time I stumble on the rocky ground underfoot, I see the soldiers bending over him, roughly pulling him to his feet. I see his eyes boring into me as if I'm not some hopeless girl whose death would never be mourned. He could have easily slipped through the door and left. But he pulled me along, even when I slowed him down.

So I don't slow down again. I owe him that much.

When nothing but the wind howls in my ears, I pause and look back, only to confirm what I already know: the soldier is long gone. But I don't stop until I pass the rows and rows of homes and slam my door shut and collapse on the floor.

Moonlight filters through the grimy window, illuminating a square foot of space. Words, fears, thoughts pound in my mind like the soldiers' fists on our door three nights ago. I heave breath after breath of oxygen, now that the addicting air of Jutaire is gone. Every door seals tight as soon as it closes and almost immediately oxygen flows into our noses.

Gradually, my breathing slows to a normal pace. In the dark, images flicker one after the other. Father's thin neck, secured in frayed rope. The boy and his intense eyes. The lies hidden in the Chamber. The pale-eyed soldier, calling me back—not *ordering*, I realize, but *calling*.

I left the safety of my home to steal something that could get me killed and possibly prove Earth exists.

Where did that courage come from?

A muffled cry shatters the silence. I start and look around, but only my pulse races in this room. The sound was my own.

I release a shuddering breath, and feel the loneliness like a weight pressing over me. Even when Father was alive I was lonely, with him stuck in his books, teaching himself to write and read. But *this*, this inexplicable emptiness in my heart and in my life, is different.

The sand coating the ground scratches against the soles of my feet when I shuffle to my bed. I don't bother to light a candle before I pull the sheets over my head and disappear. Not even the tiny yellow flames like those on Earth can give me comfort now.

I pull my mask from my pocket and place it beside me, rubbing absently over the grimy, dusty surface of the Louen. It's ironic that we owe our existence to the Jute, who we see as cruel and hurtful. Without them, we wouldn't have Louen for our masks.

My breath catches. The boy, the soldiers—

They saw me without my mask.

They'll come for me. The soldier with the pale eyes. Chancellor Kole. They'll mistake me for a Jute and drag me to the border of human territory, to die beneath the acidic rain.

Does it matter?

I squash the thought down with a clench of my jaw. It *does* matter. I have to complete what Father started. I need to go back to the Chamber, steal the metal and glass I couldn't steal tonight, make a scope and gather people. Together, we have a chance of building a ship. I have to believe that.

I sit up.

The boy. His straight nose, his perfect lips mouthing that one word. He didn't have a mask. He was breathing the toxic air just as I was.

Could he be like me? Deep inside, I know I'm not Jute – I can breathe oxygen, while Jute cannot. Maybe he isn't Jute either. We haven't seen one in human territory in years. He might know what we are.

We.

Nervousness trills through my veins as my resolve grows. If I can risk my life once, I can risk it again. If the boy is anything like me, then he could have answers. About what I am, Earth, and Father's redemption—which will all have to wait.

3

THREE NIGHTS AGO, GALILEO SAW THE Earth. With a scope of metal and glass, stolen goods that in turn stole his life. I saw it too, when I stood beside him beneath the sky so dark. I saw the colors swirling unto one another, white, blue, green. Colors that don't exist here.

I was his daughter. Was, because he denounced me when I denied him. Was, because he is dead and I am alive.

That night, Father and I trekked up the hill, where anything and everything seemed possible. There's a sense of freedom that comes at such a height. It tingled through me as I leaned back against a boulder, fully aware of the dust and sand that would layer my back when I stood. The dust seemed to cling to our every breath, and as much as I hated it, I was used to it being a part of our lives. Besides, nothing could stop me from looking up at the depthless, beautiful night sky.

There's nothing more beautiful to me than the stars. There's something magical about them, and strong. They survive in a sea of black, shining and glowing despite the smothering darkness.

I've been trying to do the same. To survive, despite the harshness of our world, where food is scarce, rain is deadly, and life is bleak. Sometimes, though, it's hard. Sometimes, I want to be like the stars that burst free.

Father said from Earth, some stars formed constellations. A picture to show us humans where to go or signs of societies past. On Jutaire, they are a mess of dots. Clusters here, scatterings there. But they are stars, something Jutaire shares with Earth, and that is enough for me.

From where I sat that night, the houses spread to my left and the Chamber stood isolated far to my right. Ahead of me was the market, the gallows in its center, bathed in moonlight. Behind the empty market stalls were the crophouses, a semi-circle of life from Earth.

This was my world.

So small, so uniform, so incomplete.

That night, Father set up the scope I didn't even know he had made, took me by the hand, and wordlessly showed it to me: the planet Earth. It was real. It hadn't exploded as the rumors whispered. It hadn't shattered into a billion bits that the universe swallowed whole. A planet that should have been destroyed, that didn't exist, now *did*. It made me lightheaded.

And I tripped.

The mask fell from my skin.

Who thinks before breathing?

I inhaled.

Heartbeats are all it takes for a human to find death once the air of Jutaire touches their lungs. But my heart was beating in my chest. I was still breathing. I wasn't choking to death.

I could have sworn the particles were wreaking havoc inside my quivering body. But even as I sat there, reeling with incomprehension and fear, I knew something was wrong.

And for the first time, I felt exposed on the hill where I had always felt free. The world would know I breathed the air and did not die.

Worse, something in the way Father turned his face before I could meet his eyes told me this wasn't a surprise to him.

I wrapped my arms around myself and shivered, despite the warm breeze. I didn't dare breathe again. It was an accident and I was sure I wouldn't be so lucky a second time. But I couldn't stop myself. This air was different. As unbreathable as it should be, I needed it, desperately *wanted* it. It was a living thing, caressing my lips, coaxing them open. It wanted to suffocate me. Fill me. Complete me.

Some part of me was sober enough to pick up my mask with trembling fingers and push it against my skin. The internal shield signaled on, shattering my lust. Cool oxygen blew against my skin as it came rushing in through tiny unseen tubes. I sucked in breath after breath. Never had I been so happy to breathe oxygen.

But.

I didn't *want* to breathe it. It was bland, defined by nothing. I wanted to yank off my mask and inhale breath after breath of this new air.

"I'm Jute," I whispered, my voice coarse. Father watched me for a few long heartbeats, each one ticking louder than my harsh breathing. He set aside the scope and sat beside me, eyes alight with something I couldn't read. He cupped my face in his hands, ten pinpoints of heat on my skin.

"No." His voice was firm. I'd never had reason to doubt him before. But how could he be certain when proof breathed right beside him?

"Then?" The scope lay discarded a few feet away. The very thought of touching it made me nauseous. Everything I loved about the hill and the night disturbed me. Even the sky was suffocating me, pressing down in black, black, black.

"You are something greater. You are *you*," he said, and stood. He walked to the scope, picked it up, looked through it. My discovery was nothing compared to seeing Earth, but disappointment raged through me all the same.

"Fath–" I started.

He held up his hand. Strands of his graying blond hair fell over his high forehead when he looked at me.

"Don't ask, Lissa. What you are is greater than man, greater than Jute." He spoke the words as if he was reading them off a page. He tucked the scope under one arm and held the other out to me, before looking up to the night sky. "It won't be long before they come for me."

I stared at his outstretched hand. He was telling me the subject was closed.

"I know," I finally sighed. His expression gave away nothing, and I couldn't bring myself to ask him anything more.

I would ask him the next day. I had the whole night to think. He wrapped his arm around my shoulders. *There's time*, I told myself.

They came that same night.

Soldiers, fully clothed in rich uniforms emulating the night sky. Such thick material is hard to come by.

The masks over their mouths and noses were made of the finest Louen, so their breath would never cloud over and suffocate their skin. They never took them off, though oxygen roams inside every home.

Perhaps it was because they knew, they've had experience after all. For as soon as they set foot inside our small home, the air became stuffy, claustrophobic. The walls were suddenly pressing closer and I had to force myself to breathe. Their eyes were cold and hard. Father always said you could glimpse inside a person's soul through their eyes.

And these souls knew nothing of mercy.

Father stole from the Chamber, an act punishable by death. But without a word, he ran to his room, leaving me alone under the harsh glares of the three men. The tiny flames swayed in the wake of his presence and his bare feet kicked up the dust we never swept in our candle-lit rooms. With a life so short and pointless, what was the point of cleaning?

He stumbled back with the scope, ready to show them we had a reason to live, that he had seen the Earth.

For a moment, everything was silent. The walls held their breath with me, as all eyes fixated on the shaky contraption.

Heartbeats passed before anyone moved. In a flash, the closest soldier ripped the scope from Father's hands. A snarl echoed in the room. His pale eyes met Father's and in the dark, I couldn't see his emotions. Were his eyes as wild as his actions? Did he feel the slightest pity as he threw the scope to the floor? I stopped myself—it didn't matter how the soldier felt. I stared as the glass shattered and the metal scattered. My heart pounded and my mind whirred.

Anger surged inside me, something I had never felt before. I ached to step forward, do something, *anything*. But I couldn't. My fear rooted me to the spot.

The same soldier broke the shocked silence with orders to the two beside him. Blood roared through my ears, and I heard nothing but the cadence of his voice. They grabbed Father by his arms, while he stared at the broken pieces on the floor. For all the years I had lived with him, I had never seen defeat on his face.

As they pulled him out the door, his head hung limp against his chest. They dragged him along the road because he didn't bother to walk. The fire flickering in him was destroyed, along with the very scope that lit it.

The pale-eyed soldier didn't even glance at me before pocketing the metal and jogging off behind them. He didn't care who saw him stealing from a thief.

There was nothing I could do. I was raised within these four walls, breathing, reading, and not much else.

But Father needed me. Despite the hope he had thrown away, a part of him would count on me. I quickly pressed my mask against my face and dragged myself out the door, before fear and reason could hold me back.

The pounding of my feet synchronized with my heartbeat. There was no sound other than the protesting wind. No chirping of bugs, no shuffling of animals like on Earth. Humans and Jute are all there is on Jutaire.

Up ahead, the faint shadows of three men stalked the ground as they passed the rows and rows of houses. Moonlight lit up Father's fair hair. No one spoke.

My breath hitched when I realized where they were going. I stumbled. *No.* They were going to the Tower, the place Father wove terrifying stories about. Where the four Chancellors lived and worked. But subconsciously, I knew it was inevitable. Where else would they go?

I slowed to a brisk walk when they stopped at the top of the five stairs, and someone rapped against the Tower door. They all fell silent as the door swung open with a slow creak.

Soft yellow light spilt forth, revealing Chancellor Kole's gaunt face, his eyes hollow pits of darkness. Shivers ran up my spine, like icy fingers dancing up and down the expanse of my back.

Everyone was wary of Chancellor Kole, even the well-dressed soldiers. The man had sentenced more people to hang than anyone can remember. He looked deathly, his face a pale, ghostly white.

As if all the lives he had stolen had taken him closer to the threshold of death.

I ducked beneath the shadows of two large boulders by the closest row of houses. There is nothing aside from rocks and rusty dirt in the barren landscape to offer hiding.

The Chancellor's gravelly voice carried on the dry wind. I held my breath and strained to pick out the words he enunciated in his painfully slow way. "Act... Earth... punishable."

Each word sent my heart beating faster and faster, louder and louder. In the end, only one word mattered.

Death.

I didn't need to hear the rest. I choked on the air brushing against my skin. Darkness edged into my mind, threatened to shut me down.

The door slammed shut. The meager light was gone. I looked up slowly from behind the boulder. Father was gone too.

I sank to the ground, the sudden weight of it all holding me down. It was real. It was happening. No matter how many times Father had told me they would come, it always sounded like something that *could* happen, not something that *would*.

Father had less than a day, *one day*, to live. Years of seeing his face, hearing his breath, listening to his voice. And tomorrow there would be nothing. I shuddered.

I heard a snap and my heart picked up speed. I forced myself to my feet. With one last glance at the Tower, helplessness stinging my chest, I turned back.

My hands were covered in red from the boulder, as if Father's blood already stained my hands, my heart, my life. I passed house after house, all uniform and small. I shivered at the single windows glinting at me, dim yellow eyes relishing my anguish.

When I finally climbed into bed, I expected tears, overwhelming fear and the shadows of soldiers looming on the walls.

But when I pulled the sheets over me, all I felt was a numbness encasing me from head to toe.

And a thought: I could save him.

I tumbled out of bed the next morning, knowing I only had till noon. Every beat of my heart brought Father's closer to eternal silence.

But I didn't find Father until noon, on the threshold of death.

It was a different kind of hanging. Chancellor Kole sought me out. He was calling Father's sighting of Earth a lie that would disrupt the peace and it took everything in me to stop the tears from spilling.

Disgusted people shoved me helplessly through the crowd until the tips of my boots were pressed against the ring of stones surrounding the gallows.

"Did you see the Earth with him last night?" Chancellor Kole's voice rumbled through the silent people.

I was stunned, because questions are never asked at hangings. No one is ever granted the privilege to speak. Even so, Chancellor Kole's dark eyes pinned me with loathing, forcing me to say yes.

Beside him on the scaffold, Father's neck was secured in the tattered rope, his hands tied behind him. His pale hair shone in the midday sun, reminding me of how we never looked alike.

I shivered at his blank stare, loneliness already aching between my ribs. His eyes didn't speak the words they usually did. A sob lodged in my throat and I looked back at Chancellor Kole.

"No," I whispered. The lie slipped easily from my mouth and I felt nothing. Fear eased the guilt of lying.

My voice gave Father life. He looked at me, eyes strangely focused. My heart quaked as it always did before Father told me something important.

"You are not my daughter."

My breath rushed from my lungs.

Chancellor Kole smirked and my legs nearly gave out beneath me. Remorse creased the edges of Father's mouth before he opened it again. But I didn't want to hear more. Anymore and I would have collapsed in the ring of stones and joined him.

I blinked in a vain attempt to hold back tears. Blood splattered against the white-washed wood before I turned and—

4

I WAKE WITH A START.

It takes a few moments for me to remember I am in my room, not in the Tower or in front of the gallows.

There's a pounding in my skull, and my head feels heavy when I force open my eyes. Outside, the sky is still dark, though splotches of red will soon creep over the horizon, tainting a blue sky. The stars will still shine beside the sun, dimmer, but there.

The blood from the day of Father's death clings to my mind, refreshed from my dream. I just don't understand. Hangings are bloodless, but Father bled on the day of his death.

Father's rickety desk leans against the foot of my bed, stacks of books from Earth decaying against the wall. Everywhere I look, I see Father. I rub at my eyes and slip out of bed. I need to get to the gallows early if I'm to save the boy. *Attempt* to save the boy.

I hear it again.

The pounding.

I slowly raise my gaze to the rattling door. The pounding was never in my head. No, *no*. I stumble to my boots and pull them on with trembling fingers. I've heard this pounding before.

I touch the mask plastered against my face, making sure it's there. It used to be comforting, in days past. Now, it's an annoyance, an obstacle.

And a reminder of how similar I am to the Jute.

There's nowhere to run. Two small rooms, one excuse for a kitchen, and one small, sealed window that if I can somehow open, I can barely fit my head through. It's either I open the door, or they break it down. I jump when the door rattles again.

With a deep breath, I reach for the rusted handle with shaky fingers.

First, I see his silhouette against the waking sun. Then, I see his deep brown hair, the shade so much like mine, and the black suit of a soldier. I lock my eyes on his.

Pale.

That's all I register before his hand clamps over my open mouth and darkness clouds my vision.

Many nights ago, I sat in front of a fire with Father. The sky was dark and I could barely make out the Chamber in the distance.

"Tell me something," I whispered to him. Because the silence of the world around me was harsh.

He sat back on his heels. "Tell you what?"

I shrugged. About my mother. About why I was secluded. But I didn't say any of those things. Father never answered those questions no matter how much I pushed.

"I don't know." But as soon as the words left my lips, a thought struck. "Tell me about the Jute."

My curiosity is too great for my own good, he would sometimes say. He leaned into the fire and stirred the water, coaxing it to boil.

"Cunning," he whispered. He looked at me, but his eyes were elsewhere. "They're cunning and beautiful. Every one of them is breathtaking so it's easier to lure you in."

He stirred the water faster and faster. It sloshed in circles, drowning him in its depths. I reached out and stopped. There were times when Father got lost in a dark world I never wanted to see. I dropped my hand in my lap. Restless, I undid my hair and ran my fingers through the tangled brown strands. Chocolate, Father called it. They had chocolate on Earth, he said. It was bitter and sweet at once. Impossible, I would say. He would shrug, because he had never tasted it, only read about it.

But on Earth, anything is possible.

I wanted to ask Father more. But if I've learned anything, it's silence. Silence brings out all. Father would speak when he was ready.

The fire crackled. On Jutaire, without oxygen, the fire is different. Fed by different air. Maybe it wishes it were orange, for it sputters and reaches up to the sky with angry fists of blue and purple. It still doesn't know we can't all get what we want.

Father spoke. "Never listen to what they say. Some are good, of course, but most are not. Everything they do is for their benefit."

"Which is why you don't want to stay on Jutaire," I said, silently urging him to continue. I tied off my braid and tossed it behind me.

"Yes," he said. "And no. I don't want to stay because of many things. But that is one reason. They aren't letting us stay on Jutaire out of hospitality, Lissa. That isn't how they are. We are here for something else."

His eyes looked past me, into the distance where the Jute lived. Jutaire is empty save for our settlement and theirs, though I've never seen it. We haven't seen a Jute in human territory in years. And while many took it as a good sign, Father did not.

His eyes were blank, glinting in the blue firelight. He was lost in his thoughts again, in the swirl of oblivion plaguing his mind.

Just as we are lost in a dark world.

I open my eyes to that darkness and part my lips. But if I scream, no one will come. There's something about being the daughter of a dead criminal that makes people ignore me.

I don't even know where I am.

I sit up and scramble back against something cool and hard. A wall. My shuffling shatters the silence and light blinds my vision.

Light like the sun, not the candlelight I've lived with for years. I glance up and immediately look away from its unnatural brightness. It has to be the solar energy I've read of in the books Father owned. The books I now own. Light must be another privilege given to the soldiers.

"You're awake."

The soldier's voice is softer than I expect, almost gentle. He's sitting cross-legged on the floor across from me, barely five feet away. I stare at him, unblinking because if I so much as breathe, fear will take over me.

I expect a grin. A glint in his eyes that says he has won. But his eyes are wary. His mouth is one flat line, like the ground beneath me. He studies me, as if he can read my mind by looking at me right.

He's strangely handsome, with an edge to his features than can only come with age. His unnerving pale gray eyes barely reflect the starkness of his black uniform. I've never seen eyes so light.

"Lissa," he says finally. My name sounds strangled as it falls from his lips.

I don't understand. I don't understand how he knows my name, how saying the name of the daughter of a man you murdered could be so hard.

"You killed him." My voice is choked and breathless. Like his, I realize. He shakes his head.

"You don't understand, Liss-"

"Don't," I say in a rush of surprising anger. I bite the words. "Don't say my name."

Something dangerously close to remorse flickers in his eyes and a muscle twitches in his jaw.

"What do you want with me?" I ask.

"He wasn't your father," he says hesitantly. Our eyes lock.

"Galileo, Gage, he wasn't your father," he says, more urgently this time.

"You're in no position to tell me who my father is. You're a murderer. A soldier," I say. The words feel foul in my mouth.

"I might be a soldier, but he wasn't your father."

I scoff. "He was my father. Until you killed him."

"No, Lissa," he says, ignoring my glare. "He never had a child. You knew him. He was too engrossed in his work—in science—to want a child."

That was the truth. And I remember Father's words. *You are not my daughter.* The weakest edge of my steel-hard belief crumbles.

"And you know," I say with a pause, "who my father is?"

A strangled sound escapes his lips. "Yes."

He knows I don't believe him. That no matter what he says I won't believe him.

"I know you can breathe the toxic air," he says instead. "And I know you're not Jute."

I stiffen. Of course he'd know I can breathe Jutaire's air—he was in the Chamber when my mask was in my hand and not on my face. But how would he know if I'm Jute or not?

The soldier sighs. My pulse pounds.

"My name is Slate. Gage was my brother," he says flatly.

Brother. Father had a brother. And a name other than Galileo that he never told me of.

Why didn't he tell me? Why couldn't he trust me with something so simple? What else did he keep from me?

The soldier, Slate, looks at me like he wants to say something else but decides against it with a defeated shake of his head.

"There's something I want to show you."

"You're not going to explain?" I ask without moving.

"Would you believe me? No. So no, I'm not going to explain. Not yet."

I consider sitting still, but if he can drug me and bring me here, wherever we are, then fighting him won't make a difference. More than anything else, I can learn something from him. Something about Father, who might not even *be* my father.

I slowly unfold my legs and stand.

He releases a deep breath and opens the door. I follow him down a long hall. Compared to the room, it's dim, but still lit with something other than a candle. I can tell we're in a house, but when I try to imagine it on the outside, I can't remember anything as long.

He stops at the end of the hall, in front of a sliding door.

"I can't give you back Gage," he says. His eyes are sad. "But I will give you what I can."

He speaks as if he knows me. In truth, he does. But he speaks like he has known me all my life as a friend, maybe more. But I've only known him for days as an enemy.

I stare at him, until the resolve to hate him crumbles inside me.

But there is nothing he can give me. There is nothing I expect to see on the other side that will fix anything in my ruined life. But when he opens the door, I realize there is something I'd like. The knowledge that someone didn't die because of me.

The boy from the Chamber.

5

THE SMALL BED PUSHED AGAINST THE dirty wall groans as the boy scrambles to his feet. His lean, pale arms are a stark contrast to the short sleeves of his black shirt.

There is nothing to show the pain he endured since last night, aside from a dirty bandage wrapped around his forearm, where I'm guessing glass must have cut through.

He's breathing. He's alive.

But I don't know how he's here. I don't know why the soldier would protect him in a room with a bed where he can rest. The boy runs a nervous hand through his hair.

"Lissa?"

My lips part in surprise. Even *he* knows my name.

"I was there," he hurries to explain. "On the day of your father's trial when Chancellor Kole called you out in front of everyone."

I stifle the ridiculous urge to snort. On Jutaire, trial is a fancy word for dragging people to a noose and letting their bodies dangle for the world to see. Though what happened to Father was a trial, of sorts. For me.

"Lissa?" The boy says again, pulling me away from the blood dripping down Father's only white shirt.

"I didn't realize you were there," I say.

It seemed to be Father, Chancellor Kole, and me. Everything else was in the background, fuzzy and blurry. But everyone was there, everyone knows me.

"And you are?" I trail off.

"Julian," he replies softly.

And then: "What were you doing in the Chamber last night?"

I catch the slight undercurrent of accusation in his voice. It was my fault he was caught, though clearly he was saved. Slate steps inside before I can answer and Julian looks away.

"Did you find her?" Julian asks him. His easy tone and the way they look at each other tell me they know each other well.

"Who?" Slate raises his eyebrows.

"Your daughter," he replies as if the answer is obvious.

Slate stiffens. "No."

Julian heaves an exasperated sigh. "You said you had a lead. You said you knew—"

"Stop." Slate's voice echoes in the room. Julian freezes, and tension rises, heavy and thick.

"When I find her, you'll know," Slate says softly and the tension disappears into the crevices between every little crack in the walls around us.

Julian mutters something inaudible and rakes his long fingers through his hair again. Each strand is a fine line of the night sky. I memorize this way to read him, because I know he is nervous. He catches me looking.

I look away quickly. Father taught me to control my eyes and voice. But he never told me how to stop the color from blossoming on my face.

I throw a glance up. The boy still isn't wearing a mask. Then again, I'm sure there's oxygen inside the house, though Slate and I still wear our masks.

But Julian wasn't wearing a mask last night. What if he's Jute and I mistakenly thought he was like me? But if there's oxygen here, inside the house, then he could be like me.

I'm confused more than anything else.

If I'm not Jute or human, then what *am* I? I shiver at the question. What am I? Three simple words, one easy question. And the person with the answer is dead.

"Are you alright?" Julian asks me.

"Yes," I lie. Because I don't think I will ever be okay. But my answer seems to satisfy him.

"What were you doing in the Chamber last night?" He is adamant.

"I"—pause and choose words carefully—"I went there to steal metal and glass."

He clenches his jaw and narrows his eyes. Because there's nothing else in the Chamber. He knows I went there to steal.

He wants to know *why*.

I take a deep breath, and when I speak, I'm not here, standing in this small, small room with two strangers. I'm elsewhere, with Father, looking through his scope.

I struggle on his name. *Gage*. But I can't say it. Nor can I say *Father* when Slate so strongly believes otherwise. So I settle for the name he chose for himself.

"Galileo... made a scope and saw the Earth."

I nearly choke on the words I've never spoken aloud. But they have heard this story—everyone has. There was magic in those words before Chancellor Kole made them deadly and hated in everyone's eyes. "And now he's dead. I need... to avenge him somehow, and the best way is to show everyone that Earth exists. That we have a reason to live. That we can do something other than wait for death. I saw it-"

"You saw it?" Two voices explode. Julian's eyes bulge out of his skull. The soldier stiffens beside me.

I want to reach out and pluck the words from their ears.

I saw the Earth, yes. I saw the colors so magnificent, so vivid, so real. It was hope so large and round, green and blue. Hope was tangible until Slate and the other soldiers came.

But only Father and I know what I saw.

"I-I," I sputter. My heart is pounding. Pounding. Pounding.

"You can trust us." My heart breaks at the simplicity of Julian's words. His voice is still and penetrating. As if the world knows when he is about to speak and silences all else.

It hits me like a gust of dry Jutaire wind.

Father betrayed me. I could have handled the truth. He could have told me about his brother, he could have told me he wasn't my father. Instead, he misused my trust and told me I'm not his daughter moments before his death. Did he denounce me? Or tell me one final truth?

"Lissa, you can trust us," Slate says softly, and rests his hand on my shoulder. On impulse, I flinch. On impulse, he grimaces. Pain flickers across his face, disappearing before I can breathe.

But Julian noticed. I hear his sharp intake of air. My eyes widen when Slate looks at him with barely concealed fear.

"You knew, didn't you?" Julian's voice is painfully accusing. Anger flashes in his eyes. He isn't referring to Earth. "You've known for years."

"No," Slate says, eyes cast down. His voice is choked when he looks back up at Julian. "Not years. Days."

"Tell her-"

But Slate isn't finished. In a heartbeat, he switches to the soldier who broke Father's scope with a snarl. "Don't you *dare*."

Silence drops like the bombs that had supposedly destroyed Earth decades ago. The tension reaches up again, sinewy and long, ready to snap.

"I'm not ready yet," Slate says, more to himself. And before Julian can respond, he leaves. I stare as he slides the door closed again.

If Julian notices my confusion, he doesn't let on. In fact, he swiftly switches topic. "Did you really see the Earth?"

"Yes." The word flies free from my lips. The outburst between Julian and Slate disappears from my mind. I'm light-headed, filled with a giddy happiness, at the thought of having another person to trust, despite the tendrils of warning fear.

"What's it like?"

For a moment, I think he's asking about trust. But when I meet his eyes, I know. Only one thing in our dwindling world can lighten and brighten a person's eyes to full awe.

"Earth?" I ask anyway. He nods and excitement builds in my chest. I've never spoken to anyone about Earth. It's a secret that could take me straight to the gallows. But right now, I don't care. "It really is green and blue and white, but different. Alive, almost."

His eyes light up and I want to grab his hand and push away the sun, entice the moon into the sky so I can show him Earth. But I don't have a scope. I don't have the courage to reach for his hand.

"It's a perfect round thing floating in a universe of darkness. When you've heard all your life that it doesn't exist, that it isn't real, seeing it for the first time shatters everything else. Everything you thought you knew is a lie."

"Seeing it in the sky for barely a heartbeat is all you need. Nothing else matters, you know?"

My question echoes in awkward silence. I finger the hem of my shirt and when I meet his eyes, he's staring at me with an expression I can't place. His eyes are a mixture of dark and light and I can't bring myself to look away.

Heat creeps up my cheeks. With a jolt, I realize I'm sitting alone in a room, too close to a boy.

"What?" My voice is barely a whisper.

"Nothing." He shakes his head. His voice is even softer, close to my whisper. Despite his answer, I can see the words waiting to be said.

"It's so many millions of miles away"—he pauses and searches my face—"and look what it's done to you."

He's right. I can feel it, like a beacon of light inside me, spreading all the way to the tips of my fingers. Even before I saw the Earth, I felt it.

Only Earth could do that to me. At least, that's what I thought when I saw it that night. But when he looks at me, I think… I think I feel it too. When he speaks, he seems to understand. I've been isolated for seventeen years, knowing no one but Father, who knew me all my life, who never truly understood me. Julian has known me for less than a day and he knows. I'm a person in his eyes. Not a shadow who became a criminal's daughter.

"Do you remember me?" He asks suddenly. "From the market?"

My breath catches when I meet his eyes.

So he *does* remember me from that bustling day in the market. It was months ago, when the wind was at its wildest, covering the market in gritty red sand and layering everything in dust.

Father always went to the market, not me. But that day, he needed a piece of pure Louen for an experiment. I ducked under the hooded tents and passed vendors and mothers and fathers and screaming children. Annoyance crept through my veins at the clutter and churning voices.

Behind the market stalls were the wide crophouses, their walls made entirely of Louen, clear and strong. From outside, it looked dark and dangerous. I slipped inside, where it was different. The smell hit me first - fresh and free, with recycled dirt from Earth.

The snickering hit me next.

"Did you find the Earth?" A voice asked. I peered through the foliage as another voice laughed.

I crept deeper into the crophouse, towards the emptiness in the center. I heard a pair of shears being dragged across the ground and the exaggerated sounds of the blades screeching against one another.

Three boys stepped from the taller plants. One of them bore a scar across his cheek.

"That stupid father of yours figure anything out?" He asked me.

"Or is he too busy babysitting you?" The other asked.

The one in the center cut them both off, shaking a mop of light curls away from his eyes. "Tell *Galileo* to hurry up. My dad's going crazy. Any day now he'll be hanging from that noose and it'll be all your fault."

"Let's pass him a message." The scarred one sneered. He clipped the shears again and my heart seized.

The others laughed, slowly coming closer. I took one step back, pressing my lips against a whimper. And for the first time, I wished Father was normal, that he wasn't trying to prove something that couldn't possibly be true. Something brushed against my hand and I jumped.

It was a leaf.

I turned and ran. Their shouts echoed behind me and I ran faster. Some small part of me lamented the loss of the plants I knocked over in my scramble. A door opened somewhere. Someone grabbed me and I slammed against the ridges of a chest. I looked up, but against the blinding light of the sun behind him, his features were as shaded as his dark hair. He lowered his head and searched my eyes. I could see him clearly then, his long nose, the fullness of his lips, the breathtaking shade of his eyes. I had never been so close to anyone in my life. I had never felt as alive as I did in those moments.

The boys skidded to a halt behind me and the blue-eyed boy looked up.

"Leave. Or I'll make sure you're all next at the gallows."

He stared, unmoving, until their footsteps receded and the door on the other end clicked shut.

"Are you alright?" He asked me. There was a hushed quality to his voice that reached inside of me and I couldn't bear it. I couldn't bear to be looked at as if I meant something, because I knew I would never see him again.

It was Julian. I meet his eyes, remembering the heat of his chest, the strength of his arms. He leans back against the pillows on the small bed with a soft exhale and it's a struggle to look at him.

"I went to the crophouses every day after that. But I never saw you again. I didn't even know who you were. You ran before I could ask."

"You looked for me?" I ask. Father never let me out after he heard what had happened. But I never told him about Julian.

He shrugs, suddenly shy. "I would have liked to know who I saved."

"Those boys knew me."

"I rarely go to the market. I rarely leave the Tower. I was... lucky that day."

"You? Or me?"

He holds my gaze. "Me. I was lucky."

My cheeks warm and I break away from his gaze. "Do you live in the Tower?"

"My mother was Chancellor Evan's sister, so yes, I do. I like it there, I guess," he says, but his voice faltered at the word *was*. His mother is dead.

The door slides open behind me.

UN*breath*ABLE

"Lissa," Slate calls. I turn. His eyes are bloodshot. "We have to go."

"Where?" I ask.

"Trust me," he says quietly. He drugged me, he killed Father. But he let me live after he saw me in the Chamber. He let Julian live after taking him in.

Take chances, Father once said. I stand.

"Lead the way."

6

I FOLLOW SLATE BACK THROUGH THE HALL,
which opens to a foyer. Sunlight filters in through the two
windows ahead of me, the door to the outside between
them. There's a series of cupboards along one wall and an
old seating area pushed against the other. Slate motions
for me to sit.

"But… I thought we were leaving," I say.

"First, I-can you please sit down?" He asks. I sit. The
color has drained from his face.

"You need to understand that Gage wasn't your
father," he says slowly.

I don't speak.

"What he did was wrong and I'll always hate him for
it, even if he was my brother," he continues. I keep my face
carefully neutral. I don't want to tell him he's repeating
himself.

"Do you know who my father is?" I ask. I still don't
know if I should trust him, but I can always give him a
chance.

He doesn't answer right away. He stares at me with an expression I can't place and it makes my chest tight. He whispers something, his voice so soft, I'm not even sure he spoke until the words register in my mind.

"Me. I'm your father."

My mouth opens, but shock has stolen my voice. All I can muster is a dying wheeze.

How many times had I looked at Father and wondered why we were so different? How many times did I repeat his last words and wonder if they are true? Father never lied.

"Y-you expect me to believe you?" I ask anyway, finally understanding why he wanted me to sit.

"No," Slate says, voice crushed in sorrow. We have the same hair, I realize. But then, couldn't we have the same hair if I was his niece? "I *want* you to believe me, but I know it will take time. And proving."

"You killed your own brother." I don't want a murderer for a father.

He shakes his head. "There's so much you don't understand yet. There's more to this than you, me, Gage, and the blood we share."

"What more can there be?" I say, but he's already leaving. Running, almost.

"Stay here," he says quickly. "I'll be back."

I lean back against the rough cushions and breathe. Inhale, exhale. Could Slate really be my father?

Restlessness makes its way into my veins, so I stand and pace the room. I keep hearing Father's last words: *You are not my daughter.* And Slate's proclamation: *Me. I'm your father.*

A small portrait on the wall beside the cupboard catches my attention. It's covered in shadows, almost as if Slate wants to remember and forget at the same time.

I cross the room. The colors are vibrant and alive, made by Jute, no doubt. Only they have such materials, close to what people had on Earth.

The portrait itself is of a woman, sitting on a throne that seems plain in comparison to her. A robe of navy blue, accented in gold, is wrapped around her slender shoulders. Her skin is a flawless, pale ivory. Her lips are a brilliant red. My mind flashes to the blood on Father's shirt and a shiver trembles up my spine. The woman's features are sharp, from the slant of her nose to the line of her jaw. But her eyes are what catch my attention the most. They're odd, the color reflecting everything around her, even paler than Slate's gray. I lean closer.

"Beautiful, isn't she?"

I straighten and turn. A ghost of a smile crosses Slate's lips. He scratches the side of his head.

"And cruel." Pain underlines his words. His eyes drift to the portrait, and finally to some distant place.

"Who is she?" I ask.

He looks surprised. "You don't know?" I shake my head. All I can think is: this man could be my father. "The queen. Queen Rhea."

"Of the Jute?" I ask. He nods.

I turn back to the portrait and carefully trace the billows of her lush robe. I've never seen a Jute before. In my mind they were feral, ugly creatures and all they wanted was to see me dead. But she is the opposite of that, cruel or not.

"She's been ruling for decades. Jute live long lifespans."

"Have you," I pause. "Met her?"

He laughs softly. "I have."

I want to know more. I want to know why he laughed. Why he chose now to say he is my father. Why, why, why.

"We can leave now," he says after a moment, without meeting my eyes. I have time, I decide. I can ask him later.

When we step outside, the ground is as dark as fresh blood. The Tower's shadow casts everything in a hushed gloom. From its nearness, I estimate we're roughly twenty rows from my own house, where the Tower is far enough that I don't have to worry about it. Mostly soldiers live this close to the spiral of pure black, with dark windows glinting like watchful eyes. Soldier houses are longer than ours, though they're still small with sloping roofs and red doors.

Everything on Jutaire is red.

"Where are we going?" I ask.

In answer, he looks up to the Tower. I stop.

"No," I burst out. "I'm not going there." Chancellor Kole is there. Power is there. I don't want to be mixed in this anymore.

I committed a crime last night.

Then it hits me: Slate is trying to take me in.

He sees the thought strike and lunges for me, sending a flurry of dust and sand flying between us. I stare at his hand around my wrist.

"You wanted answers, Lissa. I'm not going to hurt you," he says. Could the desperation in his voice be an act? "Please. Everything you've been taught is wrong. The Chancellors aren't the bad guys here."

Then who is? I want to ask. Instead, I ask something else, something that instantly makes me feel selfish.

"Will you tell me why I was raised by your brother?" I stumble on the word *brother*. But my words do nothing to acknowledge his claim of being my father.

"Yes." He drops my hand and starts walking. I sigh when he doesn't elaborate and follow him, because he will give me answers.

"Why is it so important that I come?"

A door slams far behind me and I turn to see Julian jogging toward us. Beside another house, kids laugh and run in the dust. They're all jutting bones and sun-kissed skin.

Slate takes the time to choose his words carefully. "Gage's death triggered a lot of irreversible things— including attention that's zeroed in on you. You're special, Lissa. No one else can safely breathe oxygen and Jutaire's air."

"But Julian?" I ask. I hold my breath.

He shakes his head sadly. No. I really am alone.

"Then, what am I?" I ask softly.

"Would you believe me?" He counters as we pass another row of houses. We're almost there. I can see the Tower door. He sighs when I don't answer. In truth, I don't know how to answer.

"You're half-human, half-Jute. The only hybrid on Jutaire."

I stop walking. Half-Jute. Half-Human. Half, not whole. I am nothing.

I wrap my arms around myself and think of Father, *Gage*, who said nothing. Who didn't think I was worth being truthful to. Julian catches up to us and Slate keeps his distance, watching me with his hands fisted by his sides. My limbs weaken at the possibility of him actually being my father. With the possibility of hope. Of not being alone.

"Tell me," I whisper.

The day of my birth was supposedly the night of my death. My skin was tinged a sickly blue and my eyes were swollen shut. For as long as they watched, I didn't take a single breath. This was why there were no other hybrids. They all came to this world like I did, blue and unbreathing. They were buried before they had a chance to live.

Slate set out with Gage to lay me to rest. There was no funeral—I came to this world dead, who was there to mourn me?

Slate left me there in his grief. He couldn't bear to look at his dead child any longer. Gage stayed behind. He knew more than anyone on Jutaire and when he checked for my pulse, he felt it. When he rested his ear on my chest, he knew the heart inside was beating, even if barely.

But Gage never told Slate. When Gage couldn't keep Slate away from his house, Slate saw me. Gage said he had an affair and that I was the result. Though Slate didn't think such a thing was possible, he believed him. How could he think his daughter was alive when he saw her still body?

"I never knew until I took him in that day," he whispers. There are tears running down his cheeks, glistening with the rays of the midday sun. Our shadows waver.

"Why did you leave me there?" I ask. I'm afraid my voice will break, but it's smooth and even. Encouraging.

He closes his eyes. And when he opens them again, he isn't here. He's elsewhere, seventeen years ago. "You were dead. Everyone said you were dead and I...I saw it too. I was young, barely seventeen. I trusted my older brother more than anyone, more than myself, because he was so learned."

Julian places a hand on Slate's shoulder and Slate smiles sadly. I almost forgot Julian was here.

"He didn't want to hang," he says, looking at me. I push away the pain making its way to my heart. If I let it stay, it will grow, spread. Consume me. And there is no turning away from such grief. "He begged me. He wanted me to give him a bloody death."

My breath hitches, snatched away by his words.

"So I did."

The confession is whispered. So soft, so inaudible. But in my ears, they boom, they echo and they pound.

"But why? Death is death," I force the words from my mouth. Julian glances at Slate and I get the sense that he knows why.

Slate shakes his head and continues walking, as if moving forward will rid us of our pasts. "It's not. You have to understand, there are some things worse than death."

I stare at him, but he continues staring ahead as if he doesn't notice me.

"Then my mother, who is she?" I ask.

He bristles, but doesn't stop walking. His hand is on the Tower door when he finally answers me. "She's gone."

I can tell he's lying. And if I can tell he is lying now, whatever he said before was true.

Maybe he really *is* my father.

Maybe I'm not truly alone.

7

THE INSIDE OF THE TOWER IS NOTHING like the outside. Everything is blinding white, from the floors to the walls, and surprisingly empty. I expected to see soldiers roaming the halls, to hear doors slamming and voices echoing.

The same shimmering ten-pointed star emblazoned on the Chamber's wall is here too, ingrained in the white floor. It's white too, and hard to see unless you really look. I wonder what it means, but I don't feel like asking. There are more important things to worry about.

Like my father being alive, and me being the only one of my kind.

Slate leads me to a room with nothing but a shaggy brown rug thrown in its center. My fingers itch to straighten it, to align the edges with those of the room's, but I clasp my hands together when he turns to me.

"I'll be back soon. This is pretty much the only room where you'll be left alone," he says with an apologetic smile and closes the door behind him.

I sink to the ground. The shag of the carpet brushes against the skin of my ankles that peek from beneath my pants.

I'm in the Tower, the last place I ever expected to be. Julian is alive. The man who I thought was my father could be my uncle. The soldier who killed the man I lived with for seventeen years could be my father. A shuddering breath escapes my lips.

I peel the mask off my face and rub at the spot where it itched against my skin, inhaling the sweet air. Oxygen doesn't fuel the Tower.

The air is a reminder: I'm half-human, half-Jute. Translation: not human, not Jute.

I am nothing. I belong nowhere. My lips part in a silent cry. My eyes burn.

The door opens and I quickly wipe my eyes and press the mask back on. But it isn't Slate with his sympathetic gray eyes. It's Julian. The only three buttons at the top of his shirt are unbuttoned, his chin shadowing a v-shaped portion of his neck. He sits down and doesn't speak.

"Are you like me? Half-human, half-Jute?" I break the silence first. He isn't wearing a mask. I know Slate said otherwise, but I want to hear the answer from him.

"Yes and no." He sounds distant, like he'd rather talk about anything but this.

"There can't be a yes and no," I pause and my brow furrows, "we must be the same.

He sighs and clenches his jaw.

"We're similar, but not the same. Jute women are stronger than men. Their genetics are different. Your mother is Jute, mine was human."

"Oh," is all I say, because I don't understand why that makes us different. His eyes soften at my voice.

"You're supposed to come with me."

"Where?" I ask, standing. A part of me just wants to hear his voice, the softness of it, the stillness. I trust him, I realize. He's saved me twice, and I have to believe that means he will never hurt me.

"You'll see."

I follow him down the hall. His shirt clings to his shoulders and he walks almost soundlessly, despite the boots hidden beneath his dark pants. When he opens a door, a smell hits me, tangy and acidic. Like blood.

But when the light flickers on, I don't see blood. I see metal. Weapons of every shape, size and lethality line the walls. I step inside and turn a full circle. Weapons to my right and left. Targets straight ahead. Carpet across the floor.

"Metal isn't scarce, is it?" I say dryly.

He shakes his head, but doesn't say anymore. Why was *he* in the Chamber last night?

I run my hand along the weapons lining the walls. There are daggers in various sizes. Some with the most intricately carved handles. Staves tipped with blades and jet-black bows with metal arrows. There are rows of shock guns docked beneath a solar panel. I've never seen so many weapons. Weapons are for killing. For protecting.

What do they need protection from?

"Why did you want to show me this?" I ask slowly.

He stills and turns back to me, a knife in either hand. "This room. It's where you'll spend the majority of the next month or so. In training." He sounds confused.

I stare at him. "Training? I don't need to train for anything. And I'm not staying here." I'm going home, I don't say.

He sets the knives down and steps closer, eyes narrowed. "But—how about Slate? I thought, now that you know he's your father—"

"Being my father has nothing to do with training. Or living here. Biological or not, he will never be Galileo."

Julian's eyes flash. "No, he won't. Because he isn't." There's a dangerous edge to his voice that makes me ignore the logic of his words.

"I've gone seventeen years without him. I have no need, no reason—" I can't say the words I want to say. I don't know what to say.

Because really, I'm afraid. Afraid to trust another person the way I trusted... Gage. And I'm afraid—what if he *isn't* my father?

We hear it at the same time. The shift. The sharp inhale. I jerk my head to the door as Slate takes a step back, face contorted in a sorrow and pain.

And worse, understanding.

"Wait!" I rush after him. "That isn't what I meant."

"No, you're right." Slate turns and smiles sadly at me. His lips tremble, a testament to how much I mean to him, the daughter he didn't know he had for seventeen years. He reaches for me, but his hand freezes midair. "I will never be Gage."

His body shudders when turns and sulks slowly down the hall. When the pain edging into my chest becomes too much to bear, I turn too. Guilt and regret heat my face.

And I run.

I ignore Julian's frantic calls as my feet echo down the hall. I shove past a surprised soldier and throw open the door before hurrying down the steps.

I have no reason to train. I never had to worry about being safe. But I never should have said what I said.

"Don't you want to know who's after you?"

I jump. Julian stands right behind me, eyes ablaze. My heart races. It relishes every moment when I am alone with him. My heart feels too many things at the wrong times.

"No." I surprise myself with the force of my voice.

He stares at me before clenching his jaw. And finally, finally, he turns away without a word.

Rejection. That's what I feel like a heavy weight in my chest. And guilt.

I walk, weariness underscoring my every step. Despite the pang I feel when I realize I probably won't see Julian or Slate again, I have no intention of returning again. Ever.

Far to my right, somewhere unseen, is Jute territory. Was my mother as cruel as the Jute are supposed to be? Or was that another lie Father—Gage—told me?

Maybe the Jute are like us. Maybe my mother cried for my blue corpse, as Slate did.

He cares for me – I can see it in his eyes, in his tears, in the pain burning on his face. Somehow, I know he isn't bluffing, just as I know he lied about my mother being gone. I never saw so much emotion in Father. Slate is what Father was not. I stop walking.

Slate is my father.

And isn't that what he told me, on the threshold of death? *You are not my daughter.*

Like a shock blast, it hits me. My father is alive. Slate, a gray-eyed, chestnut-haired soldier barely over thirty, is my father.

I try to make sense of it all. Half-Jute, half-human. Father—no, *Gage*—keeping me away from my own father, his own brother. Julian insisting I should train.

A soft, animal sound shatters my thoughts.

I stop walking when I hear it again. Something *breathing*.

Shadows fall over me. I look up slowly, as my pulse quickens.

Five creatures surround me. Translucent, sickly, white. Mutants. Creatures that only existed in the stories Gage would tell me at night. They're like the breathtaking horses of Earth, only uglier, *because the Jute needed ugliness in their beautiful lives*, he had said. The creatures stare at me with blood-red eyes and wheeze, a guttural sound nothing like the whiny of a horse I've read so much about.

I shudder in disgust and take a step back. And slowly, holding my breath, I raise my gaze. Atop each mutant is a man. Their faces are unmasked, their beauty is striking—perfectly smooth skin, profound features. Like Julian, like Earth. I know what they are.

Jute.

I struggle to breathe and take another step back. My hands shake. One of them laughs.

I will never be strong enough to stand up for myself. So I do the only thing I can.

Turn and run.

A

THE MUTANTS ARE FAST. THEY SURROUND
me in a flurry before I have a chance to make it a few feet. I
glance helplessly down the nearest row of houses as three
women hurry into a house, one of them carrying a toddler
against her hip. They whisper and throw nervous glances
my way before the door slams shut. I'll find no help here.

I scan the faces of the Jute. Other than their
unmasked faces and uncanny beauty, there isn't a way to
tell they aren't human.

But I can tell one thing: the dark-haired Jute in the
center is the leader of the five. His long coat, rich and dark,
billows behind him in the wind. The others stand slightly
behind him, their clothes faded compared to his, but new
compared to my own. He stands out. His features look
familiar, but I'm too far to tell for sure.

"We aren't here to hurt you," he calls.

His voice reminds me of Julian. Maybe it's because
I've heard very few young men speak before.

I think of the countless weapons in the training room.

Why did I run?

"What do you want with me?" My voice cracks.

He laughs, the sound deep. "You. I want you."

"Leave her alone, Rowan." Someone shouts behind me. Julian. Relief floods my veins. He raises a black bow, and I hear the sharp slice of metal as he draws an arrow back.

"Didn't think I'd see you again in this life," Rowan shouts back with a one-sided grin.

Their voices. Rowan. Julian. The same.

Julian narrows his eyes. "I said leave. Or they're all dead."

Rowan moves his mutant forward and his hair ruffles in the wind. He holds his arms out in mock defiance.

There's a swoosh of air behind me, followed by another. One by one, the Jute on either side of Rowan fall and oxygen seizes in my chest. The mutants groan and take off into the emptiness beyond human land.

Rowan surveys the fallen bodies lazily. Carelessly. "I need her. Not them."

"Leave, or I'll shoot," Julian says. His voice is tight.

But the same arrow is nocked in his bow. Someone else killed Rowan's men.

Rowan jumps down from the creature. "You. Shoot me?" He laughs. "No, Jules, not even if your life depended on it. But I—"

He falls when two blasts of blue hit him square in the chest. His body jerks in silent spasms. Not dead.

I turn to Julian, my eyes wide. The wind howls suddenly.

"Teach me," I say with a wheeze. Neither of us says anything else.

I tremble as I walk. Julian looks at me with sympathy and I hate it. But I keep walking. The farther away I can get from the Jute named Rowan and his dead crew, the better. Every few steps, Julian glances back, as if he expects something. Someone.

I just want to clear my mind. I just want answers. I *need* them.

"You knew him," I say. Fear pulses in my veins. Rowan wanted me.

Julian clenches his jaw. "Yes."

An arrow sinks into the dust ahead of me and a cloud of red explodes over my clothes. I jump with a gasp but Julian stills as a defiant laugh sounds behind us.

A girl about my age and height walks toward us. Her eyes are dark shards of glass. I've seen penetrating eyes like those before. Her pitch-black clothes are tight and her stark white hair is cut short, falling in messy strands over her right eye. Everything about her screams pride. She strolls past us and plucks her arrow from the dirt. Julian throws a nervous glance at me before facing her.

"Dena. What are you doing here?" He sounds wary.

"What, no 'thank you'?" She places one hand on her hip and waves the arrow with the other.

"Thanks for what? Killing them? For immobilizing Rowan? I could have done that." But his voice lacks the conviction of his words.

The girl, Dena, doesn't even spare me a glance before sauntering over to him. Close to him. Closer than close. She presses her body against his and leans in, so their faces are barely breaths apart.

"No, Julian," she breathes. He leans away, but she leans closer. "For saving you from my father."

I blink.

That's where I've seen those eyes. She's Chancellor Kole's daughter. My sliver of dislike increases tenfold. That's why Julian wasn't at the gallows. *She* saved him from Chancellor Kole. Not Slate. Not me, like I wanted to.

The tips of Julian's ears turn pink and he opens his mouth. She raises her finger and traces his lips. "Shh, don't give me that 'I wanted to die' crap again."

I inhale sharply. Julian was trying to get himself killed in the Chamber. The reality of that hits me in the stomach.

They stare at each other in silence.

Dena's gaze flickers to his lips and my cheeks burn. I don't want to see anymore. I wipe my sweaty palms down my pants and hurry towards the Tower.

It wasn't Julian who saved me. It was Dena. I don't feel afraid anymore. No, this is disgust. And anger at my cowardice.

I hear Dena screech and Julian sigh. I want to cover my ears and wash my eyes.

"Lissa, wait!" Julian calls. I stop, but don't turn around.

"Thank you saving me," I say. He flinches at my monotone.

"It's not what you think."

"I don't *think* anything. It's none of my business," I say. Even I'm surprised at the bitterness in my voice.

By the time we near the Tower, my anger has faded, and every heartbeat of silence makes me more embarrassed.

Julian looks at me. "There was one point in my life when I wanted so many things, her included. I thought I loved her."

I purse my lips and stare ahead. But he knows I'm listening.

"Then my mom died." His voice is a soft, pained whisper. "I loved her so much. More than anything. And I-I couldn't save her." He chokes off in a humorless laugh.

"I didn't want anything after that. Not Dena, not Earth, not even my life. Life lost its meaning. I've been trying to join my mom ever since. And Dena—"

"It wasn't love."

"What?" He stops.

"You never loved Dena," I say, facing him. "Or you would love her now, even more so. Love only gets stronger through hardship and pain."

He stares at me and his gaze softens. I laugh softly, and continue walking. "Not that I know anything of love."

"You loved Gage," he says after a moment.

I shake my head. "I thought I did. I thought he loved me. But I was a hungry creature he was able to feed with Earth and lies. When Slate looks at me—*that* is love. Until then, I had no idea what it looked like."

The sharp tang of acid flits into my nose, and though there are no clouds in the sky, it's only a matter of time before the sky will split and rain will spill.

They say Jutaire is red because of the rain. When humans first came to Jutaire, there were many of us. They spread their arms and welcomed the rain to wash over them. But they didn't know.

Standing in the rain is suicide.

Each raindrop is a bullet. A wound that leaves blood trailing down your skin. They say half our race was murdered by the sky. Their blood seeped into the ground and stained the land red for eternity.

Gage said on Earth, rain was as clean as the water in our basins, which we boil long after the rain has passed. On Jutaire, the scent that reeks in my nose is a warning and a reminder, to me and everyone else.

Rain is deadly.

"You're going to train." Julian breaks through my thoughts.

I nod. I don't have a choice, I don't say.

But I can't be vulnerable anymore. I can't run from every little thing that scares me. "Why are they after me? Why now?"

"They need you. We're not sure why yet. As for why *now*, I've got a theory."

"Tell me," I say, climbing up the steps behind him. He turns back with his hand on the Tower door.

"The metal and glass are locked up because of Earth. There were people before Gage who tried to build scopes, too. If humans knew Earth existed, they would draw courage from it's existence, they would fight back," he says softly. My eyebrows furrow. "The Jute want to make sure we stay here. They want to keep us contained until they leave."

"Leave?" I ask. *Fight back?* I want to ask.

He meets my eyes. "For Earth. They have a ship, fuel, provisions. They lack one thing."

A ship. The Jute want to live on Earth, which belongs to humans.

"Gage wanted Earth more than anything. The Jute need one person more than anything. If you ask me, it's the perfect trade."

Everything clicks then. The Jute coming after me. Gage keeping me a secret from my own father.

"More than anything. More than me," I whisper.

He would have traded me for passage to Earth.

"I'm sorry, Lissa."

But I don't understand. They have everything they need to get to Earth—a ship, provisions, fuel. So why me?

The man with the answer is dead.

9

I STARE OUT THE TINTED WINDOW AT THE
rain that falls for the first time since Gage's death. Maybe
the sky has finally remembered to mourn his loss, for it falls
in the thickest torrents I've ever seen.

I mourn him even now, knowing what he would have
done to me. Would he have mourned me this same way,
after handing me over to the Jute he always cautioned me
from?

I shake my head. It doesn't matter. I look around to
distract myself, but my mind drifts to Rowan and the ship
Julian spoke of. How can their entire mission depend on
me?

The room door opens and closes.

I meet Slate's eyes.

"You were an experiment to Gage," he says before I
can part my lips to apologize.

I gasp. I never liked gasping, betraying so much in a
single inhale. But I can't help it now.

"It isn't nearly as bad as it sounds. He told me the night I arrested him. He studied you, took blood samples every day." He studies my reaction, which is nothing but an empty stare. "You never knew?"

I shake my head. But how did he take it without me knowing? He drugged me. He had to have. Where did he have the equipment to test it? There are so many snippets of new knowledge I have to embed into my head, and so much more I need to know.

"He studied your bone structure, your lungs. He studied the others too, half-breeds like Julian. Where their lungs are weakened by excessive amounts of oxygen, yours aren't. You can breathe both without consequence."

Which explains why Julian never wears a mask.

"I'm sorry for what I said earlier," I say.

"It's okay," he whispers. He steps forward and I hold my breath. He raises his hand slowly and trails his fingers through the hair that has come loose from my braid. I can't imagine how much this simple gesture means to him. A breathy laugh escapes his lips. "You have my hair, my nose. You're so... beautiful. Mine. My daughter."

His eyes fill with anguish. "I will never see you grow up. Take your first steps, say your first word, read your first line."

I bite the inside of my cheek. This is all Gage's fault. How could he be so selfish?

"You'll see her do other things." I freeze as Chancellor Kole steps into the room, his dark eyes glued to me. "Like maybe, I don't know, try to save us all."

This is the first time I've seen him since Gage's death, and he is just as frightening as always.

"Yeah, right," Dena snorts and walks in behind him. "You should've seen her back there, she nearly peed her pants."

Chancellor Kole chuckles. They all stare at me, even Slate. I want to tear the mask off my face and curl up in a ball and disappear.

"Her strength lies in her mind. Gage made sure of that." There's an edge to Slate's voice.

"Right." Dena rolls her eyes and leaves.

Chancellor Kole continues to stare at me. I can feel him sifting through my mind, learning everything in my silence.

"You killed Gage." I surprise myself by blurting out. It's far from the truth, I know now, but he did hang him.

He shrugs, nonchalant. "Someone has to do the killing. Better me than them."

Chancellor Kole's voice is constant in my mind as I try to find the training room, where Slate said Julian is waiting for me. Every hall looks the same, with unfeeling white walls and smooth unblemished floors.

After I take the wrong turn thrice, stumbling on a stern-faced soldier each time, I find it.

I push open the door and step inside. But it isn't Julian standing before me. A one-sided smile lifts

Chancellor Kole's gaunt face. His black suit hangs from his shoulders, and makes him look like he has sticks instead of legs.

"You're scared of me, aren't you?" He asks. His voice reaches the soles of my feet before my ears.

"No," I say. I am terrified. And my voice betrays that.

"Do you know why Gage wanted Slate to kill him? He was going to hang anyway—what difference is there?"

I asked the same question. I have no answer.

Chancellor Kole clasps his hands behind him and slowly walks closer, just as he does when he strides onto the platform to announce another crime and death.

"You see, Lissa, the Jute have a ship." He pulls a small ball out of his pocket. I look at it without giving him the satisfaction of my interest. Blue and green, with hints of white. A replica of Earth.

Earth in his pocket.

"How? How did they build a ship?" I ask.

He shrugs. "Something about dust making metal and sand making glass. I wouldn't know. But that's aside from my point. We don't have gas or oil. Where would they get fuel?"

"I don't know," I say when he stares at me.

"Humans breathe oxygen. Our main component is oxygen—of course you know that, don't you?" Sarcasm drips from his voice. It's true. After Gage, I know more than the average human on Jutaire will ever know. "The clever, cunning Jute found a way to convert human bodies into fuel. No one wants a bloody body. Hence the bloodless hangings."

He leans forward, so our eyes are level. "Hence Gage's plea to be killed rather than hung. His final—and *only*, if I should say—act of defiance."

"And now the Jute are furious. Gage knew of the consequences for such an act. Not for his dead body, but for the entire human race. And the bastard didn't care."

Chancellor Kole takes in the surprise on my face. "Not so perfect now, was he?"

No. Not even close.

"Criminals are the easiest to hang, we can justify their deaths. We could easily get away with a dead body every other week. But because of Gage's stupidity, the Jute are demanding more."

"Why listen?" I ask quietly.

He shrugs. "It's their planet. We follow their orders and they let us live. A body a week, sometimes more, lock up the metal and the glass, and the majority of us gets to live."

The Jute are more tangled in our lives than I thought.

"I didn't want this job, you know." I meet his flickering dark eyes. "They took my wife. Threatened to take Dena. So I became the bad guy. The people I hang is a way of letting us all live."

"I'm sorry," I say. I try to sound like I mean it, but I can't.

"I don't need your sympathy." His voice raises the hair on the back of my neck. "All I want is for Dena to live.

And if I can ensure her safety by handing you over to the Jute, I will. So be careful."

The door opens and Julian slips inside.

"I was leaving," Chancellor Kole says brightly, though his eyes still burn on my skin. He smirks.

"Are you alright?" Julian asks once he leaves. I force air through my nose. Inhale. Exhale. "You look pale."

"I'm fine," I whisper.

He gives me a look that says he doesn't believe me but thankfully lets it slide. He slips knives from his boots and sets them on the table lining the wall and I wonder if he was with Dena. If he changed his mind about love.

"We're going to do some basic stretches and loosen up first. Are you ready?"

I nod, though I can't meet his eyes.

"Then let's do this."

I'm drenched in sweat and embarrassment. Julian doesn't seem to notice when he guides my arm back behind my neck.

My hand trembles beneath his touch. My heart races so fast, I'm afraid it will explode from overheating like the motors I've read about. Julian notices. My breath catches at the intensity in his gaze.

"Clear your head, Lissa," he says softly.

I swallow. His hand closes around mine again and my whole body pulses with my heart.

"Pull your hand back, like this." He pulls my hand back toward my shoulder.

"Focus on the target and nothing else. Then throw." His voice is lulling. I can't focus on anything but my thrumming heart, my hand pulsing beneath his, and my body, slick with sweat. How can I focus when he is so close?

But when my breathing synchronizes with his, my pulse slows. My mind clears. Julian releases my arm.

And the faded red and white target is all I see. I think of all the physics Gage taught me. The rules of trajectory paths. I close my eyes for a brief heartbeat, expecting to hear his voice and see his face, but all I see is the target.

I open my eyes and throw. My arm swings forward and my fingers release the knife. I hold my breath.

And watch as it sticks into the cushioned wall between two targets.

Just as the door opens. And Dena laughs.

I think I might die from humiliation.

"You did good for your first try," Julian says, but his voice is tight. I could have done better. Especially because she was here to see it.

Dena pulls the dagger from the wall and twirls it her hand.

"I bet you need a break, Jules." Her voice is suggestive.

Julian's eyes dart to me. "No, I don't. Just leave, Dena."

UN*breath*ABLE

She scoffs. "Can't you see how pathetic she is? Why bother? Let the Jute do whatever they want with her. At least they're good-looking. Better than good, I should say."

Julian clenches his jaw. His voice drops. "Dena. Leave."

Dena looks at me for the first time. She opens her mouth.

And I can't take it anymore. Because anger is stronger than fear. Because I finally snap. "Did anyone ever tell you to take a hike? On Earth, that meant shut up and leave, no one wants your condescension."

I clamp my mouth shut, heat exploding across my face. Julian snorts and barely covers it with a cough. Dena turns bright red and glares at him.

"You don't want to die anymore, do you, Julian?" She takes in his stricken face before she storms out, slamming the door behind her.

My hands shake when I retrieve the dagger from the floor.

"I'm sorry," I can barely say.

He scoffs. "Sorry? That was—I didn't think you had it in you. And besides, Dena deserved it."

I struggle to change the subject. "Can I keep this with me?"

He doesn't answer right away. Finally, he blinks. "Oh yeah, sure. Tomorrow then?"

"Tomorrow," I say.

He hurries out, leaving me surrounded by a multitude of weapons I can't even use. I stare at the knife in my hand.

Jute learn as fast as they heal, Julian said.

Pathetic, Dena said.

I'm not. I step back and angle my arm. I'll show her I'm not. I throw the knife. It lands an embarrassing length away from target, worse than before. I pull it free and release a shuddering breath. Anger still pulses through my veins. It is new to me, this anger.

I let it stay, fuel me. And I throw the knife again.

And again and again.

My room is across from Julian's.

"If you need anything," he adds quickly.

"And Lissa?" He says, opening the door to my room again. "You're safe here. I won't let anyone hurt you."

"You can't always be here," I say.

His eyes hold mine, dark and penetrating. "I will. Always."

"Who's Rowan?" I ask, before I can stop myself.

"He works for the Queen," he says slowly, and that's all.

"So the Queen wants me." I tilt my head. "But no one knows why."

He nods. "Not even the Queen knows why."

And with that, he closes the door behind him.

The bed is large, satiny blue, inviting me with plush pillows. A folded nightgown is set on one corner and a small bowl of colorless porridge sits on the bedside stand. A few steps to my left is a door leading to a small bath.

I eat, wash and climb into bed with a sigh, relieving my aching limbs.

The full moon casts a ghostly white glow in the room, making me feel like I'm elsewhere. I turn so I can see the moon in the distance, an oddly shaped round. It's nothing like Earth's dimmer moon, a perfect round riddled with craters.

One hundred and fifty years ago, humans came to Jutaire when Earth became too dangerous for life. They came on a ship, Gage had said, the ruins of which still exist close to Jute territory. Days after they landed, rain spilt from the sky.

They welcomed it as they did on Earth and it killed them. I've listened to the story from Gage's lips nearly every rainfall. And each time I stared out the window as the rain splattered on the glass, and wondered—why didn't the Jute warn us?

Half the human race bled beneath the crying skies. Of the half remaining, Gage had said, yet another half disappeared without a trace. I looked at his face, as the full moon glowed across his sharp features and pale hair.

"Where did they go?" I was younger then, much younger.

"The Lost Colony? It's too long of a story for me, Lissa," he said. He leaned against his rickety desk and scribbled something on a fraying sheet of paper. He gestured toward the dingy shelves lining the wall. "It's all in the books."

But it wasn't. I scoured every single book in search of the Lost Colony. There's nothing that tells of the humans who disappeared. But they can't have died. No, something else happened to them. I just know it.

And only now, days after he has died, do I remember: He lied.

He knew of the Lost Colony. And he died with his secret.

10

IT TAKES ONE MONTH.

I've perfected the use of a dagger, a bow, and a double-bladed staff and learned how to fight with my bare hands. Of them all, I prefer a dagger the most, and enjoy a bow the least. The way the curve of the dagger handle fits into my palm and moves as I do gives me a feeling of control, unlike a bow.

I've grown accustomed to expecting the feeling I get when Julian looks at me, stands near me, and breathes near me. But I will never grow accustomed to the feeling itself. It always feels new, fresh. I can't get enough of it.

We part ways wordlessly at the hall. He was quiet today, his eyes dark and brooding.

I wash up and sink into bed, feeling the impact of my exhaustion only when the comfort of my covers envelops me. As always, I tuck two daggers beneath my pillow.

They make me feel safe, and now that I know how to use them, they will keep me safe too.

I stare at the ceiling, and remember my first night here, beneath another full moon. And in the blank, ethereal white glow, I see my thoughts.

The Jute, who want me.

My mother, who my father claims is dead.

Slate, who wants to be with the daughter he lost.

Chancellor Kole, who will do anything to protect his daughter.

Dena, who will do anything to get rid of me, and get Julian back.

And Julian, who gets more and more distant with each passing day. Something bothers him. I wish he would share his burden. I wish I knew what he wanted.

And me. *What do I want?* I ask my beating heart.

It whispers. Because it is afraid to want what it wants. Because so many have died for it and many more will. I sigh and turn to my side. We can't all get what we want.

Yet when I close my eyes, I don't see darkness. I see blue and green and white.

Earth.

I wake to the sound of my name in the middle of the night. I slide my hand beneath my pillow and close my fingers around the hilt of a dagger as a figure moves into the moonlight.

"It's me." Relief rushes through me when I hear the soft sound of Julian's voice. His messy hair glows in the moonlight.

"What is it? What's wrong?" I whisper. My voice is thick with sleep.

He stares at me in silence. "I wanted to ask you something."

"Oh." I sit up. His eyes slip to my bare shoulders and linger before they jump back to my face. Everywhere he looks, my skin tingles, as if his gaze is a tangible thing. I hear him shift in the dark and warmth rushes to my face.

"How would you know," he breathes, "if you loved someone?"

I blink. I remember telling him his love for Dena was not love.

"I guess, you would know, in your heart. You wouldn't be able to close your eyes without seeing her face, hearing her voice and imagining her smile. And you wouldn't be able to leave her, no matter how much you tried. When you see her smile and laugh and hear her voice, whispering words just for you, it'll feel like the world is at your feet. Like nothing could ever go wrong."

I snort softly. "I don't know really. It's all in my mind."

He runs his fingers through his hair. "How would you tell them? Her."

"That you love her?" I ask. "I-I guess you wouldn't need to. If she loved you back, you would both feel it, know it, and that itself will bring you together."

But there was one word I had found in my water-damaged copy of the English dictionary that could describe love.

"Love is magic," I say.

My eyes burn and I rub at the ache in my chest. I speak as if I know, but I do not. This is only what I think. What I want.

For a moment, I think he has fallen asleep, bored by my words. But after a moment, I he whispers.

"Thank you, Lissa."

I hear his soft footfalls. I see the door open. And before sleep finds me again, I think I hear his voice, a lullaby in the dark.

"Sweet dreams."

And I think, maybe, just maybe, I dreamt it all.

The door to the training room is ajar the next day. My legs ache with every step. But any day now, the Jute might come, and I need to be ready.

It's odd, how my life has changed in the span of little more than a month. I have gone from an orphan living in a sea of dying humans to a daughter, a prized possession needed so the Jute can get to Earth.

I slip silently into the room. Sunlight shines through the wide windows, casting the weapons in shades of brilliant gold. Beautiful and deadly.

I almost don't see Julian sitting in the corner, leaning over something. He doesn't see me come in, and it's hard not to stare without his attention on me.

His face is calm though his long fingers move. There's a ridge on the bridge of his nose that I didn't notice before. A crescent-shaped scar, the length of my thumbnail curves along the side of his left eye. I force my eyes down to his lips, full and a bruised dark pink, as if he spends too much time chewing them in nervousness.

He isn't as perfect as I first thought.

He looks up through the hair dusting his forehead and I want to brush them away with the tips of my fingers. Amusement touches his irises as if he can read my mind.

And he smiles. His lips curve up and I feel as if this is the first time I've seen a smile. My heart ricochets inside my ribcage and threatens to burst free.

And I realize, in all the seventeen years of my life, I have never felt this way. Ever.

"This is for you," he says softly, reminding me to breathe. He holds up two daggers. The black hilts are carved in gold and white lines, swirling unto one another. Like the colors of Earth. And in the midst of the looping swirls, I see five letters. My name.

"It's beautiful," I say breathlessly. My fingers brush against his when I take them from him. My breath hitches. He notices, and when his eyes find mine, the corners of his lips are still turned up in a smile.

I smile back. His eyes trace the curve of my lips. "You should smile more often, it looks good on you."

I want to laugh and at the same time, fade into the wall behind me. But I find courage somewhere inside me. "You should too."

He laughs and I almost forget to breathe. I want to grab ahold of his laughter and tuck it into my pocket to keep forever. "I'll keep that in mind."

"Am I interrupting anything?" I scramble to my feet as Slate steps in. His gray eyes are alight with the smile on his face.

"No," I say too quickly. Julian watches me, offering nothing. It only makes every breath harder.

"Mm-hmm," Slate teases. My neck is on fire and I don't know what to say.

"Alright, alright," he laughs, raising his hands. But the knowing smile is still on his face. He looks between Julian and me. And when neither of us offers a word, he leans back. "Lissa, can you come with me?"

"Of course," I say, tucking the daggers into the sheaths that are almost permanent around my waist. I glance back at Julian before following Slate out the door. We walk in silence for a few moments before I break it. "Where are we going?"

"To eat," he says simply.

"We usually eat in the training room," I say slowly. For the past month, it's been Julian, him, and me. He tilts his head.

"I know," he says with a smile as we climb up a flight of stairs. "But today, you're eating where the others eat."

He leads me to a wide room with an elongated round white table in its center, large enough to seat at least fourteen or so people. The iridescent ten-pointed star in a glossier white spans from one end to the other. But what takes my breath away is the wall behind it. The wall in front of me.

It's completely glass.

Slate chuckles softly when I cross the room, unable to hold my jaw up as everything, *everything*, spills open before me. From here, at the top of the Tower, even the hill where I felt so free looks minuscule. The rows and rows of houses look as small as me, and the Chamber looks like a cube I can fit in my hand. I can see the people in the market, like sticks darting to and fro. Everyone avoids the gallows, though children run up and down the platform's rickety steps.

Everything between, around, and beyond our small settlement is red.

"It's quite a sight, isn't it?" Slate asks. I nod quickly.

I turn to him. "Is this where we're going to have lunch?"

"Along with the Chancellors, yes," he says.

My eyes widen. "But-I-why?"

He fixes me with his gray stare, his expression serious. "The Chancellors have no power, Lissa. Everything they do, every life they take, it's all because of the Jute, and more importantly, Queen Rhea. They don't deserve your fear or hatred. They're only trying to keep as many of us alive as they can."

"They know Earth exists. They've known even before Gage saw it," I say flatly. My eyes stray to the hill, where I stared into the sky on countless nights.

"They have no choice but to hide the truth. The Jute are capable, Lissa. The humans who came to Jutaire came prepared with countless amenities and supplies. They came here with the purpose of living here, not dying out. The

Jute took it all. Fighting back is pointless." He sighs and steps back toward the table, sinking into one of the chairs just as the door opens.

Chancellor Kole walks in, followed by three other men—the other Chancellors. I've only seen Chancellor Kole because he meets the people, even if only to kill us.

"You look different," he says flatly. I haven't seen him in a month. I pretend I don't hear him and creep closer to Slate.

One of the others, a pale-haired man with ice-blue eyes offers me a kind smile and crosses the room to shake my hand. "Evan. It's nice to meet you, Lissa." Chancellor Evan. So this is Julian's uncle.

The youngest of the group is a dark-skinned, scrawny man, who looks to be in his twenties. He's the newest of the Chancellors. Abel, I think. I remember Chancellor Kole announcing it at a hanging a few months before Gage died.

It's funny how easily I can think of Gage's hanging now. But wasn't it his fault? He knew of Earth through the Jute, but he still wanted to see it himself. And in the end, his greed cost him his life.

"She *is* different," Slate speaks up. "Stronger, more beautiful, but still my daughter."

I flush when the four of them stare at me. And of course, Dena chooses that exact moment to saunter in.

"What's everyone staring at?" She asks loudly. She has a bowl of food in her hand and doesn't even glance at me before dropping into one of the chairs with a snort. "I bet Julian is finally getting some time to himself."

"It's only fair for us to meet the girl we're protecting, yes?" Abel says, ignoring her. His voice is scratchy and sharp. He winks and I'm grateful for his interruption.

"I agree," the brown-haired one says, reaching for my hand. His face is carefully neutral and I wish it wasn't. But I catch the slight disgust in the way he eyes the bare skin on my face where a mask should be. He doesn't know I haven't worn a mask since I started living here. "Chancellor Willem."

"It's nice to meet all of you," I say slowly, taking a small step back. Soldiers trickle in, laughing as they set the table. I feel vaguely smug that the Chancellors have to eat the same bland porridge I do, along with the rest of our dying race.

"We're not protecting her for nothing," Chancellor Kole says. I look away from his stare. "She'll return the favor. Eventually."

I sit beside Slate and reach for one of the bowls. I eat as quickly as I can, despite the one thing evident in the Chancellors' stares. Expectancy.

That's when I realize Slate is wrong. We do stand a chance against the Jute.

We just need to take it.

11

A HAND. ON MY SHOULDER.

My eyes fly open. My bed creaks as I dig my nails into soft flesh and twist the arm of—

"It's me," Julian rasps.

I let go and shoot up, the sheets a swirl around my legs. "I'm so sorry."

"Shh, it's fine." He rubs his arm, and in the soft moonlight, I see his eyes dart to my closed door. His stance is wrong, too nervous.

"What is it?"

"Shh," he says again, eyes wide. He rushes over to the door and presses his ear against it.

"They're here," he says in a worried whisper. My eyes widen. "The Jute. They're due tomorrow to pick up a body, but someone spotted them. They never come at night. Something's up."

I slide off the bed, but Julian shakes his head. "You have to stay here. I wanted you awake, just in case."

And he's gone.

The moment he leaves, I pull out my daggers and sheaths. I'm about to change out of my nightgown when the door opens.

Slate slips inside. Soft moonlight shines off his mask. Worry gnaws at my mind.

"Where's Julian? Is he okay?" I ask.

"He can take care of himself. We have to go. Now." He throws a package my way. I catch it. "I didn't see a point in giving you another set of daggers, so I got you something that will make you look like the warrior that you are."

I shake the dark material from the package onto the bed.

A black body suit slips out, it's stretchy and form fitting. There's a tunic too, it glints when I hold it up. Thin shiny scales, each one about the size of a small tooth line it, shimmering in the flickering light.

When Slate turns away, I slip into the body suit and hold my breath as I pull on the tunic, watching as the hem drops right at mid-length of my thighs. I slip into my boots, which reach up to my knees.

There's a hood and an extra ring of fabric around my neck, lined in even smaller scales, making it more flexible. It stretches when I pull it up.

It's a mask. It covers my mouth and my nose, ending beneath my eyes. To protect me from dust. I pull on the supple gloves and spread my arms, marveling at my armor.

"But I'm not a warrior," I whisper.

"You are mine," he says softly. He looks me up and down and hands me a belt. It's slotted with small knives, each one an inch apart. I strap it around my waist, but it's too big, made for a man like him, so it hangs lopsided around me.

I take a deep breath and look up at him when I'm done. He smiles warily. "Are you ready?"

"Never been more," I say. And I mean it. Because for once, I am. The familiar quaking of fear isn't there anymore.

The halls are lit only by the soft glow of the waning solar bulbs. We run, our footsteps light on the smooth floor. Him and me, father and daughter. Something shifts in my chest when I think of us that way.

Father and daughter.

He touches my wrist when we pause at the corner. I'm envious of his calmness. His every glance is calculated, measured. This is what a soldier is—a trained protector.

Gage taught me differently, that soldiers are dangerous, ruthless, heartless creatures with shells of bodies and zero souls. And yes, they can be that. But not to the ones they protect and love.

"Don't get distracted," Slate says. But he stops too. His eyes are soft in the dim light. Why couldn't I have had gray eyes like his? "What is it?"

"You love me," I say, as if the notion is impossible. My chest tightens.

He exhales and cradles my cheek with the palm of his hand, calloused and warm. "Of course I do. I've been loving you for seventeen years as my dead child. Why stop when you're alive?"

Footsteps sound down the end of the hall. He drops his hand to the shock gun at his waist and edges silently toward the sound. I hold my breath and follow.

The light brightens. There's a flash of white hair. A blur of dark. A thud.

And I bite back a gasp when a body falls to the ground.

"'Bout time, Slate," Dena drawls, wiping a wicked blade across the dead Jute. A machete. Dena carries an actual *machete*. It makes my dagger look like child's play. She assesses my outfit with a watchful eye and smirks.

He clears his throat and she raises an eyebrow at him. "Babysitting's over. You're needed elsewhere. I'll make sure your burden of love - or is that bundle of love? - doesn't get hurt."

"I don't need your protection," I say.

"If she gets hurt—" Slate starts. Dena rolls her eyes, cutting him off.

"Yeah, yeah. Here's the thing: she won't," she says. Her back stiffens and in that instant, she's a completely different person. She scans the area around us before fixing her dark gaze impatiently on Slate again. "Bye?"

He turns to leave and turns back, remembering something. Me. He tucks the hair that came loose from my messy braid behind my ear.

"Be careful," he breathes. "I can't lose you again." I part my lips. But before I can say a word, he pulls me close and presses his masked face to my forehead. And when I think of Father, I no longer see those wise brown eyes, so much like mine, I see gray, pale gray so unusual only one person can have them.

My arms are clenched as I lift them, and slowly, slowly wrap them around him. When one fist touches the other, I am complete. Inside, a gaping black hole is filled. Tears burn at the edge of my vision.

"I love you, Lissa." He pulls back. Gage never said those words to me.

I need Slate. I need to see his smile, hear his voice. I need him to be there for me the way Gage never was. My reply is there, on the edge of my lips.

"I love you too," I whisper, hesitant and soft. But it's too late, he's already gone.

Dena snorts after a moment. "So much for being able to protect yourself. Stop dreaming."

I turn with a sigh and walk past her, clenching my teeth when the sound of her laugh grates on my nerves.

And because of that, neither of us is prepared when four figures jump from either side of the intersecting hall.

"Now we're talking." In a flash, Dena's machete is in her hand, her back to me. I pull my daggers into either hand, an odd calm settling over me.

Dena and Gage were right—the Jute *are* all unnervingly beautiful. Enough to distract you. These men have silky scraps of cloth tied around their mouths and noses. Louen, I realize, to lessen the absorption of oxygen. Slate said Jute aren't harmed with one breath as humans are, but oxygen is dangerous nonetheless. Don't they realize the air in the Tower isn't oxygen? Maybe it's a precaution, maybe there's a way for the Chancellors to allow oxygen to work in here.

The Jute to my right lunges. He's fast, but I'm faster. I dart to the side as another Jute swipes a kick to my legs and I barely leap out of the way. I throw a kick at the burlier one, and when he bends over with a gasp, I whack the back of his head with the hilt of my dagger. He falls with a groan, temporarily unconscious.

A lean arm wraps around my neck. The Jute chuckles in my ear and drags me back. My heels drag helplessly along the smooth ground. I dig my nails into his flesh, but I'm nothing against his brute strength. He swiftly shoves me against the wall, pressing a blade against my back. He releases my neck and I gasp desperately for air.

"Only cowards… kill… from behind," I wheeze. He chuckles.

I gather as much strength as I can muster and shove him off me. Duck and swerve. I drop one dagger and use both hands to drive the length of my other one deep into his chest. Surprise flickers across his face, widens his gold eyes. There's a clatter as his knife drops to the ground. He sputters and drops to his knees, then onto his back. Blood trickles between his fingers clawing at his chest. I watch as the life slowly leaves his eyes.

His chest stops moving. His eyes stop seeing.

I sink to the ground. The dead Jute's white shirt is soaked in dark blood, more pouring from around the dagger still in him. The dagger with my name written on its hilt, like some disgusting joke.

I killed him. Who am I to take the life of another person? Julian taught me so much. But not this. Someone shuffles behind me. Dena struggles in front of me.

But I hear nothing. See nothing. Feel nothing.

I killed someone.

Sharp pain explodes in my back and I cry out. I'm thrown flat on my stomach and my limbs scream when an immovable weight collapses on me.

My chest heaves. I struggle to breathe. I don't have my daggers. One is by the wall feet away, the other in the body of a corpse. I try to wiggle free, but the pain only increases. The bones in my back crunch beneath what feels like a boot and my lips part in a silent scream. I hear the *swoosh* of an unsheathing blade.

"She may need you alive, but she didn't say all in one piece," the Jute hisses.

And he falls on me.

I

Can't

Breathe.

12

I WHEEZE AND COUGH. BREATHING FEELS like pushing a boulder with all my weight.

Dena laughs at me. I roll my head against the wall and look away.

"You're good for nothing," she says. I bite my lip against the angry, meaningless words waiting on my tongue.

I didn't ask her to save me. Then again, I would have died if it weren't for her. Died because a boulder of a Jute fell on me. I almost laugh.

"Are you done yet? I don't have time for this crap."

"Will you ever shut up?" I stand and rub the back of my hand along my ribs with a wince. I pick up my daggers. I'm grateful that she cleaned them, but I'm not ready to thank her for it.

"I'm not the one who expects half the human race to die for her." Her voice is bitter. She starts walking and I don't bother with a comeback.

I'm not that girl either.

I don't expect anyone to die for me.

But Earth. The Jute have a ship. And the only way to get it is by force.

I shake away the thoughts plaguing my conscience and follow her. This time, I keep my eyes peeled for Jute. The sooner we get out of the Tower, the better. It doesn't help that my room was on a higher floor.

"It's too quiet," Dena says after a moment. She narrows her eyes at me and I have to pause, because she rarely ever looks me in the eye. "Run."

I don't need to be told twice. We run side by side down the hall, our boots squeaking on the glistening floor. We run as if we're a team, when really, I'm sure Dena would kill me herself if she could.

I skid to a stop, my boots squealing before I slam into the person standing in my path. My hand instinctively tightens around a dagger. But Dena smirks and tosses her head, so her hair falls perfectly over her right eye.

I recognize Julian right away. He turns away from his companion to face me, his eyes wide in surprise. Dena crosses her arms.

"Dena, Lissa, what are you doing here?" There's a nervous jerk to his words.

"What-" I start, but words fail me.

Because past Julian, is a man not much older than me. He's dark-haired, a black knee-length coat swathing his figure, with skin a pale contrast to his clothes. His lips twist into an arrogant, amused smirk.

Rowan. The Jute whose voice was so much like Julian's. He looked familiar because he *is* familiar.

When I meet his eyes, I can't stop my lips from parting.

Brilliant, beautiful, shimmering blue.

He's an exact replica, a slightly *darker* replica, of Julian.

My heart hammers in my chest. My gaze flickers to Julian. He reads my eyes as easily as I can read the helplessness in his. And before I have a chance to react, he dives. His body crashes against mine.

And the wall swallows us whole.

I realize two things when the impact of my fall on the soft carpet racks my bones.

One. The Tower only seemed to have a solid post in its center, marked with vertical lines. Every vertical line is actually an opening to this round room, so that the room is surrounded by doors. Doors that are hidden, keeping the room hidden and safe. In the event of an escape, like now, one can simply disappear into the wall.

Two. Julian's full weight is on me. His right knee is between my legs, his left is beside my thigh. His arms are around my stomach. My body is on fire.

If freedom had a scent, it would be his. It reminds me of my nights on the hill, my run in the crophouses.

His ragged breath tickles my neck and I meet his eyes, struggling not to get lost in the depthless blue.

In this moment, nothing exists but him. Us. I hold his gaze, and through the edge of my eyes, I see his tongue slide across his lower lip. I don't look. I don't let my eyes falls to his lips because I'm afraid of the quiver that will slide across my own.

He exhales and moves away, quickly slamming his fist against a flat button on the wall, which I'm guessing will lock the door. The buzzing in my body fades to a faint hum. But I tremble, everything else temporarily forgotten as I yearn for his touch. He must have felt the same way.

He must have.

He runs his fingers through his hair and clenches his jaw.

I sit up and cross my legs as the anger rushes back. I trusted him with everything. Yet he couldn't trust me enough to tell me?

"Who's Rowan?"

He knows I saw the resemblance between them.

"I-I," he begins to say, and stops himself. He runs his hands down his face and his lips press into one line. "My brother."

Brother. Confusion replaces my anger.

I can only associate Rowan with evil. But Julian, despite his dark looks and rare smiles, I know he's good inside.

He's quiet, waiting for my reaction, but when I don't speak, he does. "He says he's here for the body, but he rarely comes."

I stand because the anger pumping through my veins will make me say something I'll regret. He rises to his feet just as fast.

"Why are you changing the subject? Do you work for the Queen too? As a spy?"

With each of my questions, I see him shrink back. His eyes freeze in pain. I bite my lip, and it takes everything in my power not to look away.

"No. I don't work for her. I never will. And"—he pauses—"even if wanted to, I can't."

My eyes narrow to slits. "Why not?"

His eyes fall to the floor. "I'm a half-breed. I'm worth nothing in the eyes of anyone. To the Jute, I'm lower than a servant, even lower than a human. Rowan and I are half-brothers and he's Jute, through and through."

His words hold no emotion, but I finally understand why he never spoke about our differences. Because despite us both being half-human, we're at opposite ends of the Jute spectrum—he's useless, I'm prized.

He is nothing, and I am everything.

Silence falls. The space between our bodies is feet. The space between our minds is leagues.

The walls rattle and shouts echo on the other side, breaking Julian's daze and my thoughts.

He looks up, and I see the fearlessness he tried to instill in me. He angles his face back to me, like he did in the Chamber and in the crophouses months before.

"You need to get out of here," he says.

"Where would I go?" I ask. My anger is giving way to panic.

"Julian!" The voice that vibrates through the wall sounds so much like Julian's that I jump.

His eyes widen a fraction and words fall out in a rush.

"Leave through that door, go down the flight of stairs. Take the first door on the right and keep going until you reach the outside. And go straight to Slate's house."

"Can't you come with me?" I ask. My eyes flicker to the wall rattling beneath Rowan's pounding fists. Julian shakes his head.

"Rowan is mad. He has a notion that includes you and I need to make sure he doesn't follow you. We need you to be safe. *I* need you to be safe."

"Okay," I say softly, and turn away from the pain in his eyes before it makes me stay. *They're brothers*, I tell myself. I stumble through the door and into darkness.

Light and dark should have no weight, but now, this impenetrable darkness does. I feel as though I'm trudging through water. I've never stood in so much water before—there isn't enough for that on Jutaire. But I've lived through books for so many years, and to me, that counts as experience.

A small part of me is trying to reason. Darkness is simply that. Darkness is massless.

But I can't breathe. Sweat trickles down my skin and for a heartbeat, I imagine fingers trailing down my back. I shudder when Rowan's face flickers in my mind. Julian's brother. Rowan is mad. Rowan wants me.

I swallow the scream building in my chest and run, blindly feeling against the walls and stumbling on my own feet.

Until a hand clamps around my mouth.

"Don't say a word, girly," Dena breathes in my ear. "They're all over the place."

I nod quickly against her and she lets go. I can only see the whites of her eyes. She laughs, low and dark. "They have no idea how easy you are to catch."

I don't have the time or the mind for her bickering. Brother or not, Julian could be risking his life.

"Come on," she says quickly, and I wonder if she had the same thought I just did.

I don't need to relay Julian's instructions to her, and I'm ashamed at the relief I feel because I'm not completely alone.

We find the flight of stairs in silence. Dena slips in behind me and eases the door closed.

Just as another door slams further down.

The stairwell explodes with light and a shock blast flies toward us.

"Oh, crap," Dena shouts, whipping out her machete. She presses her back against the wall and I do the same on the opposite side. As soon as the blast hits the door inches away from us, everything goes quiet.

"We need to make it to the corner," she whispers. I follow her gaze down to where the stairs change direction. It's a blind spot.

I nod and rush down the stairs.

Right when a Jute rushes up.

I see my dagger digging into his chest. His heart ceasing to beat. His life. Gone. The Jute from earlier, in the hall.

And I. Can't. Move.

The Jute's eyes lock on mine, and I realize it's a woman. Her hair is a deep shade of gold, and her eyes are slanted teardrops, in a beautiful shade of brown. She's gorgeous.

Her beauty shatters when her lips twist into a snarl, but I still can't move. I can't imagine her heart unbeating because of me. Muttering a curse, Dena rushes past me and swings her machete. The Jute's sword connects with hers in a reverberating clang. It echoes in the enclosed space, and I suck in a breath and throw a glance behind us, but we're alone. For now.

I hear a soft cry and turn as the Jute sinks to the ground, clawing at her neck as deep red stains her flawless skin. Dena steps over her before she even dies.

I swallow and carefully step around the body, keeping my eyes on the gray wall. It's like me. Helplessly witnessing death and grief in bitter silence.

"Stop dreaming. We need to work together if we're going to get through this alive. I know you're all that matters, but I kinda want to live a little longer." She sounds tired, and when she glances at me, I'm taken aback when she meets my eyes again.

"What happened back there anyway?"

She sounds genuinely curious, and I'm genuinely dumbstruck.

Maybe she's giving me a chance, and maybe I need to give her one too.

"I- when I see them, I can't help but think about who they are. If they have children who'll be parentless, mothers who'll be childless, spouses who'll be widows or widowers." I force air through my nose. "And I can't do it."

Dena doesn't answer. I'm so used to her unnecessary jibes that her silence is unexpected.

"I used to think the same way until they murdered my mom," she says finally, her voice quieter, more thoughtful, than usual. "But they deserve everything they get. No one forces them to do all this pointless killing. I stopped caring about who they *were*, and started looking at them as who they had *become*."

She bites her lip. "Right. Sob fest's over. Let's go. I'm betting they're waiting for us somewhere."

Dena struck me as someone who lives in the moment, who doesn't care about anyone but herself. But maybe she's broken inside, like so many of us are.

At the corner where the stairwell turns again, she peeks over the wall with a frown. "Clear."

The pattering of our boots on the concrete echoes along the close walls.

At the bottom of the stairs, feet away from the door, Dena drops to her knees with a sigh and leans against the short ledge on the side, resting to adjust her mask.

And that's when I see the Jute behind her.

He raises a knife to Dena's neck. Her eyes widen, but she's otherwise still. She doesn't even struggle. She stares at me, breathing carefully neutral. Fresh sweat breaks out along my hairline and my heart beats faster.

"Don't want your bestie to die now, do we?" The Jute asks in a throaty voice, the pale brown silk around his face puffs with his words.

Breathe, I remind myself. I slowly reach for one of the small knives around my waist. My heart thuds and it takes me a moment to realize I'm afraid. I haven't felt afraid in so long, the feeling is almost foreign.

But I'm not afraid for myself or for Dena. But for the Jute.

He presses the blade harder against her soft flesh and chuckles. And before I can think, I pull back my arm and throw. The tiny blade disappears into his flesh.

"No," I say, standing as he drops to his knees. He chokes and sputters and his knife clatters to the floor. "We don't."

Dena grabs the doorknob without a word. I look back up the stairwell, adrenaline still pumping through my veins, but it's empty.

Dena turns the knob and pauses, glancing back at me, almost shyly, unable to meet my eyes. "Thanks."

Surprise steals my ability to speak. Dena *thanked* me.

The world around us is eerily quiet when we step into the early morning light. The red ground is so much different than the pristine white floors I've come to know so well. I haven't set foot outside the Tower since I ran from

Rowan all those weeks ago. I'm sickened by the thought of my cowardice and fear.

I lift my eyes. And see them first.

Jute, covered from head to toe in black to protect themselves from the dusty, gritty wind.

There are guns in their hands, each of them pointed straight at us.

I throw up my arm to stop Dena. She shouts.

I drop to the floor and roll towards the wall of the house to our left. Their shouts are immediate. And so is the gunfire. Real, actual gunfire.

And Dena falls as a bullet rips into her.

13

I READ SOMEWHERE THAT ON EARTH, TWO people died every second. When humans came to Jutaire, they lost track of time, but I'm certain one second is nearly equivalent to two heartbeats.

Which meant that for every heartbeat, there was one death. One heart ceased to beat while the rest went on, unfazed. Likewise, for every two heartbeats, four new souls entered their perfect world.

It's fascinating how much death touched the lives of those on Earth. Death was everywhere, occurred with every breath of their lives, yet they found a way to be happy, to thrive. Death isn't as constant here on Jutaire, though with only so many of us left, one death a week is enough.

Too much.

Today, so many Jute die because I kill them all. My hands are a blur as I throw the small knives, one after the other. They won't hurt me because they need me alive.

I'm terrified. Because as the Jute fall, I feel nothing. Not even an ounce of pity for the lives I take.

Dena moans in the sudden silence. I rush to her side when I'm certain all the Jute have fallen. And I realize they only differentiated between us because of her mask. The mask that is supposed to save her life nearly killed her.

Her head lolls over to face me and her dark eyes are wild. "They have guns. Real ones."

She sounds like a child.

"They did." I meet her eyes briefly and unbutton her tight jacket. I pull her sleeveless shirt back to the hollow beneath her shoulder. My breath catches at the sticky mess of blood.

"I've always"—she gasps—"wanted a real gun."

"I didn't know," I say quickly. My eyes burn at the innocence in her voice. She's nothing like the girl who grated on my nerves.

"I'm dying, aren't I?" She wheezes. "You killed them all, didn't you?"

"No. And yes" I press my fingers against her wound and she gasps. The bullet needs to come out.

I need to take it out.

"The bullet—"

"Shh, I know." I take a deep breath and before I can rethink my decision, I press my fingers into her ripped flesh. My fingers squelch and my insides scream. She cries out, her body arching in pain, and I want to get away. Far, far away. Run to my dark home and hide away.

But those are the thoughts of the old Lissa. The meek girl who faded away in the span of a month.

My fingers close around the stub of metal and I pull it out as Dena's cries ring in my ears.

A shadow falls over me and I reach for my dagger with bloody hands.

"It's me," Julian says. He crouches down beside me, his eyes frantic. "You're supposed to be at Slate's house."

"Dena—"

"I'll take care of Dena. Go. Now." His voice rises with every word. My blood runs cold at the fear coating his voice. Because Julian is never this afraid, and somehow, I'm certain his fear has nothing to do with Rowan. They *are* brothers, after all.

"I don't even know where his house is."

"The second road, seventh house on the left." He answers without pause, taking a satchel of water from the pack slung over his back. Dena hisses as he douses the wound, but she stays still.

I envy her strength, her calm. Maybe I'm still not strong enough. Maybe I'll always be the girl Gage wanted trade over like a shiny object.

"This is worse than I thought," Julian says softly and turns to me. For a moment, I think he means Dena's bullet wound. "We don't have much time."

He snorts softly, contradicting his words with a sideways smile. I swallow. Julian never knows when to smile, but when he does, it's like Earth. He reaches for my face tentatively and I hold my breath as he brushes away my stray hair with the back of his cool fingers. He whispers something softly, a strange look on his face.

I stumble to my feet, and pry my eyes from his. I yank one of the guns from the fallen Jute, for Dena, and collect my bloody knives, tucking them back into my belt.

And I run, letting the morning air cool my burning cheeks. I hear his whispered words, like feathers brushing against the edges of my mind, threatening to fade away.

But I can't believe I wanted to die.

But Julian also said to run. I'll think of what he meant later. I slip the gun into my boot and turn onto Slate's road.

I count the houses as I go. My heart beats faster the closer I get, as if it knows something I do not. I wipe away the sweat collecting above my lip.

At the sixth house, I stop.

A carriage stands off to the side, the entire structure elaborate, with inhuman elegance.

My lips part when I look to Slate's house.

There, in the midst of Jute soldiers swathed in the night sky, about to enter Slate's house, is a woman.

A navy robe wraps her slender form. A crown of white sits atop her head. Her stark red lips curve into a sly smile. And her eyes shine like the moon. The portrait doesn't do her justice.

Queen Rhea.

14

"WELL. WELL. NOW THIS IS CONVENIENT," the Queen laughs, light and airy. Carefully perfected. "Very, very convenient. Don't you agree, Wren?"

She slides her gaze to one of the soldiers beside her. His Adam's apple bobs as he swallows and his eyes frantically dart about. He's the only one out of place in the calm group. "Y-yes, your majesty."

She smirks and turns her attention back to me. Her beauty is strong and her heart is dark. This I can tell by her gaze alone.

"Do you know who I am, girl?" Her voice is powerful. I don't answer. But the smart part of my mind forces my gaze down, as one should do to respect a queen. I read that somewhere once.

"Are you mute, Lissa?" I flinch at her sharp tone. And my name. She knows my name. Gage told them everything.

"No." Why my voice is a frail whisper, I do not know.

"No, you're not mute." She lifts her chin as I lift my eyes. "So I will ask you again. Do you know who I am?"

"The Queen. Queen Rhea." My voice falters. Weak, that is all I am. "o-of the Jute."

"One would be a fool not to know that," she says dismissively. I look up in confusion and meet her unnatural eyes.

"Oh, darling girl, you look lost." She comes closer, her dark robe snagging on every little rock. But if she's anything like the wasteful royalty I've read about, she won't even wear the robe again.

Her beauty is like Julian's, mesmerizing, tantalizing. Depreciating and she knows it.

She's close enough for me to see her unnaturally smooth skin—so smooth it's almost frightful—and the exact point where her ink black hair pierces her scalp, and to tell we are nearly the same height.

She extends her hand, dazzling rings glinting off her fingers. My breath trembles. I swallow. I'm afraid of an unarmed woman.

She rubs a lock of my dusty hair between her fingers and smiles. The kind of smile Gage said a cat would give a mouse on Earth. She utters three words.

And I wish I had never wanted to know.

"I'm your mother."

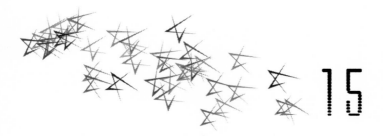

15

THE GROUND SWAYS. OR I DO.

Warm hands grip my shoulders and I look up, only mildly surprised to find my face inches away from Julian's. He's always there when I need him. As if he knows. Maybe he does. There is so much surreality in my life right now, that wouldn't be a surprise.

The Queen laughs and clasps her hands together. How many times had I imagined my mother's laugh?

"The gang's all here," she coos. "This is perfect, just perfect."

I turn and my heart sinks to the dark pit of my stomach. Slate, Dena, and Chancellor Kole are here too.

"Rhea," Slate hisses. His eyes are livid, the pale gray as dark as a stormy sky, his hands are clenched and a vein bulges in his neck. There is no love in his eyes now, no conflicting emotions. Only pure anger. Tears sting at the edges of my eyes—they're my parents.

"Did you ever think our darling daughter would live, Slate? No. The moment you saw her blue body, you assumed. You were always too... *human*. Emotional and naïve."

"I'm surprised Gage never said a word all these years," she adds flatly.

"You knew," Slate thunders, rushing forward. Chancellor Kole holds him back. Behind the Queen, the soldiers shift their weapons.

"Oh, yes," she says, unfazed by his anger. "Gage was a very smart man."

"Why keep it from him?" Julian asks, curiously. My heart skips a beat when the Queen narrows her eyes at him, her gaze darting to his hands on my shoulders.

"I know you," she muses. "You're the suicidal half-breed. The brother Rowan is always jabbering pointlessly about." She says *suicidal half-breed* as if it's a disease.

His hands slowly tighten around my shoulders and his breathing quickens. Could he have known the Queen was here when he was tending to Dena? Is that why he was so afraid?

"I have a job for you, half-breed. A way to make yourself useful to your society, wherever it is you belong." She adds the last part with a laugh and slides closer to him, closer to me. "Will you tend to my darling princess and protect her with your life? She is, after all, your future queen." Her question isn't a question. It's a threat. An order.

Princess. Me. I realize what she's doing. Where this is going.

Where *I* will be going.

"Julian, isn't it? It's time you're treated as the slave you were born as," she says smugly. His hands freeze.

Her moonlight eyes are cold and calculating. Waiting.

"I will serve her, my Queen," he says finally. His voice is flat with barely controlled anger.

"It's settled then. You, dear daughter, will be coming with me. It is finally time for you to take your place. You belong at White Plains, not here in this wretched wasteland." Her face twists in disgust.

My lips are dry. My mother is the Queen of the Jute. The Queen who wants me so she can get to Earth. I want to turn and run.

Julian said she doesn't know why she needs me, but it can't be for an heir. And she has the upper hand here, so why lie?

"You won't take her," Slate growls, coming closer. I had almost forgotten he was there. I rub my arms at his dangerous tone.

The Queen's eyes narrow to slits. "I can't take my own daughter? Is that what you're suggesting, Slate?"

"Don't call her your daughter," he spits. No one holds him back this time. The Jute soldiers drift forward like creeping shadows. "You didn't give birth to an heir. You wanted a tool. A way to get to—"

He stops. His eyes widen. "You-Gage-Both of you... you knew all along. You-you used me."

"Oh, it was fun, Slate. But the wait has taken forever." Slate has gone still. Very still. "How did you think Gage tested her blood? Where did you think he found the equipment? He was very loyal until he broke into the Chamber."

Slate pales. And I feel the blood drain from my own face. I trusted Gage with my every breath.

She laughs seductively, denying nothing. "Darling Slate, you still are dashingly handsome. And still so young." She cups her arms around his head and runs her fingers through his hair. He jerks away and storms to my side.

I stare in surprise when he shoves Julian away. Anger rages in his eyes. Shame darkens his cheeks. Fury shakes his frame.

"She's coming with me, Slate," the Queen hisses.

"No, Rhea, she isn't." His voice is low.

"Do you dare contradict me?" The wind howls in the sudden silence. No one breathes.

"Yes." His reply is firm because he doesn't care for himself. She steps forward, her soldiers mirroring her.

"No!" I cry out. Every eye turns to me. One month ago, I would have flushed and moved away in fear.

Not now.

"I'll come with you," I say hesitantly, "if you promise not to harm anyone."

Not that I have a choice. She will take me no matter what. She will take me without hurting me, hurting instead those I love.

"Now that's a good girl," she purrs. But her eyes are ablaze. No one barters with a queen.

"Do we have a deal?" I don't move. I find strength in the power of my voice. She purses her lips and her eyes flash before she hides her emotion behind another fake smile that sets my blood on fire.

"Of course we do, darling."

I exhale and close my eyes for the briefest of moments.

"Now come. I won't harm anyone." She turns with a swish of her robe and trails toward the door as a trio of soldiers slides closer to me. "But you aren't coming alone."

"Just me, or no one," I call and clamp my mouth shut. She turns, the air suddenly frigid. I suppress a shiver.

"Darling, you can most definitely come alone," she says sweetly. I release my breath and she smiles. "As long as the others die."

"No," I breathe, my legs weak.

"Exactly what I thought."

"Do you want to die?" Slate asks me, the moment she steps into the house.

"I don't want *you* to." My voice is just as hard.

"This isn't about me. I don't know what Gage told them. I don't know what they'll do to you." With each sentence his voice gets more desperate.

"There's only one way to find out," I say. "I won't watch them kill you and everyone else. They'll take me anyway. You heard her."

"I was about to say the same thing," Chancellor Kole interjects. Slate shoots him a deadly glare and wraps his fingers protectively around my arm. Chancellor Kole raises his hands in surrender. "I'm leaving, I'm leaving."

"Your Majesty," someone says. I freeze and turn, but the Queen is nowhere to be seen.

Instead, one of the three soldiers who stayed behind strides forward. He drops his hood and bows low, his brown eyes fixed on the floor.

Your Majesty. Me.

"You must accompany me to the carriage," he says. His careful monotone is jittery. Wren.

I raise my chin. "Who else?"

He doesn't acknowledge me, and I wonder if he didn't hear me. But after a silence, he speaks. "The half-breed, the old man and the platinum-haired girl."

Slate's fingers tighten around my arm. I betray nothing.

"We'll be there in a moment." I glance at the other soldiers behind him. "Can they leave?"

His eyes dart to mine. I inhale sharply as a shadow of a smile crosses his lips. He's as gorgeous as all the other Jute I've seen. He bows. "Yes, Your Majesty."

They disappear into the house and I wonder if they've cleared Slate's home of oxygen. But I don't really care.

The Queen will probably send her soldiers back outside as soon as she realizes we're alone, so I hasten to make use of our time.

"That was impressive," Dena says with a raise of her eyebrows. There's a wary shadow in her eyes. Her face is even paler from the loss of blood. She leans against her father and her shoulder is wrapped in dirty white cloth.

I guess I should feel proud. Dena's *complimenting* me. But I feel numb. My mother is alive. My mother is the Queen of the Jute.

I feel like screaming.

"Thanks to you and your mess of a child, I'm going to die," Chancellor Kole growls.

"You knew the end when you got yourself into this mess," Slate hisses back. Their voices drop to a whisper and Dena joins in.

Julian stands off to the side, lost in thought. I drift toward him.

"What if you don't come back?" I turn at the sound of Slate's pained voice.

"Gage might have been ready to hand me over," I say. "But when he was Galileo, he taught me to hope. That nothing keeps us alive but hope. And as long you hope, I'll live."

A small smile flits across his face, but he shakes his head. "You don't know Rhea."

"I will soon," I say. "And once we figure out why I'm needed, I won't let her use me."

"Those are your words. Your actions-"

"Stop." Because if I hear his doubts and worries, they will become mine.

"You said I'm your warrior," I say softly, amending my interruption. He stares at me for one long moment. The wind whistles in the silence and a door slams shut somewhere. Life goes on and on, and always will, whether we want it to or not.

"You are," he whispers, drawing me close. In my heart is a voice, sad and soft. It says I won't see him again for a very long time. His fingers trail through my hair, soft and loving. My father. If not for the mask plastered against his face, I am sure he would kiss my forehead, as he's tried so many times.

"I've known Julian longer than I've known you. Trust him," he whispers. I lean away and meet his eyes. "Do you understand?"

"Yes," I whisper.

"Lissa," Julian says suddenly. I break free from Slate's embrace as the Queen steps out of the house. Her gaze slowly flickers between us. She saw his arms around me. His fingers that trailed through my hair.

And from what little I know of her, I can tell her thoughtful silence isn't normal. Without a word, she turns and leaves.

Somehow, her silence is more frightening than if she had spoken.

16

SLATE AND THE OTHERS MAKE THEIR WAY into his house, to keep an eye on the Queen and her soldiers, though they're obviously powerless against armed Jute. They're weakened by their dependence on oxygen, and forever will be.

I stay outside, needing the freedom despite the gradually increasing heat. It penetrates the sparkling scales on my clothes and layers itself on my skin. Some ways ahead, a few soldiers are busy readying the carriage for the trip to White Plains. Where it is, I don't know.

The houses around us are silent, and I wonder if everyone is at the market now, or still asleep. I never knew anyone well, but now, I feel even more like a stranger, foreign to the rows and rows of homes.

A shadow falls to my right and my pulse instantly quickens. I turn my head to acknowledge the Queen's presence.

"Did you ever want to know your mother?" She asks. The thoughtfulness is still on her face, softening her features. Making her seem human.

It's hard not to fall for the innocence in her voice. But then I see the pain in Slate's eyes, the anger. He was used. I'm a tool. I keep my voice carefully neutral. "I might have."

Her expression remains the same. And I can't help but wonder if it's all an act.

"You have my skin. My lips. Slate's nose and hair. Gage's eyes, Slate's mother's eyes."

I press my lips together. I don't want her to speak of Slate and his mother. I don't want to hear Gage's name from her lips. I stare ahead, where the soldiers rush.

"I carried you inside me, for—"

I whirl around. Her face wavers through my stupid tears. "Why are you telling me this?"

"What wrong have I done?" She asks. I hear a hint of her normal, heady self.

"I don't know or care what you've done, but it's what you *will* do." My voice is hushed. Angry. I should stay silent.

"I won't do anything to you," she says tonelessly. "All I want is my heir. And that, unfortunately, is you." She leaves, striding towards the men readying the carriage.

What if it isn't an act? Maybe all she really wants is an heir. A daughter.

"Don't trust her."

But it isn't my conscience that speaks. Julian comes closer, squinting up at the sun. The early rays cast a warm glow across his features. "She doesn't need an heir. She's going to Earth, remember? She needs you for that. Nothing else."

"I didn't trust her," I say, stubbornly.

A flicker of a smile shadows his face. "You did. I could see it on your face."

He laughs softly when heat creeps up my cheeks. Wren steps away from the carriage and smiles warily at me.

"You may board now," he says, throwing a nervous glance towards Slate's house behind me.

The Queen steps out. "'Your Highness', you wanted to add, dear Wren." Her voice drips with sweet poison.

"Eh, yes, Your Majesty," he amends quickly, looking at her feet. He turns to me again. His voice trembles. "You may board now, Your Highness."

He bows and I feel sorry for him, pity even, that he is treated this way after all his diligence. The Queen watches me, gauging my reaction as Wren hurries away.

"After you, darling." She sweeps her hand toward the carriage. The words *thank you* rise to my lips, but I press them closed. I have nothing to thank her for.

Dena and Chancellor Kole step out of the house, Slate behind them. He holds my gaze, and I resist the painful urge to run to him. I've lived without him for seventeen years, feared him for three days, and now, I want him, my real, true father, by my side every breath of my life.

When he doesn't move any closer, I don't either. And I think it is safer that way.

I feel his eyes on me as I walk toward the carriage. No one moves, not even the Queen.

Two soldiers stand on either side of the back end, holding open the raw fabric. It shimmers in the sun, ripples like waves, like my tunic, though unlike my black clothes, this is a beautiful shade between beige and cream.

I ascend the trio of steps. Inside, the carriage reminds me of a truck, where people on Earth would load furniture and the like through the back. Only, there isn't a vehicle at the other end, there are four mutants. Translucent, pitiful excuses for horses. I turn away in disgust.

The carriage itself is more exquisite. Long, with plush extravagant seats running along either side. It's cooler, too. And despite its size, I shiver at how close we will all be to the Queen.

My mother.

I try not to think of her as that.

The floor is covered in rich velvet. Vain. The largest and seemingly comfiest seat is at the front, where the Queen will most likely sit. I run my hand along the fabric draped over the arching skeleton of the carriage. It's smooth and cool to the touch, confirming my suspicion— Louen.

It's funny how many benefits Louen offers. For human masks, to hold in oxygen and keep out Jutaire's air. For Jute protection, to reduce the absorption of oxygen.

I sink into one of the center seats as Julian climbs aboard. He doesn't even spare a glance at the grandeur surrounding us before crossing the expanse to sit beside me.

"Are you alright?" He asks me.

I nod and smile at his concern, at the reminder of the many times he has asked me that question, once before I even knew him.

His eyes are distant. He leans forward and rakes his fingers through his hair. I'm close enough to reach for his fingers and stop them. But I'm afraid to. The girl, who discovered she's the daughter of an evil queen and single-handedly killed a small army of Jute, is afraid to calm a boy.

Slate said to trust him, and I do. Somewhat. Gage said trust is earned, and once shattered, it can never be earned again. It was ironic of him to say that. But this is what I'm afraid of. Not of trusting Julian, but of never being able to trust him *again* if something happens.

Dena enters the carriage and Julian sits back. She frowns as she drinks in the lavishness around us and I don't miss the light that touches her eyes when she sees Julian.

"Thanks to you, I'll never come back," she says to me, dropping into the seat to Julian's right.

"You might," I say, remembering the gun in my boot. But I don't reach for it now. She raises an eyebrow at me. I lean back into my seat and close my eyes as she and Julian share a look.

"There are some things a person knows," she says softly to him.

"A person also knows to hope," Julian replies. And I wonder if he only says that because I did, or because he genuinely wants to comfort Dena.

And I wonder if he actually believes in what he says.

Dena snorts.

The drapes swish and Queen Rhea enters, her head held high. She crosses the carriage in slow strides. The air turns frigid the heartbeat she sits. Chancellor Kole slips in quietly, his tall frame louder than words in the enclosed space.

"We will be there soon, daughter," says my mother. She smirks at Julian and ignores Dena and Chancellor Kole. I glance at them, father and daughter.

I wonder if they both expect to die at White Plains. I wonder if they've spoken to one another of their deaths. All Chancellor Kole wants is to protect his daughter. Would he die for her safety?

In that way, he isn't much different than Slate. I shove the thought away.

The soldiers file in. Their tired, wary eyes are trained on the velvet as they take their seats.

A gray-haired Jute takes his seat by the queen. When she nods, he clucks his tongue and snaps the reins.

And we're off.

My heart jolts with my body. We're leaving, leaving the home I've known forever. I crane my neck around Julian to catch a glimpse of the outside when the Louen fabric flutters.

I expect to see Slate. Instead, there's a girl, not much older than ten. Her big round eyes stare in awe as the distance increases between us.

Every human will know of this by midday.

I wonder if Slate is watching the carriage, his eyes casting a storm. A soft touch on the back of my hand startles me and I sit back. Julian's forehead crinkles in concern and I want to reach up and smooth away his worry. *You won't be alone*, his expression seems to say, and something inside me catapults at the unspoken words. His fingers slide along the seat and close around mine. My heart explodes at the simple touch.

He looks away then, his face suddenly blank. My heart thuds a cacophony in my chest, thrumming all the way to my fingers.

Slowly, slowly, slowly, I turn my head. The Queen's moonlight eyes rest on our hands and her lips twist into a sly smile.

Nothing is worse than the chill creeping up my spine.

I don't know what time it is, though it's still light outside. One of the soldiers sealed the entrance flap shut. On the other end, I see the rears of the mutants. Through the gaps between them, I can see the ground punctuated by towering boulders. Some are double my height, others are smaller.

I shiver when the wind howls. It sounds like it's crying. For me.

With every heartbeat that passes, I feel more and more worried. I've never seen a Jute before this week, and now I'm going to the heart of their territory.

To the Queen's palace or wherever, no less.

Chancellor Kole snores softly. Dena watches Julian, her expression distant. And I wonder, despite Julian not loving Dena, if *she* loves him. Gage never spoke to me of love. In fact, when it came to being human, he spoke of nothing. It was always science, history, literature.

I know how to describe love, but I don't know how to feel it. But when I look at Slate, at the life in his eyes and the warmth of his smile, I feel something. Something that must be love. When I think of Julian, his dark looks, intense eyes, and genuine concern, I feel something too. It isn't the same as what I feel for Slate. But it is something. Something that sends exhilaration shivering through me. But I don't know how *he* feels.

If only I could read him as easily as everyone can read me.

17

THE CARRIAGE WHEELS SQUEAL TO A STOP, and my heart catapults to my lips. But when no one makes a move to leave, I know we haven't reached our destination yet.

The white-haired soldier turns and bows his head to the Queen. "Rain is coming, Your Majesty."

Sure enough, the scent of acid fills the carriage, stinging my nostrils and eyes.

"Have we covered much ground?" The Queen asks immediately.

"Half, more or less," he says with a pondering twist of his lips. "We're likely in the middle right now."

Rain. In the middle of nowhere. Bloody images flicker through my mind.

"We should be fine," Julian says under his breath. He frowns. "The fabric is pure Louen. It's the only material on Jutaire resistant to the rain."

"Then why-" I start.

"The mutants," Dena whispers.

"Someone needs to shield the horses," Queen Rhea's voice shatters my thoughts. I would snort at her use of the word *horses*, but my mind is reeling from the reality of her words.

Not all of us will make it to White Plains.

She looks at Dena with a smirk. Her every movement is deliberately slow, so not a single twitch goes unnoticed. Her eyes slide to Julian.

My throat tightens. *No.* I beg silently. Please no.

Her eyes flicker to mine and she holds my gaze. When she looks away from me, Julian whispers. "She's lying. No one needs to shield the mutants, rain doesn't affect them."

"It's a setup," Dena says as it dawns.

When the Queen turns her face to one of her soldiers, everything falls into place. This is my mother's way of showing me her power.

"Wren," she says sweetly. "Do you volunteer?"

He shoots to his feet, gripping the curving rod of the carriage for support. His knuckles are white, and his face is bloodless in fear.

He is the one who committed the harmless blunder earlier, who gave me time to speak with Slate and say my good-byes.

And because of that, he will die. Not a simple death. Nothing close to a hanging or even a slit to his throat. He will bleed beneath the open skies, his skin will tear under the pelting rain. He will suffer.

And no one will mourn him.

"Well?" Queen Rhea asks.

"I- my Queen, I have children," he begs. His voice breaks under the weight of his need to live. But his show of weakness in front of strangers is what undoes me. "Please spare me."

My legs twitch. My hands tremble. I don't know what's wrong with me. But any moment I will spring. My hands will wrap around her throat and I will strangle her. This woman who gave birth to me.

Julian's fingers tighten around my wrist.

"Don't," he whispers by my ear. "Just stay still. She *wants* you to act."

"Will your children die without you?" Queen Rhea raises one eyebrow. I certainly didn't die without her. "With the provisions they receive from me, they have enough to feed an entire neighborhood."

"That's not what I meant, Your Majesty," he stammers. "I can't leave them fatherless. Their mother is dead."

How can a mother be so cruel?

"You are of no benefit to them. As you are of no benefit to me."

Her words are final. She turns away as if she can't stand to see him any longer. A thin soldier rifles through a chest beneath his seat and brings out a sheet of the same light brown Louen lining the carriage.

Wren takes it with trembling hands. If Julian knows the mutants can survive, then surely he knows too. And if he knows that, he knows there's no point in fighting back.

We're in the middle of nowhere.

One shove and he'll be stranded. The rain will consume him.

But the rain hasn't begun yet.

A sudden spark of hope catches within me. If the mutants don't need the Louen, they don't need Wren. He can protect himself, save himself. And if he steps out now, he has enough time to shield himself before the rain begins.

But will he?

He stands hopelessly in the center of the carriage. His face is puckered, holding back tears. He draws in a shaky breath and turns.

"Wait." One word is all she says. It's like a clap of thunder in my ears.

"Not yet."

The carriage starts moving again. The rumble of its wheels along the rocky ground fills in the silence.

The acidic stench strengthens. It will pour any moment now. Why isn't the Queen letting him go? Why isn't he outside, protecting the mutants as she says we need to? My confusion must be evident on my face for Queen Rhea laughs.

"All in good time, daughter."

I hear the first drop. Like a blinding revelation in stark darkness. I hear the second drop. And suddenly, the rain is pouring. Thundering over my head in a cacophony of torrents.

"Ilen." My mother's sweet voice breaks through the rain.

The thin soldier stands, his face crumpled. He turns to Wren, who stands in front of the entrance, his eyes widening in realization when I realize it too.

Ilen shoves him. There isn't time to unfold the Louen. No time for protection. A heartbeat is all you need beneath Jutaire's murderous rain.

I hear his cry. I feel my heart wrench.

And Julian leaps after him.

18

NOT EVEN MY MOTHER HAS A WORD TO SAY.

Julian leaped. Julian is gone. Gone.

I jump to my feet, staring at the flap as if he'll materialize before me. Dena stands too, slowly, one hand against her stomach, her face pale.

I act before I can think. I rush to the flap.

"Seize her," the Queen hisses.

Three soldiers stand and two hands wrap around my arms.

I yank free and turn back. I throw a punch at the Jute. He yelps and covers his nose. The soldier named Ilen makes a move to grab me, but by the way he moves, I can tell he isn't even trying. But I throw a kick at his stomach and he takes it, falling back against the other soldier, pulling them both to the ground. I only have a moment to realize he is helping me, that I may have an ally.

But will it matter?

I pull the hood over my head and the mask over my face. A vain attempt to save myself from the rain that will kill me. I'm about to pull back the flap when someone attacks me from behind. Pain shoots down along my spine.

The soldier towers over me. As his fingers tighten around my forearms, I raise my leg without turning and kick his head.

And before anyone can stop me, I leap.

19

I LAND IN A CROUCH, ONE GLOVED HAND on the red ground. For the first time in my life, I stand beneath Jutaire's tears. I breathe in the acidic, humid stench of the bleeding world around me. And I live.

That's when I realize. My tunic, gloves, hood and mask—it was no wonder they shimmered like the carriage.

They're Louen. Slate was protecting me.

There isn't time to waste. I scan the area for Julian, but I see nothing. The rain falls in thick torrents from the sky, blurring everything in my path. Frustration creeps up my veins, taking hold of the reins in my mind. I run.

It's as if my body knows where he is. For I find him, lying beneath a towering boulder, the Louen cloth wrapped around his shivering body and Wren's still one. His shirt is soaked through. Blood streaks down the side of his face. But when he looks at me, teeth chaterring from the cold, everything is okay.

"Lissa," he whispers. I drop to my knees beside him. Blood runs down his arm, his neck, his face. "He died."

A drop of rain hits his outstretched fingers. He stares as the blood blossoms and runs down the riverbanks of his skin. I carefully tuck his hand beneath the sheet of Louen and cover his neck.

"Why?" I ask. I wonder if he can hear me over the howling wind and screeching rain.

But he hears me. He sees me like I am all that exists and hears me like I am all that is there to hear. "It hurt you. I promised you, remember? I promised I wouldn't let anyone hurt you. And I thought-I thought I could save him."

He looks down at Wren's dark hair, stained with his own blood. I'm afraid to draw back the fabric and see what's left of him. Julian looks back up at me, his eyes crazed.

"It's not your fault," I whisper, wiping the blood away from his cheek. His eyes flutter closed and he trembles. I pull the Louen over his face and wrap my arms around him, sharing my warmth. Something warms inside me, despite the rain and my pounding fear. And I feel content, whole, despite death lying beside us, lurking in our horizons.

I lie there, beside him, as his shivering slowly subsides and his breathing shallows. And I hope the rain won't penetrate the cloth saving us from our deaths.

I don't know when I fall asleep. But when I wake, the sun is barely peeking over the morning sky, the ground is dry and not a single cloud dots the sky.

As if yesterday never happened.

Julian watches me, lips slightly parted. I look around, at the barren land, and the blood-stained Louen covering what I know is Wren.

"What?" I ask, suddenly self-conscious.

"Nothing," he breathes.

"No, there is something." I insist.

He looks away and licks his lips. I tighten my fingers around one another.

"You look different when you're asleep," he says softly. His eyes are darker when they meet mine. His face is streaked with blood.

"Is that," I pause, "a bad thing?"

He laughs. "No, not a bad thing."

"It's beautiful." His expression suddenly turns serious and his eyes a level more intense as they search my face. "*You* are beautiful."

Me. Lissa. I am beautiful.

And it's as if something in me is breaking from the irrational happiness exploding inside me. The smile that cracks across my face gives life to another on his face.

"Especially when you smile," he says. His eyes speak more emotion than his words ever will. He looks at me as if nothing else is around for him to see. As if I matter, when I do not.

But I *do* matter. I know that now.

"Are you afraid?" He asks, his smile fading into reality.

"I don't know," I say truthfully. I glance at the sheet. "I didn't make much of a difference, did I?"

Wren's children are orphans now.

"You did. I would have shivered to death if it wasn't for you." He reaches for me and brushes his fingers across my cheek. His touch is searing, comforting, burning, soothing. So many things at once.

"I won't let them hurt you," he whispers. I stare into his eyes, at the pinpricks of despair dotting the vastness. He slowly leans closer and my skin burns, burns, burns.

And four wheels grind to a stop behind me.

Julian jerks away, his face falling into an expression of pain. I admire his easy acting. My own face still burns when the Queen descends the steps of the carriage alone. I look up at her and catch Dena peeking through the flaps.

The Queen's face is sharp with anger, but I only understand the extent of it when none of her soldiers follow.

"I will pretend none of this happened." Her voice is venomous. "Do you understand, half-breed?"

Julian clenches his jaw. I see his defiance waiting at the edge of his lips, but his eyes flicker to mine. "Yes, Your Majesty."

"Good. Now get in."

"He's hurt," I say, forcing her to cut her gaze to mine.

"He lives, thanks to you," she snaps. I can't tell if she is accusing me of saving him. "And that is enough."

I open my mouth but Julian groans and I take that as a plea to stay quiet. I reach down and tighten the Louen around Wren's body before helping Julian to his feet. Jutaire will forever be a darker shade of red because Queen Rhea wanted to display her power.

I meet her unfeeling eyes and walk back to the carriage. Her gaze burns into me the entire time. I don't look at Dena or Chancellor Kole when I take my seat again. I ignore them because I don't know how to answer their questions without endangering them.

One person has already died because of me.

I'm so deep in the thought of Wren's mutilated body that I flinch when Julian collapses beside me. Ilen rushes forward and helps tend to his wounds, while my mother watches, pursing her lips and saying nothing.

And before long, we are there.

20

"FINALLY!" QUEEN RHEA EXCLAIMS. SHE'S nothing like the woman who hissed a threat at Slate and ordered Wren pushed from her carriage. She stands, and the soldiers shoot to their feet, lowering their gazes in respect. "We have much to do, Lissa. Preparations must be made immediately."

She doesn't speak of my leap into the rain. She sounds like I have a future with the Jute. I feel nothing as I stand. My heart is simply a heart, beating so I exist.

But I'm a tool, as Slate said, nothing more.

A hand presses into the small of my back. I look into Julian's wary eyes. His face is dotted with bandages. "Don't think."

I swallow and nod. Ilen and another soldier unseal the Louen and hold back the flaps. Ilen's bright brown eyes are wild and I wonder if he mourns Wren.

Queen Rhea holds her head high as she crosses the carriage. Her dress trails behind her, the fabric snagging on every imperfection of the carriage floor.

As soon as she steps off, Ilen's eyes swivel to me. "Your highness."

Was he really aiding me when I tried to leap? Or did I imagine it in my crazed plight? I walk to the back of the carriage, Julian following close behind. I'm struck with a sudden thought: isn't this how a slave follows his master? That was exactly what the Queen called him—a slave. I stumble and Ilen's hand wraps around my arm.

"Careful there," he says. I meet his eyes in a gesture of gratitude and he smiles.

Maybe not all Jute are the same. Maybe they are more human than we know.

I have to shield my eyes against the midday sun when I step out. And what I see takes my breath away.

This is how man lived on Earth. This is how kingdoms sprawled across ancient lands when horses were the only means for transportation. They lived in permanence, settled and happy, because their ends never loomed in every horizon.

The land is red, the same as all of Jutaire. But that is where the resemblance ends, and where the name White Plains comes from.

Everything is white. The steeping gates surrounding us are iridescent white, like the crown atop the Queen's head. The towers, three in all, rise high into the sky, piercing through the dry red clouds. Accents of swirling gold adorn the gleaming white walls of the palace. Right above the door is the same ten-pointed star from the Chamber and the Tower. Now I know.

It's the mark of the Queen.

Directly beneath us is a plaza, where the Jute probably gather to hear the Queen's announcements. From there on, houses and shops roll away like undulating white waves.

The kingdom is circular, clearly planned before it was built. But everything is so... *alive*. The market is bustling, the houses look animated. The Jute flit about like dots so far away. They move with purpose, not blind need.

The beauty of it all is striking. Yet bitterness wells up like I've eaten something sour.

"Whoa," Dena says, resentment in her voice. Her hand clenches by her side, her skin-tight fingerless black gloves taut around her knuckles.

They have all this beauty and splendor. A reason to live, a *way* to live. And yet. They want to throw it all away and abandon us. They want to fly to Earth, which rightfully belongs to the humans. I squeeze my eyes shut.

When I open them, everything is sinister. Crumbling, fading, falling to ruins, like Rome on Earth long, long ago.

"Magnificent, isn't it?" Queen Rhea's voice is by my ear. I flinch in surprise.

"It is, yes." I say. My voice is as flat as hers, and it seems to satisfy her.

"Oh darling." I flinch again at the sudden change from lack of emotion to gushing, as if she has missed me all her life. "You must be tired. Come, come."

Her thin, elegant lips curve into a smile that doesn't reach her eyes. None of her emotions stems from her heart. I stare blankly and follow.

Because there is nothing else I can do.

The guards on either side of the double doors wear matching white coats that seem to make them camouflage into the walls. I don't notice them until they bow low, faces devoid of emotion. They remain that way for a full eye-roll conducted by Dena before they stand.

I stare at the dark void as the doors groan open. Once I enter, I may never leave. I could die here, amidst all this grand beauty.

The Queen strolls through, disappearing into the dark foyer. But I'm frozen by that realization.

Finally, I press my lips together and move forward, every step laden in lead. Every step takes me deeper and deeper into the lair of my mother, from which I may never return. I pull the dark fabric mask down from my face and drop my hood.

Cool air brushes against my skin. I can feel it desperately trying to soothe my fears while the walls laugh. I imagine my future is as bleak as this dim room, though I dared to hope otherwise while I trained in the Tower. Julian stands to my right, Dena to my left, both of them a foot behind me.

The room explodes with light.

It's more than a mere foyer, it's a grand hall. Queen Rhea sits on her throne, far beyond. But my throat tightens when I notice we aren't alone.

All of Jutaire seems to surround me.

I feel panic as the eyes scour my skin. They rake over my red-dusted Louen clothes, my bloodstained hands, my disheveled hair. I know what they must think: the Princess of the Jute isn't what they expected.

But to Julian I am beautiful, and to Slate I am a warrior, and to me that's all that matters.

"Welcome daughter, to your new home." Queen Rhea coos from her golden throne. Her voice echoes on the alabaster walls where golden accents swirl and interlock. Her hair spills neatly down her shoulders and her clothes are crisp and clean. She shows no sign of travel or weariness. She is the picture of perfection, however dark her heart may be.

When the blood-red smile curves across her face, I hear her sweet voice before she ordered Wren to be shoved from the carriage. I see Julian leap.

"Come, come, don't be shy," she sings, breaking through my thoughts.

I force one foot in front of the other and pass countless faces. These people must have been waiting to catch their first glimpse of the Jute heir.

Some of their faces are drawn and gaunt, others plump and pink, as if they've shunned the sun and warmed a couch all their life. They drink from alabaster white goblets, lips bright from whatever they sip. While a few of them dare to dress differently, almost all of them are clothed in a variety of gold and white, colors I will forever associate with my mother and her kingdom of Jute.

I stop where I think I should and look up at her, instantly feeling lowly. Her throne sits atop a white platform, the ten-pointed star in its center, a set of stairs rising from either end to meet her in the center. She peers down at me, pleased with my discomfort.

"We're right on time to meet a very, very important person. He was visiting the Chancellors in the Tower when you and I met," she says to me proudly. I almost laugh at her choice of words. "My first in command."

A man steps from the shadows. My heart stops when he looks at me with those blue eyes that don't belong to him and I want to turn around and run far, far away.

"Meet Rowan, Lissa," she says, leaning forward in her throne. Her eyes are bright with glee, and I wonder if she loves him like she would love a child. Like she should love me. "He is also the half-breed's—"

Half-breed, half- breed, half- breed. I can't take it anymore. The words tumble out before I can hold them back. "We've met."

The Queen freezes, her skin paling visibly. I flinch when something clatters to the floor in the stark silence and the temperature drops.

Drops.

Drops.

Confusion spreads in my mind. But I know enough to understand I said the wrong thing.

"Clear the room." Her voice slices through the quiet.

The hall is empty in moments, leaving Chancellor Kole, Dena, Julian, Ilen, Rowan, the Queen, and me. She raises one eyebrow at me, recovering a fraction of herself. "Ilen, lead our guests away, please."

Julian looks at me as they go, his eyes lit with concern.

"Have you now?" She asks me. I'm alone with her and Rowan. Fear edges into my mind, but I shove it away.

"When, dear Lissa?" Her voice is tight.

I glance over at Rowan. He looks so much like Julian, though they had two different mothers. But now, Rowan's lips have paled. His dark eyes flicker in what I realize is fear. Julian is never this afraid.

Realization hits like a gust of dry wind. Rowan is afraid.

I want to laugh.

I shouldn't have said we've met, not if I want to be on Rowan's good side. Because Rowan is first in command.

Rowan holds answers.

I lick my lips and meet Queen Rhea's eyes. "At the Tower, when he came to pick up the body. The same day I met you."

Was that yesterday? Two days ago?

She holds my gaze a moment longer. It's hard to stay still beneath her unnerving stare. She's exactly how Chancellor Kole was on the day of Gage's death, digging through my thoughts, detecting my lies.

"So you know about the bodies," she says finally, relief softening her voice. She picks up what she dropped.

"Just once then?"

I wonder if I imagine the undercurrent of desperation quickening her words. I don't hesitate before answering.

The lie is easy. "Yes."

My answer echoes against the walls of this vast room, again and again. The walls are a witness to my lies. I resist the urge to flinch.

But why? Why does it matter when and where I've met Rowan?

I glance back at Rowan. His relief is replaced with another smirk when he catches me looking. This time, it's knowing. He thinks he knows why I lied. But I acted on impulse. I don't think *I* even know why I lied. But I've said what he wanted.

He has more answers than we ever will. Answers that could save the human race, and maybe even me from whatever fate my mother has planned. I must get them, whatever the cost. This is what Gage turned me into, after all—a girl fueled by information and answers to questions that will never end.

"Now. You're here for more than Rowan, though it was imperative that you meet him." She pauses and I look up at her fully-recovered ease. "Tomorrow eve, you will be crowned Princess."

I keep my expression carefully neutral, though the edge of my right eye twitches. Inside, my mind is running to catch up with my life that's happening before I can even comprehend.

"Of course, every Jute who matters will be here for the event, and you will need to make yourself presentable." She scans my ensemble with a sour twist to her lips. "Most definitely not alone, you will have maids for preparing. And you must look stunning. It *is* a ceremony, after all."

I nod, my breath coming out in short puffs of air. A ceremony. Maids. A crown.

It all suggests I will live here on Jutaire. But I know my mother has no intention of crowning me as heir. Slate said so.

"But that is tomorrow, darling," she says, answering my thoughts. "Today, I have a much different task for you. Very different."

She smiles. Rowan opens a side door.

Ilen and another soldier drag a bloody Chancellor Kole toward me, Dena and Julian wide-eyed and breathless behind them.

21

"WHAT HAVE YOU DONE?" I GASP. MY HAND instinctively goes for one of the daggers around my waist.

"Cooperation is imperative," my mother says, her voice razor-sharp. Her lazy demeanor is now fierce, calculated. She doesn't even glance at my dagger as she strolls down the platform, the white fur around her neck bright. "You, of all people know that, Kole."

He hacks a cough in answer. His gray suit is stained red. The other soldier punches him in the stomach, a sick grin on his face. Dena whimpers and I feel my face pale.

I never thought I'd see Dena afraid.

"Did you retrieve the box from him?" the Queen asks. The soldier holds out a small metal box. I know what it is, but as I search through the pages in my mind, half of them have been replaced with new memories, rather than the facts I memorized over the years. But the box's darkened exterior, few frayed wires and the rusted inscriptions tell me enough: it's from Earth.

Chancellor Kole groans.

Blood trickles down a gash across his cheek.

"Leave him alone," Dena hisses, her voice is thick with tears.

The Queen turns to me. "Do you know what this is, Lissa?"

I don't answer.

"It's a voice recorder, from Earth. Gage was a very interesting man, wasn't he? He thought he could keep it from me, he thought he was smart." She laughs. Irritation flashes in her eyes when Chancellor Kole's cough cuts her short. "He's dead."

Julian silently passes the Queen and stands by my side.

"There's a problem, you see," she says. She speaks slowly, too slowly. Chancellor Kole is seeping blood, and if she drags on any longer, he'll die. What does Chancellor Kole have to do with the recorder? And Gage?

"The recorder is locked, protected. Gage, idiot that he was, configured it to recognize one voice only."

"My voice," I whisper.

"Smart girl," my mother says and strides toward me. I eagerly take the small box from her elegant fingers. I'm holding an artifact from Earth. At the thought, giddiness trembles through me.

Chancellor Kole is dying and I am thinking of Earth. My mother looks ready to rip off my head and I am thinking of Earth. I clench my jaw.

"Unlock it," she says, her voice soft and commanding.

I force air through my nose. Jutaire air. Only Chancellor Kole and Dena wear masks, no one else. In White Plains, they are the ones who stand out, not us. *Us.*

I almost laugh. I have a place where I belong and I still don't belong.

"No."

The temperature drops. "What did you say?"

"I said no." I meet her eyes as defiantly as I can. My daggers pulse against me—two around my waist, another hidden against my leg.

"Very well." She turns to Rowan. Ilen and the other soldier hold Chancellor Kole by his arms as Rowan slides a sword out from the soldier's sheath. He presses it against Chancellor Kole's neck.

Chancellor Kole looks at me, his black eyes strangely focused. "Don't," he wheezes, "do it."

Rowan presses the blade harder and Chancellor Kole shuts his eyes with a shuddering breath. Rowan glances at the Queen, and I catch a flicker of something in his eyes that makes me pause.

Remorse.

I look back at my mother, panic rising in my chest. "Leave him alone."

"Why? Wouldn't you want him dead? After what he did to your poor uncle?" She asks.

"No one deserves to die," I say, my voice quiet.

"No," she says with a humorless laugh. "No one deserves to die. Everyone is *destined* to. Unlock the box."

"Lissa, please," Dena begs. Julian remains silent.

Chancellor Kole doubles over. My breathing quickens. Rowan pulls the sword away, the tip wet with blood.

No.

"Stop!" My voice echoes. Hysteria taints my words. "How do I open it?"

"Flick the switch," the Queen says smugly.

There's a nauseating, sickening rolling in my stomach. Gage *was* smart. He wouldn't encrypt information in a precious artifact from Earth unless the situation was dire. Unless the information was of utmost importance.

My mother is right. My uncle was an idiot.

The box speaks through the three tiny slits on its side. The vibration of a voice I never thought I'd hear again tingles up my fingers.

Gage's voice. I thought I would no longer mourn him, now that I have my real father, now that I know what Gage would have done to me. But nothing can replace the years where I thought he was my father, always looking out for me.

"Lissa, if you're hearing this, it means I have failed. Moreover, it means I am dead. You likely know the truth now and Slate must finally be reunited with his daughter. And Lissa"—he pauses—"I am sorry. Very and truly."

If I ever had any doubts, I know now: Slate is my father.

The Queen scoffs, dragging me back to the reality before me.

"In this digital recorder, I've protected a file. It will open to your voice only, with a set of words I once told you. I know you more than you know yourself, Lissa. You will figure it out.

"As for what lies in the file," he trails off with a sigh laden in remorse. Julian's fingers press against my arm.

"As for what lies in the file," he starts again, "it is the truth. I would never lie to you. I've thoroughly tested what began as a theory, a speculation, and this is the conclusion."

He clears his throat. And when he speaks again, his voice is constricted with emotion. "Unlock the file, Lissa, and decide what needs to be done."

Silence. The large room is suddenly too small. I won't decide what needs to be done.

My mother will.

"Password." I flinch at the female monotone. I think of all the words Gage had told me. There are so many. Gage never said anything that didn't need to be said. Every word was uttered for a reason.

"I don't know what it is."

"Neither do we, darling," the Queen says. "But you'll figure it out. Or they'll die, one by one."

As she says the words, more soldiers enter the room. Two of them grab Dena. She screeches and struggles against them. One of them slaps her across her cheek and she stops, stunned into obedience. When they come for Julian, he doesn't even move a muscle as they pull him in front of me, where I can see him. He doesn't react at all.

Fear rolls through me. No amount of training could have prepared me for this.

I stare at the recorder, as if that will make it spill its secrets. Chancellor Kole coughs again.

"You are you," I say to it, remember Gage's words on the hill when I took my first breath of the toxic air. Nothing happens. The light is still red. The Queen stares in silence, as does Rowan. And everyone else.

There are too many eyes on me, too many.

"Well, try another, we don't have all day," one of the soldiers whines. The Queen slants her gaze at him and he straightens.

Chancellor Kole is the only one moving. Heaving, because he is dying.

"Rowan," the Queen says. I glance up and meet Rowan's eyes as he draws more blood, deepening the gash across Chancellor Kole's neck. A scream builds in the back of my throat.

"Lissa," I hear Julian whisper.

I swivel my eyes to his, my movements are jittery, too much of a display of my fear. But when I meet his eyes, there's no one but us. No blood. No death. No threat.

"You are running out of time," the Queen says. Chancellor Kole cries out. He falls to the ground when the soldiers release him. He moans and heaves.

The man who had taken countless lives, who acted as the most hated man in human eyes to protect them all, is dying. Rowan drops the sword and pulls a small dagger from his waist.

I hold my breath as the clatter of the sword echoes into silence. Everyone does. Because suddenly, no one is breathing. Suddenly, every eye is on me. The room thickens with anticipation. Even the walls grasp their breath.

I close my eyes. And there, in the dark harshness of my breathing, I hear Gage's voice on the threshold of death.

"You are not my daughter."

The red light turns green.

And Rowan plunges his dagger through Chancellor Kole's heart.

22

DENA SCREAMS AND I NEARLY DROP THE recorder as my ears explode with her bloodcurdling cry.

"Dena, *shut up*," Julian thunders. The walls yell back with his furious words. In swift movements, he kicks the soldiers away from him, twists their arms behind them until they themselves drop in pain. He's by Chancellor Kole's side in heartbeats.

"No," I breathe. I press my fingers against the edges of the recorder, letting the pain of the metal edges bite into my skin.

Julian's hands roam over Chancellor Kole's chest, which is covered in blood. It covers the tile beneath our feet and pools around him. But there is no use. He's dying.

The Queen watches with pursed lips. Rowan wipes his dagger across his thigh and drops it back in its sheath, his forehead wrinkled and eyes downcast for barely a moment before his face clears of emotion. He looks blankly at the Queen. As if nothing happened.

As if he didn't just slaughter an unarmed old man.

He's as two-faced as everyone else.

"It's no use, boy," Chancellor Kole rasps. The knees of Julian's pants are soaked in blood, his hands red. Dena tries to break free from the soldiers holding her back, but they don't budge. Chancellor Kole looks at me, his eyes losing focus. "Stupid girl. I told you, I told-"

He grabs Julian's shirt as blood sputters from his lips again. "Protect my daughter."

And those are his last words.

"You murderer." Dena breaks the silence, her voice is raw. Julian slowly lifts his head from against his chest and looks at me with pained eyes.

"Press the button," the Queen says. I blink and Chancellor Kole's body comes into focus again.

"You killed him," I say breathlessly. My body trembles with anger.

She doesn't care. "Press the button or they'll all die."

Julian is by my side in an instant. His bloody hands close around mine and gently force my finger to the button.

I bite my lip as Gage's voice spills from the wretched instrument again.

"You unlocked it," Gage says sadly. Light static fills the silence, drowned out by the rushing in my ears and the thudding in my heart. "When I said you are greater than man and Jute, I meant it. You *are* greater. And because of that, dear Lissa, you are in danger.

"The Jute are going to make Earth their home. They will leave us here to wither away and the last of the human race will fade into nothing." His voice changes and I hear the smile in his voice. I've seen it countless times—a small one, twisting the right edge of his lips while his eyes drown in sorrow. "But. There is always a but, isn't there, Lissa?"

I would have smiled at his old joke. Less of a joke, really, but it always managed to lighten gloomy stories.

But now, it's different. Now, my smiles are smothered in this harsh reality.

"But Jute cannot breathe oxygen," he says. "There is no use in going to Earth if they'll die days after they inhale.

"That's where you come in. Where your value lies, and why you must be protected at all costs. I entrusted Kole with this recorder, just as I have entrusted your life to him." His voice is low now, grave. "The Jute need you Lissa. I made a grave mistake and the Jute know they need you. But no one else knows what for."

He sighs. "So hear me carefully. The only way for them to survive on Earth is through you. Your blood holds the ability to thrive on both Jutaire and Earth.

"I'm sure you're wondering how it works. You were born with blood containing a certain amount of a special nutrient. You can harbor a certain bacteria that thrives on this planet and live in perfect symbiosis."

I stare at the recorder. I'm filled with bacteria?

"And because the bacteria can survive in both oxygen and non-oxygen states, so can you. You are a hybrid. The only one of your kind. And with one drop of your blood in each of the many Jute, they will be like you—they will breathe both oxygen and the toxic air without issue.

"But with only a finite amount of this nutrient, you, dear Lissa, will be dead."

The recording shuts off. I lean forward, closer and closer, but that's it. He's gone. The box is as silent as the room around me.

My mother doesn't intend to crown me as heir. It's an act. My mother intends to murder me.

To suck me dry.

"Ilen." My mother says with a jerk of her head. He doesn't react. He's staring at Chancellor Kole's lifeless body. She raises her voice. "Ilen."

"Yes, your Majesty." He rushes to her and bows. I try not to look at the body of the man I hated for so long.

"Prick her vein."

I shiver. The soldiers stare at me. Dena and Julian stare at me. The throne room shrinks.

She brought me out here without a word, but this was her motive all along. She may not have known exactly what she needed me for, but we both knew I would be used. Didn't I climb into her carriage knowing that?

I didn't know I would be killed.

I don't know anything anymore. My life was a lie. My mind is a muddled haze.

"Relax, daughter," she says with a humorless laugh. "We have to perform a test. Make sure you really are our Princess."

Ilen comes forward with a case. He unfolds it, pulling out a needle and two vials, each one the length of my hand. I inhale sharply at the thought of so much blood. She knows I am the Princess. My breathing is a testament to that, however vague.

Ilen swipes the inside of my arm with a wet substance. His hands tremble.

The Queen wants to test Gage's theory, to see if my blood really is more valuable than the air I breathe.

Ilen presses the needle into my arm and I suck in a breath. Beads of red slowly trickle out, forming a steady stream down the first vial.

I grit my teeth at the pull. Clench my fists. Then it hits me.

If Jute can breathe oxygen with my blood, then the effect can go both ways—humans can breathe the air of Jutaire. Lack of oxygen will no longer be a hindrance. They can fight back.

My mind begins to clear as the answer slowly clicks.

Yes. Yes, they can. We can.

The sudden weight of everything comes crashing down on me. And I fall. Darkness swallows me whole.

Because finally, finally, there is hope in the world.

2 3

I WAKE TO A VOID IN MY CHEST, EMPTY and sad. I wish Julian were here, or Slate. Or even Dena or Chancellor Kole.

My breath shudders when I see his dark eyes devoid of life and his unusual white hair stained in his own blood.

I hated him, once. I thought he was a heartless murderer. But all he wanted was to protect his daughter and his people.

Chancellor Kole would never have hung so many humans if it weren't for the Jute and their orders.

In the end, *he* was murdered.

And despite the hatred I harbored inside me against him, I forgive him. Because I know now *why* he did what he did.

And in the end, the blame lies with the Queen.

The pillow beneath my head is plush and soft, unlike anything I've ever felt before. Above me, a silken canopy of midnight blue, dusted in glittering white, drapes over the four bedposts, emulating the night sky.

I sit up. My Louen tunic and suit is gone. Someone changed me into a pale yellow nightgown. Gold and white sheets swirl at my feet, the material a caress against my mostly bare skin. The richness of the room emanates from the walls' elaborate deep brown decor. The trims are honey brown, a sunlit beacon in the dark.

On the other end of the room is an unlit fireplace, two brown chairs embossed with gold sitting on either side. To my left is the door, a slab of white against the brown wall. To my right is a dresser, sprawling with trinkets and other accessories I can't name from their silhouettes. Another smaller door, most likely leading to a bathroom, stands beside it.

It's beautiful. Rich. I lie back against the pillows with a small smile on my lips.

And immediately sit up.

No. I'm in the center of Jute territory. The man I thought my father is dead. The mother I never knew I had is the Queen of the Jute. I'm in her castle, where Julian's lookalike brother murdered Chancellor Kole before my eyes.

And my blood.

The inside of my arm prickles in reminder. They have two full vials of my blood.

The lab the Queen spoke of must be somewhere here. How else will they conduct tests? And what tests will they conduct?

I slide out of the bed. It's tall, and my feet barely skim the floor when I sit on its side.

My belt and daggers are gone and I feel vulnerable in this flimsy dress. When I move toward the door, keen on sneaking out, someone knocks. My heart catapults to my throat when I pull it open.

Julian.

The bandages dotting his face are gone, his scars barely visible. *Jute heal fast*, he had said. He looks more like Rowan now, with dress pants and a midnight blue shirt, the sleeves rolled right beneath his elbows. His messy hair glistens with droplets of water.

But when I hear his monotone, something inside me falters, stumbles and can't get up.

"The Queen requires your presence in her chambers, Princess. Her Majesty requested that you make yourself presentable."

Princess. The word feels like a slap. I stare at him, my breath frozen in my chest. Something flickers in his eyes and I wait for him to speak, to say something.

And when he doesn't, anger rushes through me, strengthening me. I press my lips closed. Inside, my heart is breaking, but I can't let that show.

"I will," I reply coolly. He flinches and lowers his eyes. And though everything inside me screams the opposite, I move to close the door. But when I touch my hand to the wood, he reacts. He reaches out on instinct, his fingers brushing against my skin and I want more. More.

What is wrong with me?

"Wait," he whispers. His voice cracks in pain. I exhale through my lips.

"Yes?" I breathe. He searches my face.

"I'll keep my promise."

And the door closes behind him.

I stare at the door after he leaves, wishing I can pull him back inside, run my hands through his hair and my fingers across his lips, the bridge of his nose, and the stubble on his cheeks. Where these thoughts come from, I don't know. But I think of his promise, *I won't let them hurt you.*

And I hurry.

I wash my face in the bathroom and drag myself to the closet. If I hadn't stepped into the bathroom, I wouldn't have even known where the closet was.

My feet move as if they've walked through this room hundreds of times before.

Behind the closet's double doors, dresses hang in a multitude of colors. Lavish reds, dark navies, and elegant greens. I wonder how long they had been preparing for me. I run my fingers over the silk of a simple black dress on the far end. I pull it from the hanger with a smile, because this is the one Queen Rhea will least expect me to wear.

Royals on Earth had maids to dress them, braid their hair, and tend to their baths. I have my own two hands. I don't need anyone to work for me.

The thought of Earth reminds me of the ship and the promise I kept to myself.

Everyone hopes for a miracle. They hide in their small homes, nibbling on whatever food they have left, their faces dirty, their homes filthy. They don't care for life anymore, their appearances say. But deep, deep inside an unseen crevice of that ever-moving mass we call a heart, hope still throbs, however faint.

Every faint heartbeat brings a human closer to death. And once one person dies, another will follow, and soon the human race will fade away to nothing.

I can save them all. Or I can bleed to death.

But first, I will meet my mother. Then take a look around. Plan.

And when I finally feel a sense of purpose, I clear my mind of everything and get ready.

I've never worn a dress. It clings to me like a second skin, accentuating every curve of my body. I long for the Louen tunic and skintight suit Slate gave me. But the dress is the least of my worries.

I step into the empty hall, which stretches from right to left, where it turns onto another hall. I turn right, because it ends with two elaborate double doors that look important. The emptiness feels odd, because in my mind, palaces are always teeming with nobles, servants, and maids.

But maybe the emptiness is a gift and I can find out more than I expect to—like the whereabouts of the lab I hope exists, and information about the ship.

I pass door after door, but I stop at none. Something tells me they are rooms much like my own, and I won't find anything in a bedroom.

"A Princess should never wander alone."

I freeze at the sound of Julian's voice. Only it isn't. This voice is dangerous. I hold my breath as his footsteps come closer.

"Hello, Lissa," Rowan says, meeting my eyes. His voice is soft like Julian's, yet arrogant. His dark lashes brush against the tops of his cheeks when he lowers his eyes. I try not to see the shimmering seas of Earth. I try not to imagine Julian's gentleness. Because this isn't Julian.

"What do you want?" I ask, holding my head high. I remember the flash of emotion that crossed his face when he plunged his dagger through Chancellor Kole.

He raises an eyebrow. "Getting haughty now, Princess?"

"I asked—"

"You lied back there."

A part of me wants to run back to my room. But I'm not a coward. I've heard of horrors worse than Rowan.

"And?" I ask.

He stills and leans closer, forcing me to look in his eyes. The sea pulls me under. "And I think I know why."

I want to laugh in his face. But the gears in my heart turn faster and faster. He is close. Too close.

He shouldn't affect me this way.

"What if you're wrong?" I ask, taking a step back. He steps closer, his body still inclined toward me. He smells sharper than Julian, spicier. The collar of his knee-length black coat reaches his scruffy jaw, swathing his long neck in shadows. Dangerous excitement trills through me.

I take another step back, my throat growing thick when he follows. *This isn't Julian*, my mind whispers. *They are the same*, says my heart.

"I am very rarely wrong, Princess," he whispers. His breath washes over my skin. Like the rare sprigs of mint from the crophouses. I can't stop my eyes from flickering to his lips.

"Rowan," someone growls. Julian. Rowan pulls away and guilt heats my face. "Lay off her."

"Why?" Rowan is amused. Not ashamed of being caught, not angry for being scolded by his half-breed brother. Amused. "What does it matter who the Princess associates herself with?"

"Associate is the wrong word," Julian spits. His eyes are livid and a vein pulses in his jaw. "Don't touch her."

Rowan laughs. "I've never seen you so angry, Julian. You're so flat most of the time, I'm impressed. As for the Princess"—Rowan turns to me, his eyes darkening—"why don't we let her choose who she *associates* herself with?"

There is no question of whom I would choose. But choosing would be dangerous in this place where Rowan is powerful. I bite my lip and meet Rowan's eyes. "If I say, it'll ruin all the fun, won't it?"

I don't wait for an answer. I don't even spare Julian a glance. I turn and head in the opposite direction, hoping Julian will follow me.

24

HE DOES. WHEN I TURN THE CORNER HE IS there.

"How?" I trail off in surprise. The edge of his lips lifts in a treacherous half-smile and I forget to breathe. There must be a shortcut, because I know he didn't follow me.

"I have my ways," he says. "I was told to escort you earlier. But I"—he runs a nervous hand through his hair—"got distracted."

"Distracted," I echo. He doesn't reply. We turn down another hall, the gleaming wood floor hard beneath my shoes.

"Dena's hysterical," he says finally.

"Oh," I say, tonelessly. Her father was brutally murdered in front of her helpless eyes. I know what that's like.

"And you," he says. His soft voice caresses my skin. "There's something you're not telling me."

I don't want false hope in his heart. So I don't answer. He looks away. Before either of us can think of words to say, we've reached the room where the Queen requires me. His hand closes around the handle and a wary shadow of a smile crosses his face.

"You're wrong, you know. It isn't fun at all."

But when I part my lips, he opens the door, leaving me beneath the Queen's stare. She sits in a chaise in a room adorned with dark walls and a crackling fireplace, sunlight filtering through the windows behind her. Her expression turns from one of boredom to amusement when she sees my darkened cheeks.

"We are making progress," she says. I wonder if she speaks of my blood or something else.

Good for you, I want to say. She raises one eyebrow as if she heard my unspoken words.

"I trust the half-breed, you know."

"Julian." My voice is quiet.

"Hmm?" Her voice is the definition of apathy.

"His name is Julian." I grit my teeth.

"I will call him what I like," she says with a wave of her hand. "I trust him, as I was saying. He had a most unusual request though."

I am silent.

"And I've decided to grant him permission. You may as well have some fun," she laughs. "Life is short."

Very, very short.

"I will have some maids sent to your room tomo—"

"When will you stop acting? Do you care about what you'll do to me? Your own daughter?" The words burst free from my lips.

The room dies. Wilts. Freezes. My stomach drops. Something crawls beneath my skin.

But my words struck. I can see it in the way her skin pales and the way her eyes freeze for the barest of moments.

"Leave." She drops the word.

I don't need to be told twice.

I slip into the hall. What did the Queen really need me for? I should have kept my blabbering mouth shut and listened.

When the thrumming in my heart finally settles down, I make my way back to my room. Like earlier, the hall is empty, but not quiet. I hear loud, booming laughs and tittering voices. They're far from here though, far enough that I'm safe from their eyes.

But the palace isn't as empty as I thought.

I trail my hand along the wall as I hurry forward. When I reach my room, I throw a glance behind me. I don't intend to go back to my room just yet.

I pause at the spot where Rowan caught me earlier, half-expecting him to materialize in front of me, his lips inches from mine.

But I don't feel disgust or fear. It's a faint thrill of something I don't understand. I shake my head, clearing my mind. I can't be found wandering around.

At the end of the hall, the double doors are closed. I don't know why I want to go in there, but something tells me I might find answers. It could be the lab. Even if it ends up being nothing more than a ballroom—if Jute dance like Earth royals did—at least my mind will be at ease.

I press my ear against it and hold my breath. When I hear nothing but my pounding pulse, I wrap my fingers around the knob and brace myself against the door.

"Don't do it."

Even muffled from the other side of the door, I recognize Julian's voice, soft and commanding. But now, it's tainted with desperation.

Rowan laughs and I slowly release the handle. "Does it pain you, brother?"

"I've stood by and watched you do so many things. Not this. Please don't do this."

Why is Julian begging?

"I'll do what I want," Rowan says, dangerously.

"Don't hurt her." Me? Dena? The Queen?

"Don't get in my way. Do I need to remind you of what will happen?" Rowan muses. His voice grows closer with the sound of his footsteps.

I look around, frantically searching for a way out. My room is too far and I won't make it in time. And the hall ends here. I catch sight of a smaller door that's almost blended into the wall to the left of the double doors. The wood is frayed, the knob rusty. It's old compared to the rest of the palace's restored beauty.

"Please." Julian tries again. His voice is hollow and desperate. He hasn't moved from wherever he is.

I stop breathing.

Rowan stops walking. "That's enough. You've never tried to get in my way before. Why start now?" He sounds genuinely curious, and so much like Julian.

"This is different," Julian says, defeated, ashamed.

Rowan laughs. Maybe he really is mad. "I can see that, Julian. And it's just what I need."

My eyes widen when I hear his weight press against the door. I can't risk it any longer. I can't wait to hear what else Julian will say.

I quickly throw open the other door and fall into darkness.

25

I SIT UP AS THE ROOM FILLS WITH LIGHT.
I'm behind an old desk. The door I entered through must not be used if there's a desk in front of it.

Sounds of struggling and shuffling break the silence, along with shoes squeaking on the tiled floor.

"Let go of me," someone spits. Dena.

My breathing shallow, I slowly sit up and peek over the table. Three soldiers struggle with Dena, pulling her toward the center of the room. She kicks one of them in the nose and he screams.

The other two soldiers force her onto a flat bed and strap her arms with metal bands while she struggles fruitlessly against them.

Test tubes surround her, some of them bubbling and emitting hazy smoke. Microscopes sit on the stark white desks pressed one beside the other. Pens and loose paper scatter their surfaces.

I squint at the familiar features of one of the soldiers. Ilen. The other two jeer at him and his cheeks darken. He reluctantly picks up an injector filled with dark liquid. Even from here I can see his hands trembling as he brings it to Dena's arm.

She stills. Her chest rises and falls in rapid breaths. He whispers something and slips the needle into her arm.

I watch as her breathing slows, fear shivering her frame. It looks unnatural on her, this fear.

Ilen, crumpled and broken, ignores her shuddering plea and follows the others out the door.

I shoot to my feet, lifting the hem of my stupid dress before swinging over the desk. I run towards her, sidestepping black bags and tables and other nameless things strewn about.

I touch the back of my hand against her forehead and my heart crashes at the iciness of her skin.

"Dena," I whisper, glancing nervously at the door. She doesn't move. She doesn't even breathe. I could be wrong, my mother could be wrong.

My blood could kill and no one knows.

Dena's face blurs in my vision and I struggle to hold back tears. I shake her. I don't know if she still hates me, but I can't hate her back.

She lost her father because of me, her mother because of the Jute. *And*, a voice whispers in my mind, *maybe even Julian because of you.*

"Dena, wake up," I plead. My fingers are slick against her skin.

UN*breath*ABLE

Her eyes flutter open, her dark eyes flashing an image of Chancellor Kole's bloodied face in my mind.

"Lissa," she sighs.

"What happened?" I ask, my voice breathy.

She shudders. "He's dead isn't he? He's really gone."

"I'm sorry," I say. And I mean it.

"I should hate you even more now," she laughs bitterly. "But my dad knew what he was doing. He knew this would be his end when he made Gage record that."

"What do you mean?" I ask quickly.

"Hmm?" She asks absently. Wild delirium flashes in her eyes. I look down at the dark dot on her arm.

"Does it hurt?" I ask, but I want to know what she meant. I want to know more about the relationship Gage and Chancellor Kole had.

"Look at my face, Lissa. Look close. Real close. Do you see my nose?"

I see her nose, yes. I see her lips. I see the contours of the mask that are forever wrought into her skin. But I don't see a mask.

"You can breathe—"

She nods before I can complete the question.

"It's sweet. Pretty cool," she says. But her voice is dead. She's a completely different person than the one I met in the Tower. "They wanted to test it, make sure it works on humans. Looks like it works, but they won't let me live."

"Why?" I ask.

She gives me a look the old Dena would have given me. "If humans knew there was a way to breathe this damn air, we would be stronger. We would actually *try*. There would be a race for Earth, not this lame one-sided battle."

"I don't understand why they want to go to Earth. They can breathe this air, they have everything," I say.

"Know what my dad used to say?" she asks. "Jutaire's resources are nothing compared to Earth. They can live here, sure, but look at it their way: if they can get Earth, why settle for this crap?"

She sounds as if she understands them, as if she sides with them. As if their want for Earth is something that can be justified. My head suddenly feels heavy.

"There can't be a race," I say quietly. She narrows her eyes at me. "There isn't time. They had everything but my blood and now they have that too."

She shakes her head. "They can't go around injecting your blood into everyone. There's a catalyst. It needs to be mixed. Made."

She meets my eyes, the gesture no longer surprising.

"We have time," she says fiercely.

I narrow my eyes. "We?"

She grins. The first I've seen on her. "Yep, *we*. They won't kill me right away."

"So you can help from in here," I say as it dawns.

She nods and wriggles her hands, frowning when the straps don't budge. "I'm not going anywhere yet. You, on the other hand, better scram."

I stand, but I don't want to leave her like this. Vulnerable, with a foreign substance running in her bloodstream, and air that could kill her if my blood decides not to work.

"So, you and Julian, huh?" She asks. I stop and turn. She says it lightly, but I can hear the pain in her voice.

"No," I say softly, "I don't- I don't think so. I don't know."

"Liar." She smirks. I twist my lips.

"I mean you don't have to tell me or anything. It's not like it's my business," she says quickly.

"We never—I don't even know," I trail off. She nods, understanding. I never expected Dena to understand me.

"He loves you though," she says softly. "After his mom died, he was like this ghost of himself. He burned all his drawings. He tried to kill himself so many times, that's what he was trying to do in the Chamber when you came. But now, his face isn't as pale, he smiles. He's... living again."

My throat is filled with a million tears of happiness.

"Drawings?" I force the word from my lips. *He loves you.*

She nods. "He's an incredible artist."

I want to say something to fill in the silence, but I can't. She watched Julian slowly distance her and slowly fall in love with me, when I didn't even notice. I doubt even *he* noticed it.

"I just... I want him to be happy," she says finally. Her face falls. "My dad wanted you to have this."

She wiggles her hand into her pocket and pulls something out with two fingers.

The replica of Earth Chancellor Kole had that day in the training room.

"He said to fight, or we won't go anywhere." Her voice breaks. "I know I was a jerk before, but"—she stops—"truth is, you're our only hope. I mean, look at me, I'm strapped to a damn table. Don't let my dad's death go wasted."

I take the ball from her hand, its tiny weight magnanimous. "I won't," I whisper.

"And Lissa?" Her dark eyes blur in my vision. "See that case over there?"

I follow her line of sight to a black bundle on a table against the wall.

"There are empty vials in there. Do you think you can fill them with blood?"

"M-my blood?" I ask, my eyes wide. She nods. "But why?"

"Just do it, there isn't time for me to spell everything out for you." I blink at her command and do as she says. I open the case. Five empty vials glint up at me, reflecting the light from above and my own pale face.

"Hurry," Dena calls. I take it to her and rest the case on her stomach, ignoring her glare.

"Can you do it?" I ask.

She rolls her eyes. "I'm strapped to a table, Lissa."

"Here," I say. I screw the needle to the top of the first vial and slip it in her hand before crouching down beside her. She snorts when I guide the needle to the inside of my arm and carefully slip it into the vein.

"You know I'm not doing anything but holding it, right?" She asks dryly.

I don't answer. I watch the needle closely. I can see the blood pulling against my skin, the vial slowly filling with dark, thick liquid. What a simple substance blood is.

I fill the rest myself, watching as the blood sloshes against the glass and the needle pucker my skin. It's almost mesmerizing.

Dena laughs when I seal the case again. "I'm glad there aren't any*more* vials or you'll sit here all day and drain your blood yourself."

I make a face. I've read that blood loss can bring fatigue and dizziness. But I feel nothing and it takes me a moment to remember Gage said my blood reproduces quickly. Chances are my body has already replaced the lost blood.

"Hide it under that table," Dena says. I go to another, matching table and slip the case beneath the three-inch gap between the table and the tile.

"What will you do with it?" I ask. She shrugs. I raise my eyebrows.

"Look, you've spent long enough in here. Go," she says. She's right. I turn quickly. "Oh, and come back tomorrow at midnight. Ilen says there's a way out of here."

Ilen *is* on our side.

"I will." After the ceremony, I will.

As I make my way to the unused, forgotten door, movement catches my eyes. A blue flame flickers inside a suspended tube, reaching higher with each of its gasps. Fire is dangerous. Risky. Like this game Dena suggests.

Queen Rhea is as unpredictable as the flame. One wrong move and she'll kill Dena without a thought—humans are abundant in her eyes.

The flame flickers in answer to my thoughts. And I hear Gage's words from long ago.

Never, ever, play with fire, Lissa.

26

I SINK INTO MY BED AND ROLL THE BALL
of Earth between my palms. I don't know what good Dena
could do strapped to a table in a room full of combustibles
and unknown things. But she said there is a catalyst. If she
knows what it is, we could use it.

A soft knock shatters my thoughts. I wouldn't have
heard it if I wasn't waiting for it. I shove the replica beneath
my pillow and drag myself off the bed, cracking the door
open the slightest bit.

"Can I come in?" Julian asks hesitantly. I let him in
and close it with a glance at the empty hall.

We're both silent for what seems like an eternity. I
can't bring myself to look at him after what Dena said, so I
look at the floor. I look at everything but him.

"Rowan," he says finally. I meet his eyes. The collar of
his shirt is open, his pale skin shadowed by his face.

"What about him?" I ask.

"Stay away from him. Far away."

I sputter a laugh. And the anger that rises suddenly surprises me. "Is that why you came here? To tell me what to do?"

His eyes widen. "No! That isn't what I meant." He sighs. "Just be careful. Rowan is treading dangerous land, and he'll pull you in too."

I want to ask him what he means. I want to ask him why the Queen was so desperate to know when I had met Rowan, why her demeanor changed when it almost never does. Julian knows something.

I want to ask him about the words he shared with Rowan in the room behind the double doors. But something keeps me quiet.

"Tomorrow night, after the ceremony, will you come with me?" He asks nervously. Is this what the Queen meant by his unusual request?

"With you?" I ask.

"Yes. There's," he pauses, his neck flushes and his eyes brighten. I've never seen Julian so unsure of himself. "There's something I want to show you."

"I would come with you anywhere," I say softly.

His lips twist into that smile I forever want to see and relief passes over his face.

"I needed to know if you'd come. If all that trouble will be worth it."

Something crashes through my chest. I know that feeling. And when I speak again, I can only whisper.

"It will be worth it."

The smile that spreads across his face is bright enough to outshine the moon. I laugh softly and shake my head.

"You're hiding something from me, aren't you?" he says after a moment. "When you fainted earlier. You figured something out."

Part of me is awed that he noticed. But when it comes to me, he notices a lot of things.

"I think... my blood goes both ways." I struggle for words. I know what to say, but I'm afraid of his reaction. Afraid of what he will think.

"You mean it'll allow humans to breathe the Jutaire air," he says. He doesn't ask. He knows.

Which reminds me: I need to tell him about Dena, stuck in the lab.

"I think so," I say. "I didn't know how to test it, but—"

"Why do you think Dena's here?" He asks, an edge to his voice. "They're one step ahead, Lissa."

He shakes his head and rubs the back of his neck.

"You said my name," I say. He stills and drops his hand by his side.

"I-I apologize. I—"

"No, no," I say, realizing how awkward this is and I wonder why I even blurted that out in the first place. "I want you to call me Lissa. Just Lissa."

He swallows and runs his tongue over his lips. And grins. I've never seen him grin before, but it makes me want to melt.

"I'll remember that."

I trail to the window, his footsteps shadowing mine. Outside, a blanket of blue spreads for as far as I can see.

Far below, I can see Jute moving about. A large reservoir sits behind the palace, filled with what looks to be about fifteen feet deep of rainwater. The Jute are efficient.

"They've already taken Dena," I say, turning to him.

Confusion flickers across his face. "Dena? But I-I saw her barely—"

"They've tested my blood on her already. It works."

"Then we don't have much time," he says, his eyes hardening.

"Dena said there's a chance of her being able to do something inside the lab."

"I have to go," he says suddenly, stepping toward the door.

"Wait," I call. He looks back at me, eyes questioning. I'm afraid to lose him. I'm selfish, I realize. "I'm sorry about Chancellor Kole."

"It's not your fault," he says.

"What could happen? If we gave my blood to"—I stop before I can say our people. Because I can't.

I belong nowhere. I'm not human, I'm not Jute. I'm stuck in between. A half-breed like Julian. And at the same time, I'm not like him.

I really am alone if I look at it that way. I shake away the thought. "The humans."

He smiles. "War."

When I think of war, I see blood. Pain and suffering. Nothing good comes from war.

But there is good. There will be an outcome. One side will find peace, solace. While the other will suffer a bitter loss.

There are two sides to the coin of war.

27

I FALL ASLEEP WITH SLATE'S VOICE IN MY head. *I've been loving you for seventeen years as my dead child. Why stop when you're alive?*

And I hope he's okay. That he isn't wallowing in grief.

There's no way to tell, but I'm sure I've been asleep long enough for the night to have shifted into day. It's odd, going a full day without watching the stars twinkle and beam down at me. I even miss the redness of the ground beneath my feet and the dust that swirls in the distance.

I slide out of bed as a soft knock sounds at the door. I bang my knee against the bed frame and yelp under my breath before limping to the door, expecting to see Julian.

But it's a girl about a year older than me, with fiery auburn hair and soft features. Her skin is the color of the rare fresh milk we used to get from the Jute.

"Can I come in?" Her voice is airy. She looks at me with fierce green eyes and strolls in as if she owns the room. The room's dark beauty seems to lighten in her wake. She pauses by the bed and turns back to me.

"Are you going to stand there?" She asks bluntly. But the way she asks it comes off as innocent curiosity. I close the door.

"I apologize," she says with a bow. The ends of her long hair brush against the carpet. "I am Mia Leen, your maid. I am humbled, Princess, to have been granted the honor to attend to you." I wonder if she was made to memorize her short speech and for a moment, all I can do is stare.

"Lissa," I finally say.

"Pardon?" She leans closer.

"Call me Lissa."

"As you wish, Princess—I mean, Lissa," she says, bowing her head.

"And please don't bow," I add.

"We've never had a princess," she says as if she didn't hear me. I imagine the green of her eyes to be like the land of Earth—lush, magnificent, never-ending.

"Well, I've never been a princess," I say dryly.

She laughs, the sound chiming in the air. She's carefree, like Dena, but at the same time, completely different.

"You're upset." She tilts her head to the side and fixes me with a stare that reminds me of the little birds I've read about.

I study her soft features. She's a stranger, a sweet stranger, but a stranger still. "I'm nervous, is all."

She nods, and I wonder if she sees through me the way Julian does.

"Are you Jute?" The moment the question escapes my lips, I regret it. It didn't sound as rude in my head.

But Mia is unfazed. She tilts her head again. "It is quite obvious. I don't wear a mask like humans do."

"Right. Sorry," I say.

"No need to be." She smiles and I smile back.

And after a moment: "You're not like her."

"Like who?" I ask, though I know full well. But I need to know what she thinks of my mother. I need to know if Mia is more human than Jute inside her heart.

Which brings another thought: what difference is there, between humans and Jute?

"Your mother, Her Majesty the Queen."

"How so?" I ask, playing with the edge of my dress sleeves.

"In more ways than one." She stares at me until I meet her eyes.

It's too early to call her an ally, but she isn't a foe.

"Now then," she says, gliding to the bed. She drops a group of bags onto the sheets and exhales. I feel sheepish for not noticing her load.

Her eyes brighten. "The ceremony is this evening! You must be excited, Lissa. You'll be the Princess!"

Her enthusiasm stretches a smile across my face. But I don't say a word.

How can I, when all I feel is dread spreading through me, threatening to paralyze my mind, numb my limbs, and tear a scream from my lungs?

"You're not excited," Mia says. She turns to her bags, pulling out colorful ribbons and powders, pastes and liquids. Makeup. Yet another something I've only read about.

It's silly, really. Women, and sometimes men, dabbing artificialities on their faces, hiding away their true beauty. Sometimes flawlessness is defined from within. Not from the pallor of your skin.

Certainly not when your skin isn't real.

"Why are you dressed like that?" she asks, her clatter ceasing for a moment. "Like you're going for a funeral?"

She tilts her head. Her own dress is a soft green. "Are you?"

Funeral. She doesn't know that until recently, I had no idea what happens to our dead once they hang. Only I had a funeral—and I was alive.

"I felt daring." I force a grin.

She grins back. "Welcome to the life, Lissa."

Everything is a blur. More maids flutter in and out of the room. Some of them are broken, limping, their smiles toothy with gaping holes where pearly white teeth should be. None of them are as beautiful as Mia. All of them bow and smile and profess their love for me, their soon-to-be Princess. Clearly, my mother makes them happy, despite the impossibility of the idea.

Mia sets five dresses across the bed, each a different color. I sit in a chair where a small girl weaves through my hair, pinning and twisting the strands with sure fingers almost as fast as my heartbeat. I lean forward to catch a glimpse of the dresses despite her sharp protests, though I'm certain I won't have a say in which one I wear.

The red one reminds me of Jutaire, a never-ending sea of blood. The blue one reminds me of Julian and hopeless despair. The green one reminds me of the land on Earth, lush and endless, something I fear I will never see. The white one reminds me of a world of light, beauty, and happiness, a world our one will never be.

The cream one with a warm brown sash reminds me of myself, lost between the shades of life, just as the color is a mixture of so many, lost in the shades and hues of the spectrum. Belonging somewhere, but nowhere.

I am lost in a world I have no place in. A world that has suddenly claimed me as heir, to a kingdom where I don't belong.

If I had a choice, that would be my dress.

The girl's fingers fall from my hair. Her thin lips curve into a smile and she brushes dark strands from her dark forehead. "All done, Princess."

I murmur a thank you and stand, about to turn to the mirror.

"No!" Mia shouts. I whirl around to face her, instinctively reaching for my nonexistent daggers. She laughs when she sees my expression and I can't stop the irritation from surging through my veins. "Not yet! Don't look in the glass 'til we're done."

I raise an eyebrow and give her a look, for which she chuckles a laugh. I run my fingers over the dresses. "Which one will I wear?"

"I don't know," Mia breathes. "But they're all gorgeous."

"Yes," I say, tilting my head. "Do I get to choose?"

In answer, the door opens. The maids freeze. Their friendly babbles cease. Queen Rhea steps into the room and the air instantly turns frigid.

"Hello, daughter."

"Hello," I say, realizing this is the first time I've actually greeted her. I wonder if I should bow, but I settle on dropping my eyes to the ground.

I do this for Dena's sake. For Julian's sake. And for my real father's sake. Because I have no respect for her, mother or not.

"These are the dresses, girl?" She turns to Mia. Her milky skin pales under the Queen's stare.

"Yes, your Majesty."

"They will do." Her tone is condescending.

"Which one do you like, darling?" She asks me.

When she looks at me, I see Chancellor Kole, dead. Dena, dying. What is it like to know you won't see the sunrise tomorrow? What is it like to know you'll die alone?

One of the maids sniffles in the silence of the Queen's words. I blink. Dena's dark eyes fade into the Queen's pale moonlight ones, waiting for my answer.

"I like them all," I say, flinching at the breathlessness in my voice. She won't let me wear what I like. She will always defy me as I will always want to defy her. She gives me a tight smile and I wonder if her eyes will ever reflect her lips.

"As do I, daughter, as do I." She trails her fingers across the dresses. Left to right. Right to left. The walls around us pulse with my heartbeat. The silence is heavy, heavy, smothering.

Her fingers touch the red one. "Bloody."

Her fingers tighten around the blue one. "Bright."

Her nails wrinkle the green one. "Lush."

Her eyes sweep past the white one. "Pure."

She stops at the cream one. "Perfect."

My breath swooshes out, confusing me. Why does it matter what dress I wear? But sweat trickles down my back and I realize it does matter. I am more vain than I thought.

Mia runs for the dress and picks it up. "Yes, your Majesty."

Queen Rhea turns and leaves. She doesn't even spare me a glance.

Why should she? I'll be dead in a few days.

For a few moments, the silence is kept. Everyone stares everywhere. The younger maids wring their hands as if the Queen sentenced them all to death. I was wrong about my mother keeping them happy. They fear her. And it's a wonder they don't fear me the same.

"All right, back to work," Mia sighs and the world spins again. Their voices pick up as one and my ears sing with the cacophony of their cadences. I lock eyes with Mia and hope she sees the silent gratitude in my eyes.

"You will look stunning, Lissa," she says excitedly, leaning close and squeezing my hand. I allow myself to smile, to let in her enthusiasm. To indulge. Because at least once before my death I want that.

And while the maids flutter around me in a flurry of color, my smile widens. And inside my heart, a weight softens.

"Wear this," Mia says when a maid sets a tray of jewelry on the bed between us.

I sift through the shimmering jewels and shiny chains as she reaches into the pocket of her simple dress and pulls out a handful of gold. At the end of the linked gold chain hangs an emerald square, the edges lined in swirling gold. Emerald and gold from deep within Earth.

"Where did you find that?" I ask, fingering the gem.

Her smile is full of remorse. "It was my mother's. It was all she had left before she lost her life."

I look up. I know nothing of her or her mother. "She had you."

She shakes her head and the green of her eyes turns liquid. She bites her lip. It's the first time I've seen her enthusiasm snuffed. "No. She lost me before the jewel."

"What happened, Mia?" I ask softly.

"I can't say," she says so softly. She raises the necklace and with it, her voice. "Wear it."

I gently push away her outstretched hands. "No. What if I lose it?"

She smiles as if she knows something I do not. "You won't. I need you to keep it safe. I need you to wear it."

I am silenced by the fierceness in her eyes that won't allow me to contradict her as she slips the chain around my neck. I see a ten-pointed star, this one in gold, before the gem kisses the hollow of my bare neck with cold lips. When she clasps the chain, it falls lower. She pulls it from beneath my dress and drops it in front of me. Another maid pushes Mia away and brushes something on my cheeks.

I close my eyes for the briefest of heartbeats and I feel the weight of the jewel in my heart more than my neck.

"Done."

Mia's exclamation sets my heart pounding. And when I part the curtains, I see that night has darkened the sky. We're right on time. It's confusing how my heart decides to accelerate. The maids titter around, all gasps and *ooh*'s and *ahh*'s. A blush explodes across my face, competing with the rose powder they brushed onto my pale skin.

"You look stunning. I told you so," she says with a smile. Two girls, twins I decide, judging by their matching olive skin and stunning hazel eyes, run to the bathroom. They come back, hefting a long mirror between them, wide grins stretching their faces. Mia turns to me with a grin of her own. "Now for the glass."

The set it on the bed and step back.

I see the girl in the mirror, her dress illuminating every inch of her exposed skin. I see her shimmering neck. Her chocolate brown eyes sparkle beneath dark lashes. I see her hair, two braids disappearing to the back of her head, pinned in a bun behind her skull. I see her lips, pink, soft, lush. I see someone beautiful. Breathtaking.

I see someone I never thought I could be.

I see myself.

But at the same time, I see my mother.

28

THE MAIDS LEAVE IN A FLURRY OF excited whispers. When the door closes behind them, Mia turns to me.

"You think this is all a lie, don't you?" She tilts her head and fixes me with that bird-like stare.

"You know more than you let on, don't you?" I tease. But I'm already nurturing the possibility that I have someone who could understand.

She breathes a laugh. I look in her eyes and for a moment, there are no Jute, there are no humans. There is no difference. We are all the same.

It's our hearts and souls that change us, define us, ruin us. Nothing else.

"I know of your blood, of the girl in the lab. I know many things, Lissa." She sounds tired.

The door opens before I can speak, and Rowan steps in, his open black coat reaching down to his knees, the shirt beneath it a silky midnight blue. A grin stretches across the side of his face. I meet his depthless blue eyes and wonder where his brother is.

"It's time, Princess," he says, flourishing a bow. His eyes flick to Mia and the disgust is clear on his face. But why? She is beautiful, both inside and out. I glance at her, wanting desperately to offer something. But she doesn't need anything. Her chin is raised and her eyes are strong. She doesn't care, her stance says.

"I was asked to escort you to the throne room," he says.

"Bye. And thank you, for everything," I say to Mia. She smiles and bows.

"Good-bye, Princess."

Rowan loops his arm through mine. Tingles spread through his touch and I want to pull away and press closer to him at the same time. Before we leave the room, I meet Mia's eyes one last time and I'm struck with a sudden sorrow pulling deep inside my heart. What if I never see her again?

The door closes, shutting away the thought.

"You look stunning," Rowan's voice is low in my ear. This time, I lean away from his face that is inches from mine and hope my smile is sweet. "I won't let you out of my sight. Queen's orders."

We walk down a flight of stairs and I realize why my hall was so empty. Everyone is on the lower floor.

"So many people," I whisper. He nods.

We push through the crowd, heading to the throne, where my mother sits wearing a dress of shimmering white.

Pure, she had said, when she fingered the white dress made for me.

She is stunning, not I. And I shiver at the reminder that we are more alike than I first thought.

As Rowan half-drags me through the crowd, eyes sweep past me. A hushed quiet passes through the crowd. Some think I'm another party invitee. Others blink when they realize who I am, but I pass them before they have a chance to grab my arm and voice their thoughts.

"Princess Lissa," the Queen calls from her throne, and the crowd falls silent. I look up at her as Rowan pulls me to the side, where steps rise up to her platform.

"Go on. Don't worry," he urges me, his face serious. In that moment, he isn't mad or evil—he's just a boy, like Julian. He smiles for the first time, a real smile. Maybe it's because the Queen can see him. Maybe it's because the crowd has silenced and every eye has turned to me. But I feel reassured by him. When I finally remember to breathe, I break away from his gaze and climb the steps.

Maybe he isn't as evil as Julian says he is. Maybe he only does what he is forced to do, like Chancellor Kole was.

Every eye is on me as I take the steps. Sweat trickles down my back. My heart pounds as if I am running for my life.

When I reach the top, the Queen hisses and her face pales. "Where did you get that?"

"What?" I ask. Her eyes are on the chain around my neck. Hundreds of eyes are on me.

"You know full well what I ask of. Tell me." Why is she so adamant and afraid? I study her stricken expression, my tongue suddenly dry.

"It was with the jewelry you sent for me. I adore it," I lie smoothly. I rub my fingers on the stone and smile at her.

She stares at me a moment longer, and finally pulls on a fake, razor-sharp smile.

"It is stunning, darling. Now come"—she raises her voice—"let us crown our heir."

The crowd roars in agreement, some hooting and howling, others murmuring to those standing beside them. The Queen watches them while I stand beside her, ready to shrink into the golden platform. My mind replays the desperation in her voice, the fear edging into her face.

Queen Rhea stands and walks to a dark-skinned man behind us, who holds a gold pillow in his hands. An alabaster tiara sits serenely on the cushion. It's small compared to the Queen's crown, made of metal twisting around a moonstone in the shape of a ten-pointed star that glints in its center. She picks it up with graceful fingers and a hushed quiet falls over the Jute swarming below us.

I feel nothing as she comes forward with an insensitive smile on her beautiful face. I notice the same star on her crown. What does it mean? It was on the Chamber, in the Tower, on the platform—what significance does it hold for my mother to carry it on her head?

And there's a matching one in gold on the emerald jewel around my neck. Why?

I feel nothing as the crown's weight descends on my head. But the crowd gasps and stares as if I have sprouted wings.

"People of White Plains, your Princess," Queen Rhea calls, settling into her throne. "Let the festivities begin."

I talk to so many people I don't know whose face is whose. Everything is a blur of voices and movement.

After what feels like years, I stumble down the steps, drunk from all the attention. Hands grasp my shoulders before I fall. I see the bottom of his coat and I lean into Rowan as he helps me stand, too exhausted to care about anything but a familiar face.

But the touch is too soft. Caring. Gentle. I look into his eyes. His wounds are gone. He looks different in the dark knee-length coat, more tamed.

His eyes darken. They miss nothing, not the jewel around my neck or the pearls in my ears, not even the shimmering of my neck. My heart races so fast, I'm afraid it will jump free from my ribcage.

"Hello," Julian says. "You look... amazing."

I blush and stand, slipping away from his hands burning into my bare skin. I struggle to say something, anything, to change the subject before I explode in a burst of red. "Are we going?"

"Oh, yes," he says, his lips quirking up in amusement. "In fact, we can leave now."

He cranes his neck and searches over the sea of heads around us. He drops his voice and flashes me a grin that sends my pulse racing. "Before Rowan gets here."

He says we must see the Queen first, and we hurry back up to her throne. This time, I don't feel countless eyes watching me, because everyone is enjoying the festivities. Queen Rhea raises a single eyebrow to acknowledge our presence and Julian bows.

"May we leave, your Majesty?" He asks. His voice is flat.

She ignores him, fixing me with her moonlight gaze instead. "I trust the half-breed. You may go." She smiles, her lips a crescent of blood.

"But be careful. Keep that in mind before you do anything dangerous, darling. I've already lost you once."

When I leaped from the carriage or when I was declared a dead baby?

"Thank you," I say instead and hope my gratitude is clear without sounding desperate. And I have the sudden urge to add something at the end.

"Mother."

My breath hitches when her eyes widen, and for the second time tonight, her features are stricken, her face frozen. The word affects her as much as it affects me.

"Let's go," Julian murmurs beside me, sensing the sudden tension. I let him lead me away, but I glance back. The Queen whispers something to the dark-skinned man beside her, but her face is still pale, her eyes distant.

We're almost by the door when hands fall around my waist. I gasp and whirl around.

"Princess," Rowan says. He bows and quickly shakes away the hair that falls over his eyes. It's longer than Julian's, curling at the nape of his neck, making him look older. His coat is gone. His eyes flick to Julian and he inclines his head. "Thank you for keeping an eye out for the Princess while I was away."

When I think Julian will stay quiet and leave, he snorts. A laugh threatens to burst from my lips. But I press my lips together and take in Rowan's surprise.

"I wasn't doing anything for you. We were leaving." He reaches for my hand. I let his fingers twine with mine and suddenly wish this were different. That Julian was slipping his fingers between mine because he wanted to, not because he was saving me from his brother.

I remember that day so long ago in the Chamber, when I was afraid to be touched. Now I want it more than anything.

"I don't think the Queen wants her precious daughter running off with a servant. In fact, I wonder what she'll say about this rendezvous." Rowan steps back. Julian's face transforms into one of mock horror. Again, I have to stifle a laugh. My arms tremble from the effort and he gives my fingers a tight squeeze.

Rowan pushes through the crowd, making his way to the Queen. Julian laughs and my pulse quickens as he pulls me in the opposite direction, toward the palace doors. The guards on either side move to stop him and he drops my hand, the smile fading from his face.

"Let them through," a third guard calls. Ilen. He bows his head slightly and when our eyes meet, he winks. My heart feels light.

The doors open, stealing my full attention. I hear them groan from the effort, and a little part of me feels sorry for them, forever swinging their massive weight back and forth.

Only when the night greets me do I remember: I was supposed to meet Dena.

29

THE NIGHT IS COOL AND THE STARS ARE bright. They shine down on me as if they are happy to see me. As if they missed me as much as I missed them.

I want to spread my arms beneath the cloudless night, because I'm finally free. But I force myself to walk calmly beside Julian.

I glance at him, the words rushing to my lips. *Dena is in danger.* But when I see his face, the words die away. He seems calm, happy even. There's a brightness to his face I haven't seen before and I don't want Dena to ruin this moment.

I am selfish. My bare skin glows in the moonlight. I've never bared so much skin.

"I've always wanted this. A moment where nothing else matters," Julian says, looking at me. I love the stillness of his voice.

The wind blows, running its fingers through his hair and tossing it over his eyes as he watches me intently. It whistles through the loops of the crown atop my head. Its soft fingers tug and pull, trying to yank it away, trying to tell me I don't belong in a palace. I want to tell the wind I don't belong on Jutaire, either.

"We'll have to walk there. I know how much you hate the mutants," he says, his tone apologetic.

Until now, I never thought to ask him where *there* is. "Where are we going?"

"Somewhere," he says with a quick clench to his jaw. "You'll like it."

How can I like something that pains him?

We walk in companionable silence. The white houses and shops are silent, the Jute either asleep or in the palace. Julian asks me questions, at times, and I answer, but mostly we are quiet. I learn that his father owns a plantation in the outskirts of White Plains. I learn that he and Rowan are only months apart. Rowan's mother is Jute, while Julian's was human.

I absently rub my fingers across the stone around my neck. Julian catches the movement.

"The Queen didn't like to see this," I say.

"There's a rumor of an emerald stone her sister once owned. That could be why."

"What happened to her?" I ask.

He shrugs nonchalantly. But his eyes rove up and down the houses and buildings around us. "Rumors, I don't know. They say she was murdered."

"By whom?" I stop walking.

"It doesn't matter."

I don't move. "Who did it? What do the rumors say?"

He turns to me and struggles for words. "For once, Lissa, *once*, can you ignore everything else and just... be? Pretend nothing is wrong for one night?"

He doesn't wait for my answer. I blink. I upset him.

"I'm sorry," I say, catching up to him.

He nods and bites his lip, but he doesn't look at me. "Queen Rhea."

"What?"

"They say it was the Queen."

My heart skips a beat. My mother murdered her own blood, her own *sister*.

I'm about to ask if she had any children.

A daughter. Mia.

But he speaks first. "Don't go looking for more trouble. Please, Lissa. We're already counting down to the day."

The day of my death.

"What will happen? When they take my blood."

"They'll suck you dry. Every bit, because they need some for everyone. Even if your blood multiplies quickly. Lissa—"

"I know, I know. Tonight isn't for the future." Because I have no future.

But I have hope. It's what moves me forward, step after step, breath after breath. Because there could be a future – despite what I know.

His lips curve into a small smile, as if he knows what goes through my mind. "We're almost there."

Eventually, the buildings and signs of civilization thin and towering, frightening boulders are all that dot the vast emptiness. The ground beneath me rises as we climb a hill.

Julian stops a few feet ahead and turns back with a grin. "This is it."

I look at the boulders around us. "This?" I ask in amusement.

"No. Come on."

His fingers slip between mine. One by one they close around each of my own and I forget to breathe. Every millimeter of my skin that touches his burns like the electricity from a soldier's barrel.

He gently pulls me forward and all of Jute territory unfolds before me.

I am on top of it all, watching down at the world that has claimed me to die on its lands.

The palace lights shine and twinkle like stars. The white walls radiate in the moonlight. The lights of the houses and shops glow like eyes.

"Not that. This." His hushed voice washes over my ear. I turn with a gasp.

The Ruins.

The remains of the ship the first humans came on. The ship that had crashed. The scraps of metal that started this all.

Julian watches me expectantly.

"I thought they were encrusted in sand." I say finally, recalling Gage's words.

Julian's hand shoots to his hair. "I-uh. They used to be."

I turn to face him. "You cleaned them all?"

"Is it so impossible to believe?" He asks and I look away. Because his question asks much more.

The ship was silver, though time has worn it down to a matte gray. Streaks of red and blue shoot down several areas, a placid adornment. It really *is* in ruins. Part of a wing juts out of the ground to my right, another one far to my left. Domed pieces from the body dot the area.

Nothing from the interior remains, only the outside pieces entombed forever in the ground.

The wind is quiet and the world is hushed. As if the surrounding area will always mourn the people and the ship we lost.

In a way, the sight *is* breathtaking. Julian was right—I do like it.

"It's beautiful," I say, my voice echoes strangely. He smiles.

"Sometimes," he says softly, his fingers trailing along the wing, "you only see the beauty of something once it's broken."

His face is somber, sad almost. He means more than the ship.

"You're sad," I say, because I don't want him to be. "We can leave."

"No!" He comes closer and holds out his hand. I hesitate before reaching out, and his fingers slip between mine. He leads me deeper into the Ruins, toward a curving piece of the ship's body, rising like a small hill on the ground. We climb it, him steadying me as I go.

"My mother used to bring me here," he says. He's never spoken to me about his mother. He stretches his long legs and leans back on his hands. I wrap my arms around my legs, my dress flowing around me.

"What happened to her?" I ask.

"She had a fever," he says. He looks out into the night and I wonder if his thoughts are plagued with happiness that will only reside in his memories.

"I didn't"—he stops and exhales—"I didn't want to give her up. To the Jute.

"Chancellor Kole let us bury her, not far from here." He draws a path down the metal with his finger. "Rowan knows."

He looks up at me. "It's why he holds so much leverage over me."

"But why?" I ask. I don't want to offend him, but her body is already gone.

"The body's gone," he says, as if he can read my mind, "but we defied orders. If word gets to the Queen there would be trouble."

I think of that girl, with barely enough cloth to cover her sun-kissed shoulders, staring as the carriage rolled away. What would it be like to die because of something that happened years before you were even born?

Julian's hand slides over mine.

"It won't happen," he says softly. But he can't know that.

"They're so heartless. I can't understand why they want what isn't theirs."

"We can't blame them for wanting. Without wants, nothing would ever happen. It's the methods we use to get them that are the problem."

"I guess," I say, making a face. To me, there's nothing to justify what they will do.

He laughs, a beautiful sound that shatters the dark world around us, and jumps down, holding out his hand. "And you? What do you want?"

I drop down beside him and think, closing my eyes. In the darkness of my closed eyelids and the hushed silence of the night, I see one object.

Round and green and white and blue.

"Earth." My voice is soft. I turn in time to see something flicker in his eyes. "What about you? What do you want?"

He meets my eyes. Intense. A million words in one penetrating look.

"You."

The world pauses. The wind ruffles his hair but the world is still and silent.

I take a step back before I can think. He gently pushes me against the broken wing jutting out of the ground, his touch searing through my nerves. My heart thuds in my chest, thrums in my ears. My body pulses with energy.

His fingers brush the hair away from my face and my heart stops. My cheeks burn, burn, burn. And then he is there. Here. He lowers his head to mine.

"You, Lissa. I just didn't know it."

His lips close over mine.

Soft.

Hesitant.

They taste as free as his scent. Heat shoots up my stomach, tendrils of want and need. My heart explodes in my chest. The shards melting away in the heat of his touch.

My head angles to the right. His to the left. It's as if we've done this so many times before. When really, I have never even touched another soul like this before him.

There's suddenly too much space between us. No space at all. Everywhere his body touches mine, I ignite. He pushes against me, our bodies fitting together as if we were meant to be. I can feel his heart racing against my chest. He runs his hands up and down my bare arms. Like flint against flint, electricity courses from him to me. Me to him. His lips press harder. Desperate. And we're both gasping for air.

His hair tickles my forehead. I reach up, and the silk is unlike anything I've ever felt before. I wrap my fingers around the dark strands and pull him closer, closer, though there is no space between us. He groans against my lips, his breath against my skin, my chest and my stomach pulsing. Throbbing. His fingers press against my back, holding me against him, ten pinpoints of searing heat.

I gasp and he leans away, staring at me with dark intensity before his lips touch mine again.

This is how I suspect humans will die without oxygen. Gasping. The way I feel I will die without Julian. Without his lips against mine.

"Julian," I whisper against his lips. He stills. His eyes open and all I see are two pools of depthless desire. He leans his forehead against mine, a gorgeous half-smile teasing his lips, and I raise my finger and trace it along the curve of his smile. I don't know where this courage comes from. Maybe it was there all along, inside me, waiting for him.

His lips are soft beneath my fingers, warm. Bruised because of my teeth.

"That's the first time you've said my name." His voice is a caress against my skin. A soft, breathless laugh spills from my lips. My body continues to hum and he chuckles softly. "So this is what it feels like to have the world at your feet."

I splay my fingers across his chest, remembering the words I said to him that night. I feel his heart racing beneath my touch. I feel the muscles laced beneath his shirt. And I feel happy. Loved. Wanted. Needed for more than my blood.

"I never thought this could happen," he says thoughtfully. He looks down at my hands, his eyes sparkling. Moonlight hits the right of his face, illuminating his blushed skin, the scar along his side, and the ridge in his nose.

He is beautiful.

"What?" I breathe. He raises his eyes back to mine. And I'm reminded of the first time I met him. The way he looked at me the way no one else ever had. Intent. Focused. As if I mattered.

"That I could fall in love," he whispers, kissing me again. And I realize I have always wanted this. Ever since he saved me in the Chamber, and before that in the crophouses, I have wanted him. I just didn't know it.

He parts his lips, slowly parting mine as he does. I shiver and he pulls away with a grin. His white teeth sparkle in the dark. A laugh bubbles from my lips and for a moment, I don't recognize it as my own. And the way his eyes flash, I know he doesn't either.

His lips graze my neck, feathering the skin Mia made sure I bared. My hands flatten on his chest and I feel the shudder that goes through him.

And he stops. He looks up at me, his eyes like the sea as it laps against the shore, lazy beneath the moon. He brings his lips to mine and places one more kiss.

Something slices through my heart, pulls tears to my eyes. Because I feel the finality in it, the sorrow. He touches his nose against mine. And I never want to be away from him. Never.

"I'm sorry, Lissa."

And I hear Julian's laugh. Only, it isn't Julian's.

30

calls, his voice full of amusement. Seven shadows of men slowly surround us.

I think I should be afraid. But I look at Julian and I still imagine it's just us. I still feel the ghost of his lips against mine. My body still hums with our magic.

The rest of me is numb.

I reach for something, anything, but my mind is drunk with Julian.

"That has to be the best act you've ever put on," Rowan laughs.

Now, I feel something. Pain cuts through my heart, shattering me. I look at Julian, my eyes holding half the accusation and betrayal my heart feels.

But he knows.

He's Julian. He will always know how I feel.

"Lissa, no." His voice is a whisper. His fingers tremble when he reaches out and I shrink back, sidestepping away from the wing. His face cracks, and with it, my soul. He stares at me for what feels like forever, and finally turns away, trembling with anger.

"Rowan, you liar," he growls and I flinch. He throws himself at Rowan. But two of Rowan's men grip him by his shoulders and hold him back. He pulls free and manages to throw a punch at one of them before they grab him again, kicking him in his groin. He groans and drops to his knees. Rowan smirks and turns to me.

I stand tall and stare back, because Julian taught me more than how to use a blade. The wind kisses my burning skin.

But inside, I am still trying to make sense of it all. Because I don't know if everything that happened between Julian and me was an act.

What if he lured me here? Away from the palace so Rowan can take me for whatever madness he wanted me for?

I shift my gaze to Julian. His eyes have been on me the entire time, watching me, reading me. He struggles against his captors. "No, Lissa. Please, don't."

I say nothing. My chest hurts. Breathing hurts. Because everything inside me shattered beneath his touch, and I can't put myself together again.

"What do you want with me, Rowan?" I ask. I raise my voice because I don't want to step closer to him.

"Julian didn't tell you?" He feigns curiosity.

"I asked you." I don't know if this is a game. I don't want him to speak of Julian.

He laughs at my tone. "You certainly aren't the same girl I met over a month ago, are you?"

I stare until he stops laughing.

"You're coming with me," he announces, stepping closer.

"Am I?" I ask.

"And Julian will go back to the palace. Alone." He looks at me pointedly, waiting for the words to sink in.

They do. Oh, they do.

When Julian shows up without me, the Queen will have him tortured. Imprisoned. Possibly killed. And he'll say nothing because of Rowan's leverage.

"I know"—Julian pants—"what you're going... to do. Don't Rowan."

Rowan barks a laugh.

"You're mad," Julian spits. He tries again to break free his captors. They don't budge. They're burly, stronger than Julian's lithe and muscle. But I've seen Julian break free from Jute soldiers, and I can tell he isn't trying enough. Or maybe he's like me, still drunk from moments ago.

"We're all mad here," Rowan muses. "Some of us just more than others."

I don't feel the men creeping up to me until their calloused hands suffocate my arms. I don't struggle against them, I hold Rowan's gaze, hoping my defiance shows in my eyes.

I try to think of what Rowan wants, but all that rolls through my head is Julian. And how he may never see tomorrow. How I may never see him again. How he may have known all along that Rowan would come for me.

Through the corner of my eyes, I see him stop struggling. Something unravels inside me, and I know what he wants, the way he always knows what crosses my mind.

He wants my eyes on his, one last time—because he may never see me again. And I give him that.

I look at him, into him, as if it is only him and me in this bleeding world.

"Give him some bruises," Rowan says. "Send him back to the palace. And Julian, please don't try anything stupid."

The men obey with low, throaty laughs. They throw punches to his stomach, they kick him in the shin. Julian groans.

They beat Julian while I watch, my body weakening with each blow. He doesn't even try to fight back. My lips tremble and my vision blurs.

"That's enough," Rowan says, his voice tight. Could he feel the ties of his blood?

I grit my teeth and clench my fists. But I if I open my mouth, words will spew out of my anger, not my conscious. Words that could worsen everything.

Rowan strolls toward me while Julian watches, heaving and sagging between the men holding him like a doll. He trails a long finger down my cheek and the men tighten their hold on me so I can't move. He looks so much like Julian.

"I hate you," I hiss, pulling away.

He smirks and drops his hand. "Then we're heading in the right direction. After all, love and hate go hand in hand."

Julian's eyes bore into me until Rowan's men drag him away. And I know it wasn't an act.

I can only hope the entire human race is worth his silence.

The freedom of the night is gone, replaced with four dark walls. I sit up when I hear breathing.

In the dark, all I can see are his dark eyes. My murky mind grasps onto a single image. Julian.

But reality rushes back. Julian isn't here. He's in the palace. Being tortured.

"Rowan?" My voice is a raw whisper. Was I screaming?

"You're awake," he says, shifting on the edge of the bed.

"Why am I here?" Why do I sound so vulnerable?

"Where are you?" He answers with a tilt to his head. Strands of darkness fall off the side of his face. His voice sounds so much like Julian's. Too much like Julian's. Their differences are only noticeable when they're together.

"I"—I frown—"I don't know."

"You're beautiful," he says, reaching for me. The bed groans beneath his shifting weight. Dangerous, nervous energy rushes through me. How did I get here? His fingers brush back the hair on my face, his touch softer than I expect. I don't flinch away. All I can do is hold my breath and stare into his eyes, seeing Julian.

"Why did you do that to him?" I whisper. I don't want to say Julian's name out loud. I have only said it once. And if I say it again, I know that one instant will flood into my mind and I will never submerge from the memory. I will drown in its grief.

"He was a distraction. I need you for myself."

He says it so simply, innocently. As if Julian was an obstacle and I am an object to be acquired by any means possible. The words are nothing to him. Julian is nothing to him.

He looks at me as if I should understand. As the Queen's first in command, he's probably used to getting whatever he wants.

"Why?" I ask slowly, hoping he will spill his plans. "Why do you need me?"

"I just do," he says. He's mad *and* smart. He runs his smallest finger down the bridge of my nose and I shiver. His lips slowly curve up in a smile and my body stills when I see Julian again.

They may as well be twins on the outside.

"Wash up and come to the hall."

He stands and leaves, and I'm irked by his command.

I lie back in bed when I'm alone. I feel the ghost of Julian's touch on my lips, my neck, my arms. I see his soft eyes. My faintly throbbing lips are still swollen. What will they do to him?

Lying here will help no one. I sit up.

Surprisingly, I do as Rowan says. But what surprises me most is this: the instant I remember Rowan's touch, a gnawing craving rises in me. Threatens to take over me. He killed Chancellor Kole before my eyes. He had his men beat Julian feet away from me. And yet, this feeling wrenches at my heart.

Maybe, just maybe, we're all mad here.

I expect a pair of pants and a top to change into. But it's another dress, deep blue and soft to the touch. As soft as Julian's hair. I dig my nails into the flesh of my arm and the memory recedes.

I slip into a larger room, which is mostly dark with an illustrated domed ceiling. I seize the chance to look around, get a glimpse of something.

Because if Rowan is the Queen's first in command, why would he hide me from her? Simply to get rid of Julian? The doubt in me is strong.

"Princess Lissa?"

I turn towards the sound of the voice, which belongs to a man with graying hair and smiling eyes. His lips are as pale as his skin. And when he smiles, it is almost as if he doesn't have lips at all.

"Rowan would like to see you," he says, clearing his throat. I study him a moment longer, because something seems off about him.

He's wearing a mask.

The clear Louen fogs with his labored breathing. He isn't Jute.

"You're human," I say, surprised.

He smiles again, the edges of his eyes crinkling. He neither accepts nor denies my statement. A true politician, Gage would say.

"Right this way," he says. I don't know where he'll take me, but I might finally get answers.

"What was your name?" I ask, following him through another door.

"I never gave you my name. But I can. It's Eli." He walks with sure steps and opens the door to another room.

"You may have a seat wherever you'd like. Rowan had business in the palace, but he'll be here shortly," he says. I nod and he leaves without another word.

I stay still for a moment, holding my breath to see if anyone else is here.

I wish I could sense Jute like Julian can. Maybe it's something that can only come from a father. At the thought, Slate's gray eyes flood my mind, swimming with love. I don't know how I spent seventeen years believing Gage was my father when he lacked Slate's love.

The room is rectangular, with a fireplace on the wall to my left. In front of it is a wide chair. The crackling fire casts a warm, inviting glow across its fabric surface. I pause.

The fire is orange, but the air isn't oxygen. I'm too tired and numb to even try to understand.

A map sits on the wall above the fireplace. Along the opposite wall is a table, stretching from one end to the other, covered in swords, shining ornaments and other things I can't make out.

The door opens and closes behind me. I turn to see Rowan, stunning as always. A pair of black pants hangs low around his waist. He has traded his usual darkness for a silky white shirt, the first few buttons opened to reveal the pale bronze skin of his neck.

He smirks when my eyes linger on his bare skin a moment too long and heat rushes to the back of my neck. I look into his eyes and see Julian. No. This isn't Julian. I focus on the differences, however small.

His hair is slightly longer than Julian's. The scruff on his jaw is more pronounced, making him look older. His stance is lazy when I know he is strong and quick, whereas Julian stands attentive and calm. Two opposites at once, always.

"You're fast." He speaks first, glancing meaningfully at my new dress. When I don't say anything, he exhales and crosses the room to the wide chair. The flames sway in the wake of his movement. He sinks into the seat.

"What are you doing, Rowan?" I blurt out, shaking my head in confusion.

He sighs and runs a hand through his hair. "Can you just not worry for once?"

I freeze. Was he there when Julian asked me the same question? No. I remember the way Julian's eyes roved the streets.

Their minds are more similar than I thought.

"What should I do then?" I ask. I need him to speak. To tell me. To trust me.

"Come, sit, talk." He shrugs like it doesn't matter.

UN*breath*ABLE

But by the way he holds himself—his carelessness tinged with uncertainty—I can tell it does matter. I matter.

I cross the room and sit on the carpet by his feet. I lean against the chair and stare into the flames until they burn inside me. I'm more comfortable here, even if we are only separated by the small elevation.

"Did you know there's a ship?" He asks. I hold my breath when he reaches for me. Through the corner of my eye I see his hesitation. It's in these small acts of uncertainty that I find humanity in him, a reason that begs to give him a chance. His fingers softly brush the hair away from my neck as if I may demolish beneath his touch.

"No," I lie. My voice is a bare whisper, because I don't want to break his thoughts. Because I can't muster anything louder.

"It's magnificent," he says in awe.

"You've seen it."

"Yes." He shifts in the chair. I glance back at him, lock eyes. I break away first.

In the fire, I see Julian. I see him gritting his teeth against the pain. I see his eyes flooding with agony.

And you? What do you want?

Earth, I said stupidly. While he wanted me.

"What's this?" Rowan's voice. Julian's voice. What is the difference? His finger trails along my cheek, wiping away a rogue tear.

"Will I see it?" I ask instead. Will Julian live? I desperately blink away my tears.

"And board it." He tilts his head.

"I don't understand," I say. Because I'm going to die, not get on that ship.

He chooses this moment to stand. He holds his hand out to me and I consider ignoring it. But I don't. I need to get out of here. I need to save Julian. I place my hand in his, ignoring the trills that shoot through me.

He pulls me up. Against him.

In a heartbeat, my body is pressed against his. His grip tightens before I can pull away in surprise. I crane my neck up to meet his eyes and my breathing quickens. His eyes darken when they fall to my neck and climb to my lips. And without meaning to, I run my tongue over them. His eyes flash. My insides pulse.

He brings his face close to mine. Julian. Rowan. Julian. Rowan. I can't stop the dangerous need spreading through me. It takes over me. This desire, as overwhelming as Jutaire's air.

Rowan missed nothing.

When he's satisfied with what he sees, he leans close. I see the flecks of black sprinkling his blue eyes. His hair brushes against my skin.

And he breathes against my lips. "I'll see you soon."

I'm only alone in my room for a moment before a soft knock sounds at the door and Eli walks in.

"My apologies, miss." He bows. "Rowan asked to bring you to the dining room. You must eat."

I'm still trembling. And angry. Angry at Rowan for doing this to me. But isn't it my fault, too? I squeeze my hands together and press them into my lap. Eli narrows his eyes, and only then do I see that they are blue.

"Are you alright, miss?" He takes a step closer.

"I'm fine," I say quickly. The words come out harsh, but he doesn't seem to notice. Or if he does, he doesn't react.

He nods like he understands. "You mustn't be late."

I swallow the bitter laugh that bubbles to my throat. I want to ask him what will happen if I'm late. Because there's nothing worse that can happen to me. Everything has been taken from me. Rowan has nothing to hold over me as he did over Julian.

And that's when it hits me. Rowan has no leverage. There's nothing he can use to blackmail me.

He needs my trust.

I slip off the bed and follow Eli down the hall.

If Rowan wants my trust before he'll share his plans, I will give it to him. Because mad or not, Rowan is smart.

And two can play at that game.

31

THE DINING ROOM IS EMPTY. SAVE FOR
Rowan sitting on one end. Eli pulls out the chair on the
other and I sit down.

It's ridiculous. Such a long hall, its grandeur evident in
the intricate moldings and the glossy finish of the carved
wooden table.

And empty.

I feel sorry for Rowan. But then, up until recently, I
was alone too.

"Eat. You'll need the energy," Rowan says from his
end. I don't ask what I need the energy for. In fact, I don't
ask anything, or even acknowledge him. I eat, because why
not?

Unlike the Chancellors and the rest of the human
race, the Jute don't eat the same bland porridge mixed
with every vegetable from the crophouses. They have fresh
leaves and colorful vegetables, something the porridge
very rarely hints at.

When my plate is clean, a flawless girl with dark hair and equally dark skin comes forward. She holds a swab in one hand, a finger prick and vial in the other.

This is what the energy is for, the sparkling needle says.

I scramble out of the chair and face Rowan. "What are you doing, Rowan?" I hiss.

"We'll need a sample. And I expect you to give it." He says simply, lazily. "Hold out your arm, Lissa."

"No," I press my hand against my chest. Rowan's eyes follow my movement.

"If you abide, I'll make sure you go to Earth."

"Why? Why do *you* need my blood?" I ask. But I hear his words. My mother would never take me to Earth. He sets his jaw, his eyes livid. But I don't care. His anger means nothing to me. He can't hurt me.

"Let's just say it's time for your mother's rein to end," he says, standing.

End. My mother's rein. The Queen of the Jute.

My breath hitches as everything clicks into place. Rowan's madness, Julian's fear, my mother's desperation when I said Rowan and I had met. The room swerves and spins. I reach out to steady myself on the table and sink into the chair beside him. He watches me, his eyes startling.

I try to look away, but I can't. Because those eyes will always have that effect on me. Julian and Rowan will always be two sides to the same stone, mirrors of one another.

Is he like Julian? Does he know what goes through my mind when my voice is silent?

I feel the prick, the pull. I feel my blood seeping into a vial I don't want to see. I don't look. I don't even move until the girl's footsteps recede into another hall.

Sorrow wells up inside me and crashes through me. Because with every breath, I get closer and closer to being sucked dry.

I went from being alone, knowing only one other soul, to something two groups needed—the Jute and the humans. Now there are three groups and the humans don't even know they need me.

Eli leads me back to my room. By the time he opens the door, the small wound has healed. He lingers a moment longer, and I take my chance to question him.

"Do you know what Rowan is going to do?" I ask. I take his hand and lead him to the chair beside my bed. His skin is papery thin and I wonder how much life he has left in him.

"I know of your blood. I know of the ship. And I know Rowan is out of his wits," he says seriously. "I don't really know the details."

"Do you know where we are?" I ask, biting my lip. Eli should know *something*.

"Not too far from the palace, if that's what you're asking. But we're past Queen Rhea's radius," he says, rubbing his chin. So that's why she didn't come after me.

"Do you ever leave?"

"Rarely. But there are a few people who come by, messengers and the like. If you want to get word to someone in the palace, I can do that." I wonder if the possibility of helping me makes him happy or wary.

"There's a girl, Mia Leen—"

His eyes widen and his face freezes. His hands clamp down on the chair, knuckles deathly white.

"Where did you hear that name?" His voice is hoarse.

"Mia?"

"Lower your voice," he hisses. I drop to my knees in front of him.

"Why? What is it?" I ask.

"You don't know?" He asks, furrowing his brow. I shake my head.

"Rumors, mostly." But he believes whatever the rumors say. I can tell he hopes they're true. He pauses, clearly deciding if he can trust me or not.

"Your mother had a sister elder to her. She was queen, by birth. When she died mysteriously, they say she was murdered by Rhea."

I nod, encouragingly. He has to have more to add to Julian's story. "Only few people know this, but it is said Queen Mina had a daughter. One she hid from her sister and the rest of the Jute world. She gave up her daughter to a merchant on the street. When he died, the girl went missing. The only piece of Queen Mina she had left was a necklace, a marked green and gold jewel that no one knows for sure exists."

But it *does* exist. I reach for my neck, though I know the emerald isn't there. It's gone, along with the cream dress I wore.

"Mia is the girl's name?" I ask. He raises his eyebrows when I say *is*.

"It was," he says.

"Mia," I pause, "is alive."

His eyes harden. "You aren't much different from him, are you? I didn't come here for your amusement. I wanted to offer whatever help I could."

"No!" I grab his hand. He sits back down, his gaze untrusting, his face closed.

And I tell him.

"So she's the true heir?" I ask. There's a light shining in my chest, filling me with giddiness. Because Mia is good, inside, outside—she is thoroughly good. And the thought of her ruling the Jute sends my flicker of hope shining like a beacon.

She is as human as a Jute can get—if only humans were as pure as the word implies.

Eli nods quickly. He's as hopeful as I am. But we both know Mia being crowned as the rightful heir is slim—there's no way Queen Rhea will allow it. And now, with Rowan a part of the mix, the complications have multiplied.

"Will you get word to her... that I'm here?" I ask. He rubs his small graying beard.

UN*breath*ABLE

"I will try. I doubt she goes by Mia, it's too dangerous," he says. I wonder again why she decided to trust *me* with her name. "But I'll try my best."

A knock sounds at the door. I glance at him before crossing the room.

"Lissa," Rowan murmurs. He steps into the room without an invitation. I step away from his closeness and he mimics me, stepping forward. I press myself against the wall and he comes closer still. I sneak a glance at Eli. Rowan notices.

"Leave, old man," he growls. Eli goes to the door, not even bristling at Rowan's tone. He stops and looks at me, his eyes worried. But he knows I am strong enough. He bows his head, not because I'm a princess, but because I'm a friend.

And he leaves me alone with Rowan.

My whole body pulses with that dangerous pull that rises whenever Rowan is near.

"Why was he here?" He asks, tilting his head. Why is Rowan so close?

"He wanted to see if my wound had closed," I say, thinking fast.

"You're Jute," he shoots back. "We heal fast."

"I'm only half Jute." I remind him.

"There's something I want to show you," he says. I want him to give me room to breathe.

"Oh?" I say.

"Oh, yes," he says with a grin. I look away when I see Julian.

Every heartbeat I waste with Rowan is a heartbeat of agony for him.

He crouches down by the bed and opens one of the three drawers along the side that I didn't see before.

He pulls out a mask and makes sure I'm watching before he presses it to his face. The mask suctions to his skin and the rush of oxygen clouds the clear Louen. I struggle to keep my face blank.

I watch as he breathes in and out. A slow grin transforms his face as oxygen surges through his system. His skin doesn't pale as it does when a Jute breathes oxygen. His eyes don't dilate.

My blood works.

It's done. There's no doubt anymore.

He pulls the mask off and breathes in the sweet air around us. "It's pretty bland, compared to this."

"This is intoxicating," I agree, but my heart is banging against my rib cage. It's happening, already. They're using my blood.

He raises one eyebrow and tosses the mask on the bed. "You?"

"I meant the air," I say flatly. His eyes fall to my throat when I swallow uneasily.

"And you," he says.

"Where is my necklace?" I ask, steering the subject away from me.

He angles his head and narrows his eyes. Does he know about Mia? "Why?"

"I liked it. I want it back." I wonder if I sound as obnoxious as he does, because you are who you associate yourself with.

"I'll give it to you," he says simply and I blink in surprise.

My heart skips a beat when his fingers reach for his neck and he begins unbuttoning his shirt, his gaze hot. I step back, but again, the wall is behind me. When every button is undone, he drops his hands by his sides and I'm thankful that he at least *left* the shirt on.

The necklace hangs around his neck.

I see the gold chain, the green stone. I see his chest too, the muscles tight and lean.

"Can I have it?" I ask. My voice is tight. Hushed.

"Take it." His eyes flash and his jaw shifts.

I take one step toward him, expecting him to move closer. Instead, he shifts so he's a foot from the wall adjacent to us, but he's otherwise still.

"Why are you doing this?" I ask. There's a plea in my voice.

"There isn't an answer for everything." He says softly with a shrug.

I stop, inches away. I look at his chest. No. I look at the jewel and reach for it, and I notice, barely, that he holds his breath too. His chest is a sculpture of stone, brushed in the light caramel I've read about. Heat creeps up my neck as I think this.

I focus on the stone.

But I can't. Our bodies are inches apart. His breath is hot on my skin. I can feel the heat of his body as if it's mine. I notice everything no matter how hard I try not to. The way his silky Louen pants hang from his bare hips. The way his shirt hides so much and bares so much. The way the collar of his shirt brushes against the scruff on his jaw. The way his jaw angles and his lips curve into a small dark smile, as if he knows something I do not.

I reach for the stone. My fingers tighten into fists when his hands close around mine and my heart explodes. He pulls me against him. Turns. And I am sandwiched between the wall and his body.

It all happens in heartbeats. I can't breathe. Danger pulsates through me.

"Rowan." My voice is soft. I can't stop seeing Julian.

"Hush," he says quietly. "Do you want the necklace?"

I swallow and nod.

"Take it," he breathes.

My hands tremble as I reach for the chain, forcing air through my lips. In, out, in, out. His breathing mixes with mine and I lose my concentration. My fingers brush against his burning skin. He watches my every move. Drinks in my every emotion. I lift the chain over his head and slip it over mine.

But he doesn't move. My eyes flicker to his, to the deep pools of darkness staring back at me. He leans close. I can almost feel his lips on mine. Barely, just barely, I lean forward, my heart throbbing.

UN*breath*ABLE

My breath shudders. Something in me desperately wants to know the feel of his lips against mine. But I don't kiss him. I can't kiss him.

I'm dying.

And after what seems to be forever, he pulls away. I breathe.

"We'll be leaving soon. You should change. There's another dress behind that door." He is as breathless as I am, and I find slight comfort in that. No, I can't find comfort at all.

"Thank you." I force the words from my mouth. They fall one by one, in a whisper. "For the jewel."

"It was never mine." He smirks and the door closes behind him.

I drop to my knees the moment he leaves. Sobs rack through my body. I nearly kissed him. I'm going mad. I am mad.

I think of Julian, somewhere in a dark place. I hear his groans of pain, see his eyes barely able to stay open.

I rock back and forth on the cool ground and clutch my stomach. I feel his pain as if it is my own. I can barely tell the difference.

There is no difference.

We're leaving, Rowan said. I force myself to my feet and make my way to the closet. I pull the lavender and gray dress from the hanger, ignoring the deepness of the neck and the buttons dropping along the front. Rowan must have chosen it for me himself.

But I change. I need to get out of here before Rowan drives me mad. I pretend I am another person and leave the room.

And I will myself to believe every step takes me closer to Julian.

32

MY CHEEKS STILL BURN AS I HURRY DOWN the hall. I head in the direction of the dining hall, hoping to see someone other than Rowan, because I don't think I can look at him.

I hear a creak as I turn the corridor. Fingers wrap around my wrist and before I can pull away, I'm jerked into darkness.

"Don't struggle."

Light floods the small space.

"Eli?" I whisper. We're in a closet with brooms, buckets, and rags strewn about.

"Did he hurt you?" His blue eyes search my face. There's something in the way his intense gaze roves my face that reminds me of Julian, though I'm sure I'm imagining the likeness. It could be the blue eyes.

I wonder if my cheeks are still flushed.

"No," I say quickly. I feel the urge to steer him away from Rowan, as if something happened between us that no one should know of. He stares at me a moment longer, deciding for himself.

"I found these," he says finally. He holds out the daggers Julian carved for me, and the gun I saved for Dena.

"How? Where?" I ask as he helps me strap one to my shoulder and one above my ankle.

"I have my ways," he says with a warm, fatherly smile.

"Thank you, Eli," I say, earnestly.

He nods and his smile fades. "I tried to get word to Mia. It might be a while."

I nod and bite my lip. "We didn't expect it to be easy."

"No, we didn't." He studies me closely. "Are you sure you're alright, Lissa?"

"I'm fine," I say quickly. I need to get away before my face betrays everything. I reach for the door.

"Be careful," he calls as I shut it behind me. I want to tell him it won't matter how much care I take.

"Where are you running to?" Rowan's voice stops me in my tracks.

The sleeves of his shirt are rolled up a quarter of the way, hands lazy in his pockets. I still feel the tickle of his hair on my face.

"I was looking for you," I say. My eyes stray to his lips. I still can't believe he nearly kissed me. That I nearly kissed him.

"Were you?" Rowan asks, amused. He studies my new dress.

"You said we were leaving." I point out.

"Ah, yes. I said that. We leave this way, not that." He points in the opposite direction.

"I don't live here," I say, defending myself.

He murmurs something to himself and leads me the other way. The hall ends in the map room with the fireplace. He tells me to wait and moves toward one of the three doors leading from here.

I crane my neck when he opens the center door. It's mostly dark inside. But I make out the large bed swathed in dark sheets and the shape of a desk on one end. Rowan's room.

I turn to the table running along the wall. I squint. They're not mere ornaments—they're artifacts from Earth. I take a step toward them when the doorknob rattles.

Rowan emerges, wearing a different shirt, this one sky blue. The pants are the same. I don't know why I notice these things, but I do.

"We can leave now," he says, but he sees me by the table, he comes near. "Do you like them?"

"What are they?" I ask. In the dark, I can't see anything but glinting metal.

Light floods the room when he pulls a chain above my head.

"It's my collection of knives," he says and I shiver, remembering the dagger running through Chancellor

Kole's heart. Every other feeling I had for him dissipates, replaced by blinding anger.

"Knives used to kill," I say, my voice is hushed with anger. I face him in time to see pain flicker across his eyes.

"I don't kill," he says softly. "I only follow orders."

His face is downcast, sad. And I don't understand how he could switch to a completely different person in mere heartbeats.

"You don't have to follow orders," I say quietly. "You don't have to do what the Queen tells you to do. You're not a tool."

Like I am.

"You have no idea what I am," he says quietly, his eyes flashing.

I bark a laugh and step away from him. But I realize something. "We're not much different. You can't say I don't understand."

He clenches his jaw in answer. Something passes over his face, something like hopelessness, before he crosses the room and opens the door on the left. I stare at his retreating figure and the slight droop in his shoulders.

My words struck.

I take a deep breath and follow him into the living room, where the door to the outside stands. It takes everything in me not to fling it open and burst into the freedom of the outdoors, however dry and bloody and barren it may be.

Rowan takes one look at my face and a sliver of a smile flashes across his face. I ignore him.

He may have me under lock and key. But my thoughts, every single one of them, are mine.

Even if they are sometimes in his favor.

33

ROWAN IS SILENT. HE PUSHES HIS HANDS
into his pockets and stares into the distance.

From where I stand, I can see the white towers of the
palace spiraling into the cloudless sky. The stars are few
tonight, and I wonder if many of them are hiding in shame,
saddened to see me with Rowan instead of his mirror.

Or maybe they're in mourning. Julian is imprisoned.
Being tortured. And here I am, dressing in lavish gowns
and following Rowan as if I am sick. Out of my mind.

Maybe I am.

"The palace isn't as pretty inside and you know it."

"It isn't," I agree. "I was just waiting for you."

Those are my words, but with my tone, I tell him I
wasn't waiting for him. I want him to know he will never
have full control over me.

He lips twist into a half-smile and he shrugs as if he
knows something I do not. I pretend it doesn't faze me. But
it does. And I want more than anything to know what lies in
his mind.

I *need* to know, if I am to save Julian.

And there's only one way to get it.

Warnings blare in my mind as I think of this new possibility. I close off the reasoning voice begging me to end the absurdity before it begins.

And make my decision on a whim.

I reach up, entwining my arms around his slender neck, pulling him close. It's an act. It means nothing. But my heart races, my insides tremble.

He's rigid for a moment before he exhales, coming close until there's barely an inch between us. He doesn't move any closer.

He waits. This is the third time he's waited for me to make the first move. For all his madness, Rowan is smart.

I think of Julian, somewhere, out there. He was taken because of me. Rowan holds every answer I'll need.

I *will* get Rowan to trust me.

I smile a sly, half smile.

And touch my lips to his.

For a moment, Rowan is deathly still. As if he can't understand what's happening.

Neither can I.

The still moment is over in a flash and Rowan's lips move against mine. Trills of excitement rush through me, up and down my body in never-ending loops. All I feel is him. My body against his, his lips against mine. And I realize with panic, *I want him.*

"I think, I think I love you," I whisper, pulling away the slightest bit. *It's a lie*, I tell myself. I hate him.

He exhales and I feel his lips curve against mine. "So you say."

"I wonder what Julian will say," I muse.

He kisses me harder. Harder. Unlike Julian at all. Rowan's kisses are hungry, his fingers desperate. His need reverberates through his whole body.

My lips part. His desperation becomes my own. I wrap my fingers in his hair and pull him closer, closer.

Julian is soft. But Rowan is dangerous. His hands run along my arms, pulling them away from his head and lowering them to his neck. I feel the heat of his neck beneath my fingertips.

I don't want this. I don't want him. I want Julian.

I deepen the kiss.

"It doesn't matter," he says, his voice low, hoarse. I shiver. "He won't live much longer."

"You'll kill your own brother?" I ask, leaning back.

Panic momentarily overtakes every other emotion crashing through me.

"Never." He pulls back and moves me toward the house. Presses me against the cool wall. He kisses my neck. I gasp. This is real. Too real.

This wasn't what I planned.

But you want this, my heart whispers. I tremble.

He lowers his head slowly, strands of his hair feathering across my skin. His lips press down in the hollow of my neck. They brush against every inch of bare skin this ridiculously deep-necked dress reveals.

Panic pulses through me. A part of me wants him to keep going. But there is still some part of me that's sane, realistic. With trembling fingers, I press my hands against the sides of his burning face and pull him up. The darkness makes me stronger.

"Then?" I force the word from my lips. He studies me. His eyes are hungry, dark, feverous. But I can sense his hesitance. A part of him isn't drunk with me as I am wholly with him.

I need to distract him. I reach for his shirt, my hands trembling as I undo a single button. I struggle on the next. He pushes my hands away, and in heartbeats, his shirt is on the ground. Moonlight glistens across his chest and shoulders. But he still hasn't answered.

My body aches. It shouldn't be this way. I shouldn't want him. I shouldn't relish his lips on mine. I shouldn't want to run my hands across his chest. I shouldn't. This is an act. A way to get information.

But it isn't. Julian's kiss was love, Rowan's is lust.

Yet I feel disgust. Guilt. Anger at myself.

He kisses me again. And again. His kisses begin to trail down my neck again. His hands begin to stray and I want this to stop.

"He'll be in the palace when it catches on fire."

I freeze when his words strike. My body forgets to move.

Rowan notices. His hands fall away from my dress. "Too soon?"

I force air through my nose and catch his words. Seize the chance. I fasten the button that somehow came undone. When did it come undone? My breath shudders, my limbs shiver. "Yes."

"We have time," he whispers with a grin. His face wavers between Julian and Rowan when I meet his dark eyes.

"We do." My voice is a tight whisper. My breathing is harsh.

My lips curl in disgust.

I press my hands against his chest and push him away.

My body shudders with quiet sobs. There's something wrong with me. I know Julian suffers. I know how much I want Julian. I know how cruel Rowan is—he murdered Chancellor Kole, hurt his own brother.

But still. I wanted him.

I smooth down my hair. Rowan watches me for one long moment. In the dark, I can't see where his eyes stray and linger. He reaches down and plucks his shirt off the ground, dusting it before throwing it back on. He walks and I follow. Away from his house, away from the palace as he slowly buttons his shirt again.

"It's kind of a long walk," Rowan says, his voice is still hoarse. I touch a hand to my throbbing lips. "Julian told me how much you hate the mutants."

"Oh?" I ask, feigning interest. My mind is elsewhere. My mind keeps drifting to Rowan's plans.

"He's told me a lot about you." He pauses. I don't think I've ever heard Rowan pause. "I've wanted you even before we... formally met."

I look at him. He's been watching me the entire time. Doubt flashes across his face and I feel sorry for him. And at the same time, anger.

How can he suddenly seem so human? How, when he plans to burn down the palace, taking with it so many lives, can he sound so unsure of himself?

I look away. When will Rowan light the palace on fire? The question bubbles to my lips and I swallow and push it down. If I ask, everything will be ruined. Rowan will suspect me. All this would have been for nothing. Rowan will know why I kissed him.

But I don't even know why I kissed him.

"Where are we going?" I ask.

"To the ship," he says distantly.

I don't understand why he needs such power. Why he needs to kill the Queen when she has given him enough power to stand beside her.

Or maybe the Queen knows. Gage always said to keep your friends close and your enemies closer. Maybe that's why my mother keeps Rowan close.

"Is your mother alive?" I ask, glancing at him.

He doesn't answer. It's a simple question that warrants a simple answer. Yes. No. In the sudden silence, I hear his lips part. "The woman who gave birth to me is alive. But she was never my mother."

Silence falls again.

"It was always Julian. He wasn't even her son, but she loved him. A half-breed like him."

Sudden love for Julian wells in my heart. That's the difference between him and Rowan. The difference between my disgusting want for Rowan and my need for Julian. The difference between my lust for Rowan and my love for Julian.

"Everyone loved him. He was always the perfect one and I... hated it. Him." Rowan trails off. I wonder if it's the dark that makes him spill his past, or my presence.

"But then, he never," Rowan pauses, "he never hated me back. He looked up to me. I'm only a few months older, but he looked up to me like a king. I-I didn't know what to do."

"You ended up in the palace," I say, urging him on. I don't know why I want to hear his story. Maybe I'll find a way to justify his evil. Maybe I'll find humanity in him.

"As soon as I was old enough, I left. I met some soldiers, tried to draft with them. Days later I met the Queen. She, I don't know, liked what she saw and took me into the palace. I've been there ever since."

He looks up from the ground and meets my eyes.

"Story of my life." He adds with a laugh. But it's forced. "We're nearly there."

"Did you know Julian's mother?" I ask.

He falters and quickly straightens. And when I think he'll ignore me, he whispers. "Yes."

I have no response to his sudden plague of emotion.

"She... was a mother to me," he says finally. "She loved us both the same, equally. But she was human. She didn't belong here, and I didn't belong there.

"The Queen knew about her though, because she's Chancellor Evan's sister, and the only family he has left. And when he spared a few people from the gallows, she—" He cuts off, his voice choked. Julian said Rowan holds leverage over him. He never said this.

I never thought Rowan could feel something other than pride.

"Queen Rhea sent me to collect a body with another soldier. By the time I figured out what his task was, it was too late," he whispers.

"She was already dying."

I look out into the night, pain pinching my chest. There's no sound other than our feet on the brittle ground.

"I killed the soldier then and there," Rowan says, a harshness in his voice that dies as soon as the words leave his lips. "But I couldn't save her. I tried, but... I couldn't."

"Does Julian know?" I ask softly.

He shakes his head. "He thinks she died with a fever. I couldn't take her body back—she needed peace. I couldn't watch them convert her body into sick fuel, so we buried her."

He looks up, into the empty starless distance. I'm drowning in his tale and I have no idea where we're going. "But Julian saw the soldier, and I knew that if he suspected what had happened, he would come looking for answers. The Queen wouldn't even blink before ordering a half-breed like him killed. So I blackmailed him. I told him that I would tell the Queen we buried her instead of bringing her back, and that kept him away—he doesn't care for himself as much he cares for every innocent being. And I told the Queen the soldier shot his mother before the poison could do its job, losing a body for fuel, so I killed him.

"And I've been waiting to avenge her ever since," he finishes, looking at me.

"And you'll avenge her by ending the Queen's reign?" I ask.

"Yes." He holds my gaze.

"You don't have to do this," I say quietly. He turns to me, and I'm flooded with the sadness in his eyes. "You don't have to avenge her. Not like this."

"I do," he says. He takes a deep breath and turns away. "I'm sorry, Lissa."

The words shatter my heart. I want to wrap my arms around him and give him someone who cares, because I know he has no one. He has made everyone hate him, including his own brother. But like Rowan and Julian's mother, we don't belong together.

"Stay here," he says after a moment, and leaves me alone in the darkness. We're in the middle of nowhere. There's nothing around for as far as the eye can see.

Could it be a trap? Could his whole story be a lie? I can't doubt everything. But madness knows no bounds.

"Close your eyes," Rowan says, jogging back. I stare at him until he tilts his head to the side.

His voice softens. "You don't trust me?"

I close my eyes. For Julian's sake. For the sake of the entire human race. Because if the ship really lies here, I need to know. Then I will plan.

But I also close my eyes for Rowan, because if I can be a sliver of that person he needs, I will be.

I jump when the beep of an alarm shatters the silence. As soon as it ends, another sound crashes through. The grating of gears, the sliding of doors. I want to open my eyes.

"Open," Rowan whispers, his breath soft in my ear.

My eyes fly open. The night is suddenly day. No. The ground is opening. Parting. The sun shines from the depths of Jutaire. I rush toward it as the sounds cease. It's no wonder we never saw the ship. Because now, *beneath my feet*, it stands in all its grandeur, larger than anything I could ever imagine.

"Clever, don't you think?" Rowan asks.

"Hiding it in plain sight? In a hole?" I ask, unable to take my eyes away.

The hole goes as deep and as far as I can see. The ship itself is elliptical, like the blimps I've read about, and covered in metal, the white, ten-pointed star branded across it. Where did they find it all? Even from where I stand, I can tell the shell is thick—it has to withstand the forces of space after all.

Space. The thought sends shivers through me. This ship will carry the entire Jute race to Earth, leaving us to wither away.

"Magnificent is the word you're looking for, isn't it?" Rowan asks.

"It is," I say. I feel small compared to its massiveness. "Is it ready? I mean, where's the fuel and all?"

I try not to think of what the fuel looks like.

"It's ready to go. Fuel, food, provisions, everything. All Queen Rhea needed was your blood. And I think that will be ready soon."

"But," I suggest, knowing there's more he wants to say. I can hear it in the hesitance in his voice.

"But she won't be leaving Jutaire," Rowan says simply. "I will. With you by my side. And everyone who chooses to side with me."

He reaches for my hand and smiles. His words ricochet in my mind. He will kill the Queen. And as much as I don't care for my mother, I don't want her dead.

"But why? Why kill the Queen when she's given you enough power to stand beside her?" I ask. I only want to know.

He tilts his head and studies me for a long moment. "There's no power in killing. I kill whom she orders me to. I trusted her in the beginning, enough that she knows all about my father, about Julian. She knows how much they mean to me, how they're my weaknesses. I'm done being a slave to her whims."

He's as imprisoned as the rest of us. He gets the little things he wants, but never his own freedom. But if he cares so much for Julian, why would he let him die in the palace?

"Earth will be a fresh start. And I want to start at the top. As king. And you, dear Lissa, will be my queen."

He says it as if his words are the most logical in all of Jutaire.

I swallow and plaster on a smile. I hope with all my life it looks real.

"Does anyone keep watch?" I ask, peering down, changing the subject.

"We don't need anyone to keep watch. The humans don't know about it," he says with a shrug. "And Queen Rhea never imagined her own people to go against her. In any case, I have some of my men down there. They work for the queen of course, but their loyalties lay with me."

"You have many on your side," I say, half-questioning.

"Of course. You can't overthrow a queen with no one. I have about a tenth of the populace on my side."

A tenth. I raise my eyebrows. "That's a lot."

He grins but doesn't elaborate. "We had better head back. We start tomorrow."

Tomorrow. What starts tomorrow? I have less than a night to get word to my father. I have less than a night to save Julian and find Mia.

I have less than a night. And the way Rowan stares at me, I doubt I will get anything done.

34

WHEN WE REACH HIS HOUSE, I CAN'T HELP but glance at the wall. My heart races in reminder. Rowan pulls me close as he opens the door and looks into my eyes. I see the secrets he shared and I know he's never told anyone about Julian's mother and his real position with the Queen.

He's churning his grief into action—into revenge. And it's making him evil. Mad.

He rests my arms on his shoulders and leans closer, but I can't. I can't kiss him again.

I can't.

But I can feel his disappointment growing. He'll figure out why I kissed him to begin with. So I kiss him back and he instantly relaxes before pulling me inside the dark house.

"Rowan," I whisper. He pauses and searches my eyes, and something in me breaks. There's pain in his eyes. Not the dark desire from earlier. *Pain*. He has never had anyone who wanted him, anyone who would hold him close and whisper his name in his ear. He's pushed everyone away after Julian's mother died, all for the sake of protecting them from the Queen.

But this can never go on. I can never love him the way I would love Julian. Julian's grief led him to hurt himself, Rowan's is leading him to hurt others. Something I would never do.

He pulls me toward his room. I pull away.

"Rowan," I say again. His eyes search mine hungrily, and finally soften. In that instant, I see Julian.

"I'm sorry," he says softly. Before he closes the door, he looks back at me. My fingers are on my lips.

"Lissa?" I meet his eyes. "Don't leave me."

In that instant, I hear Julian.

I stare at the dark door, my body lit on fire. I sink into the chair by the fireplace, where the flames echo the ones inside me. Hating Rowan should have been easy. But our trip changed everything.

"You're confused." I look up in surprise as Eli steps out of the shadows. And I'm grateful for the darkness hiding my heated cheeks, bruised lips, and disheveled clothes.

"I know the horrible things he'll do." I pause as he settles beside me. My voice is soft because darkness always calls for hush. "But I feel sorry for him. A part of me, a part of me *likes* him. I feel lost."

Eli studies me a moment. "Rowan is lost too. He was never given the attention he needed, not like Julian. He doesn't know what he wants, truly. And I think, well, I think, you can show him what he needs." I turn to him with a sharp inhale. "I know how he looks at you. I know how he feels inside. He has strayed, but you can bring him back."

"How would you know?" I ask, suddenly angry. How would he know how Rowan feels when not even I know? When he looks at me, I see hunger and snippets of compassion. I didn't even know he had anything close to compassion until he spilt the truth.

"I know," he says, his voice just as angry, "because I am his father."

My jaw drops. Rowan's father. No wonder his blue eyes were familiar. And if he's Rowan's father, that means he's Julian's father, too. This man, treated by Rowan like filth on his sleeve.

I latch onto the only shred of a thought I can. "But-but you're human."

"No." He shakes his head. "But I prefer oxygen, it keeps the mind clear."

So he's a hybrid like I am.

I always thought the air of Jutaire was intoxicating, but I never thought it muddled the mind. Is that why I can't get enough of Rowan? Is the air ruining my mind?

No. I prefer this air. I prefer the sweetness because it makes my thoughts sharper.

But he can't be a hybrid. Gage and Slate said I was the only one of my kind.

"Julian," I start. I struggle to say something, but I can't. My throat is suddenly dry. But Eli understands.

"He is my son too, though he isn't as welcome in White Plains." He smiles. "He loves you very much. He's broken inside, but in a way much different to Rowan. Julian had only wanted death before you came. And for that, I thank you."

His words wrench at my heart. The fire crackling in front of me blurs in my vision.

"He's being tortured. Because of me." I manage to whisper.

Eli tilts his head, resembling Rowan. He envelops my hand between both of his. "Why? Because you were with him? No, Lissa. We find ways to blame ourselves when grief overcomes our souls. But that isn't the way. It was Rowan's fault."

But I can't help but think of how nothing would have happened if I hadn't been there. He never would have taken me to see the Ruins.

"Why do you stay here with Rowan, when he treats you so wrongly?" I ask, forcing my mind away from Julian.

"This is my home," Eli says simply.

Julian said his father owns a plantation on the outskirts of Jute territory, between the palace and human territory. I can't believe I didn't realize it myself. "It's my fault Rowan is beyond control. Had I treated him differently when he was younger, he would be different now. I will forever live in guilt. This is the only way I can cope with it."

I want to relieve him of his sorrow and pain, to tell him it isn't his fault. I want to comfort him the way he comforted me. But I can't. What is it like to have two sons, completely identical, yet completely different?

"Rowan will burn the palace down. Tomorrow, I think." My eyes are wet with tears. Is Julian even alive?

"Then you will leave now," Eli says with such force, my breath catches. In the light of the fire, determination flashes in his eyes, so much like Julian.

"I can't. I don't know what to do," I say. My voice breaks. But this show of weakness in front of Eli doesn't embarrass me.

"Head to the palace," Eli says softly. "Your heart will know what to do next."

He stands and gestures for me to follow. I stare at the flames and rub my arms. I glance at Rowan's door. *Don't leave me.* What will I do when I step outside these walls? Where will I go?

I'm the only one who knows what Rowan will do. I'm the only one who can do something, anything, to stop this madness. And there isn't much time.

With this thought, I stand and follow Eli's shadow to another room.

I stop at the threshold, and I have to grip the doorframe against the pain in my chest. The room is an exact replica of the training room in the Tower. But here, I won't find Julian carving a design into my daggers. I won't see his first smile. Or his face flushing when Slate catches us laughing.

"We have to hurry if you want to cover ground," Eli says, breaking me out of my thoughts. He digs through some drawers and pulls out a dark outfit. My outfit, the clean Louen scales shining in the light of the room.

"One of the maids gave it to me," he says when I look at him in surprise.

I move along the wall, picking weapons—daggers in various sizes, darts, and expandable staves.

"Perfect," Eli says when I've changed and fastened the weapons wherever I can. I slip the emerald jewel over my neck and tuck it beneath my shirt before hurrying with him to the back door. I quickly pin my hair into a braid and toss it behind me. "Follow the alley lights. They'll lead you the castle."

I nod and step out. The wind picks up, ruffling the loose strands of my hair. "And you? Will you be safe?"

"Rowan is my son. He'll never hurt me." His fingers close around my shoulder. I wonder if I imagine the warmth spreading from his usually cool touch. But it's real. I stare into his bright eyes and I know hope did this to him. Brought life back to his weeping soul. "Be careful, Lissa. There is more at stake than the human race."

Now, nine-tenths of the Jute populace is in danger. And despite what Gage said about the Jute, I have learned they are more similar to humans that I could ever imagine.

Eli is right. There is more at stake.

I take a deep breath to calm my heart. And run.

The wind whistles through my hair. I pull my shimmering hood over my head and the mask over my mouth and nose, following the lights. I can see the palace in the distance, the lights illuminating the white walls like a beacon for all to see. Rowan will ruin it all.

Human territory lies far behind me. I'm painfully aware that my every step takes me farther away from it. I'm aware of many things. The lone figures, the eyes following me as I run. An alley is the worst place to be, night or day. I leap over a pile of debris without pause.

It was a night like this when I met Julian first. I ran free then, confined only by the sky above my head. Now, the walls of buildings surround me. The sky is nothing but a rectangle of silky navy blue. Now, the walls of a new reality surround me, threatening to encase me forever.

I hear nothing over the rushing in my ears. My legs pump beneath me and I wonder if I was born for running.

I think this, and my mind wanders far enough that I don't sense the other presence until it's too late.

35

PAIN EXPLODES IN MY SHOULDER WHEN MY arm is wrenched in the opposite direction. I cry out at the sudden pain as a scent reeking of decay penetrates the fabric of the cloth against my face and slams into my nose. I cough and gag. Struggle to hold my breath. I'm pinned against the wall, my chest heaving.

I see a face.

My eyes widen and I want to squeeze them shut and never see again. White panic momentarily blinds my brain.

Breathe, a part of me is still sane enough to say. I breathe and grit my teeth at the stench and breathe some more.

I can't tell if the creature is male or female. I can't tell where its nose begins and where its lips end. Its dark eyes are buried deep inside the hollows of sickly white skin, veins bulging in all the wrong places.

It reminds me of a mutant. A mutant resembling a human more than a horse. I close off the horrifying thought.

"Hello pretty." It rasps. I cough and grit my teeth at the stench that shoots from its mouth.

"Let go." I spit through gritted teeth.

"Pretties and riches, I want." Its eyes scour my face. It licks its nonexistent lips with a puckered tongue and I gag again. "Something other than despair."

"I have nothing," I wheeze. It pins my arm against my chest and I gasp for air. My lungs already ache from running. Now, they scream in sheer pain. I gasp through clenched teeth. "Let me go."

It laughs, a wheezing screech that sounds like it's dying. Anger surges through my bloodstream. I've been through enough to be afraid of a deformed madman. I blink away the sweat trickling down my eyes and shove his arm away, twisting it behind him while I suck in gulps of clean air.

It stumbles back in surprise and recovers quickly, leering at me. It lowers its head and widens its stance. Matted strands of dirty white hair fall over its face as it sways back and forth.

My knives pulse against my skin. I whip one from my left arm, holding it ready. Steady. My body itches, slick with sweat.

"Leave and I won't hurt you." My voice is sharp.

"*You* hurt *me*?" The creature screeches. I flinch and it lunges. I act on instinct. Fear more than practice.

The knife flies from my hand. It sinks into the flesh by its heart and I turn away as the creature sinks to the ground.

And I know, more than hear, it has breathed its last.

I steady myself against the wall and catch my breath, pushing away the image of the creature's face seared into my mind.

I grit my teeth against the stench and take careful steps forward. In one swift pull, I grab my dagger and wipe it on its dirty coat as Dena would have done and slip it back into my sheath. With one last look at the still body, I run.

This time, I keep my mind clear and I hear nothing. But just as I felt the presence of lurking shadows earlier, I feel nothing now. Everyone has gone.

I've earned my solitude by taking another life.

The guilt hits me as soon as I leave the alley. When the sky widens before me, I feel the accusation in the dim twinkle of the stars. But they should know I acted in defense. Had I not, I don't know where I'd be now.

I tell myself I killed the creature to put it out of its misery. It clearly was a Jute once, male most likely, but despair ate him from the inside. I shudder when I think of the alternative. Could it have been a mutant?

Where do mutants come from?

I shiver and focus on the ground beneath me, and the palace, still a good distance away. But I feel safer, away from the dark confines of the alley. Though this is worse in some ways. I can easily be seen.

I pass silent houses as I run. Some have lights on, others are dark. I only pass one lone man roaming the streets, his head ducked beneath the collar of his coat. I keep my eyes glued to him until I pass.

I'm panting by the time I've climbed the palace hill. Swarms of dust burst and swirl in the gentle wind.

I pause beside a ring of boulders and scan the area. Though I don't see anyone, I know there are guards—even in broad daylight there are guards.

I creep closer, staying beneath the shadows as much as I can. There isn't a single cloud in the sky, nothing to lend to my invisibility. Moonlight illuminates my location when I'm close enough to see the swirling gold etched into the palace walls.

I tense.

I'm not alone. I whip my head up, but before I can turn, a hand tightens around my mouth.

I struggle against the person, digging my nails into the hand around me. I try to scream, but nothing penetrates the grip. Panic edges into my vision.

"Stop struggling," a man whispers. Hot breath suffocates my skin.

He pulls me toward the palace, his hand still around my mouth. A guard?

I twist and try to see who he is through the corner of my eye, but I can only see the moon.

I dig my heels into the ground. But it's no use. He drags me anyway. He's strong, though the hand around my mouth is bony.

When he drags me beneath the shadow of an eve above a smaller palace door, he lets go. I fall to the ground, panting. My hand flies to my leg and I yank out a dagger.

"It's me, Princess," the man says hurriedly. He crouches down in front of me, and moonlight illuminates his features.

"Ilen?" I ask, lowering my hand. My heart pounds loud enough for Jutaire to hear.

He nods, eyeing the knife nervously. "Where were you?"

It takes me a moment to realize all of Jutaire thinks I'm missing. Everyone thinks Julian hurt me.

"Is Julian okay?" I ask.

Ilen nods, gravely and relief floods through me. "Barely. I see him sometimes, take him whatever food I've got."

I blink in surprise. "You don't think–he didn't—"

"I know he didn't hurt you. I know all about Rowan and his plans." Ilen sighs.

"How? Does the Queen know?" I ask. My mind swarms with questions.

"I was with him in the beginning. I wanted," he pauses and frowns. In the light of the moon, he looks younger. "I wanted to go to Earth but I never thought it involved so much death. So I backed out. And no, the Queen doesn't know. I can't tell her."

He shudders and looks closely at me, as if seeing me for the first time. "Why are you here, Princess?"

Can I trust him? He knows of Rowan's madness. He knows of Julian's innocence.

"I came to save Julian. Rowan is going to burn down the palace."

"There's nothing I can do," he says, shaking his head before I can ask. "All the men here are loyal to him. I'm supposed to be, too, but I'm too scared, obviously."

Ilen sneaks me into the maid's quarters and I trust him to stay silent. He murmurs something about his shift being over and disappears.

I slip through the door and squint in the darkness, quietly creeping through the wide space.

My feet kick something soft and I nearly stumble. When I right myself, I hear a soft cry.

"Jude," a voice calls far to my right. I squint and my heart beats faster when I make out the sounds of breathing. How many Jute are in here? How many of them can see me?

A dim light brightens from above and I gasp. The wide room is filled with girls sleeping on the floor. Maids.

"Princess?" Someone whispers excitedly. I jerk my head toward the voice, recognizing the girl who dressed my hair on the eve of the ceremony.

I hold a finger quickly to my lips and everyone falls silent. "Hush. No one must know I'm here."

She presses her lips together and nods. I let my eyes scan over the rest of the girls. They stare up at me with wide, expectant eyes.

Their excitement is palpable in the air. The thrill of keeping a secret runs through their veins.

"Where's Mia?" I ask them, my voice low.

"We don't know. We haven't seen her since you went missing," an older girl says.

"Does she disappear often?" I ask, panic rushing through me.

"No," a little girl whispers, half to herself. "Mia is always here. Not anymore."

"The human, the platinum one." One of them points at another door. "She's in there."

Dena. She's safe and so close. My heart picks up speed. I walk around limbs and fingers, carefully making my way to the door on the far end. I look back at them, my hand on the door. "Thank you."

A few of them smile. The rest break out into hushed chatter. I barely hear the two girls whispering beside me.

"She said she wanted to be left alone," one says.

"But *she* isn't alone," the other whispers back, and they both break into giggles.

I step into a short hall. The bright yellow glow of a globed oxygen candle warms the room.

Just like our masks, the globes produce oxygen, allowing the flames to sputter in yellow and orange, rather than blue and purple, like Jutaire's fire.

I take three steps and pause when I see the shadows. Two heads inclined.

Dena isn't alone. I step back, ready to leave when the floorboard creaks beneath my feet and a shadow flashes to my left, where the wall should be.

A hand pulls me into a hidden room, and darkness clouds my vision.

36

FAINT MOONLIGHT BOUNCES OFF THE BLADE
of my dagger when I whip it out.

"You are dazzlingly fast, Lissa," an airy voice says
innocently. I nearly drop the dagger.

"Mia?" I blurt in surprise.

"It would help if you were a little quieter, but yes, it's
me," she says. Only Mia can be so blunt and sound utterly
innocent. A light flickers on, illuminating a small bed, an
unwrapped cloth with half-eaten food carefully set in its
center.

"What are you doing in here? Why are you hiding?" I
tuck the dagger back into my sheath. The room is so small I
can't stand fully straight. She sits cross-legged against the
bed and shrugs.

"I know you're the real princess," I say when she
doesn't answer. She chimes a small laugh.

"There are men after me. They have been for years,
but they're getting closer. I don't know how they found out
after so long, but I am slightly afraid of death."

I almost laugh at the way she says it.

"You need to come with me. You need to be crowned. You need to—"

"No, Lissa. *You* are the princess. I might be royal by blood, but that doesn't make me capable of leading anyone." She looks down at her toes. "Sometimes I wonder how I lead myself from one place to another."

I blink.

"Okay," I say, sitting in front of her. I lift the emerald from my neck but she shakes her head.

"It's yours now. It belongs to you. I just want to live a simple life. I like being the head maid and dressing up in pretty clothes. This is the life I've always wanted and I am content with it. Do you understand?"

I raise my eyebrows, but in the end, I nod.

"Will you at least come with me? I can take you someplace safe."

She smiles and chews on a chunk of bread. I wait, but she doesn't answer.

"I wanted to say good-bye and see you one last time. We didn't get a proper farewell before. So good-bye, Lissa. Farewell."

She shoves me out of the room before I can say another word and locks the door. If I had to choose one word to describe Mia, it would be crazy. Whimsical, alive, caring, gentle, sweet, yes, but in the end, crazy.

The stupid floorboard in the short hall creaks beneath my weight again.

"Princess?"

"Ilen?" I ask in surprise.

He grins, his bright hair disheveled, and points to another door on the other end of the room. He *is* young, probably not much older than me.

"Thanks for coming back at midnight," Dena says. She steps around Ilen and faces me, sarcasm dripping from her voice. Her face is flushed.

"I-I'm sorry, I—"

"Yeah, I know. Crap happened, right?" She asks with an eye roll. "Truth is, I never thought I would see you again, being in Rowan's lair and all."

I clench my jaw.

"You knew," I spit. "You knew Rowan had me, but you didn't even try to help." *You didn't want help either,* some part of me whispers.

Her eyes flash. "Help you? Strapped to a table?"

"You said you had a way out the night of the ceremony." I shoot back.

"But you didn't show up. You were busy getting cozy with Julian." A vein pulses in her neck.

"Don't talk about Julian," I say, my voice deathly still. She scoffs. Ilen gently pushes Dena aside, breaking our stare.

"I actually got Dena out late last night," he says.

Dena's quick breathing slows and she sighs, her whole body sagging.

"All of Jutaire is looking for you." I look away. I'm ashamed I let my anger control my words when Dena isn't the same person I first met.

"I'm sorry," I say quietly. Dena was in danger, Julian is still in danger.

"Why are you here?" She asks.

"Rowan is going to bring down the palace," I say flatly. She sucks in a breath and I tell them everything.

"Ilen, you need to get the maids somewhere safe. And Dena, you need to go back," I say. She meets my eyes. "To the Tower."

"And do what?" Ilen asks. I look at him and blink. I never thought of that. "There isn't much good in telling them there's a ship."

"No," Dena agrees. "But they need to prepare. Get everything together."

"If Rowan does set the palace on fire, he'll be the one to take the ship," Ilen says, stating the obvious. "The humans will stand no chance against him."

"Why not? We have more numbers than they do. He only has one-tenth of the Jute," Dena says, narrowing her eyes in confusion.

"Haven't you heard of mask tracking?" Ilen asks.

"They track our locations, we know," I say. That was what I was worried about when I broke into the Chamber. I never thought someone else would set off the Chamber's own alarm.

"There are two parts to the control. The main panel that tracks the masks and a smaller, portable control that controls the oxygen flow. It's here, unguarded, secluded, and easy to access. One flick of a switch and every mask will stop functioning. Every human will die," Ilen says.

Dena and I share a glance. Her face suddenly looks so much like Chancellor Kole's—haunted.

"Well then, there's only one thing I can do." She grins half-heartedly and unzips her leather jacket. I furrow my brow as she pulls the flaps open, revealing a clean tank top underneath.

The inside of her jacket sparkles in the candlelight. Sown carefully into the leather are rows and rows of glass vials. Filled to the brim with blood. My blood.

"You've been preparing," I say, my voice no more than a whisper.

"I told you I would help from the inside. Already mixed with the catalyst and ready to go," she says proudly.

"Can we stop wasting time?" Ilen says.

"How did you get so much?" I ask, ignoring him.

"Five vials were more than enough. Your blood multiplies faster than I thought." She shrugs.

"Then why did we think I would die?" I ask. What if we bloated everything? What if my mother never planned on killing me at all?

"The more it multiplies, the less potent it becomes," Dena says, zipping up her jacket. "There's a nutrient in hybrid blood, which, when derived, functions as the catalyst. When fresh, it's the strongest. These aren't strong enough for the Jute, but perfectly fine for humans. And yes, I kept my ears open in there too."

"Dena," Ilen groans.

"Yeah, yeah, keep your head on. I'll leave now."

"Alone?" I ask. I still see the countless vials lining her jacket. I still can't comprehend how such small bottles can save so many lives.

Ilen shakes his head. "She can go with me. There's a body I'm due to collect at sunrise. May as well get an early start."

I shudder. While I was away, humans were still being hung. I remember how much Chancellor Kole used to frighten me. I remember the limp bodies, the masks. The gaunt faces of every man, woman, and child living because there's nothing else to do. Dena reaches for my hand.

"It'll all end soon, Lissa," she says softly. No doubt she's remembering her father too. "Try to stay alive."

She crosses the short hall and turns back, eyes narrowed.

"What are you going to do, anyway?" She asks.

Does she know what happened to Julian? I'm selfish and afraid she'll want to come. I'm afraid she'll have questions that I won't be able to answer.

I let Gage die. And Chancellor Kole. It won't happen again.

"There's something I need to do," I say, letting loose a deep breath.

Ilen meets my eyes and places a hand on Dena's shoulder before she can push any further. "Come on, Dena. Let her do what she has to do."

I thank him silently and watch them leave, quickly and quietly. As soon as I'm alone, I reach for the emerald, warm from my skin, and knock on the hidden door again. Nothing. I call Mia's name. Still nothing.

I drop the stone beneath my tunic and feel it's weight against my heart.

It's a part of me now.

37

I STEP OUT OF THE MAID'S CHAMBER without a sound. The wood floor is old and withered, creaking with my misplaced steps. A musty smell tickles my nostrils as I creep through the dark corridor.

Ilen said the hall leads to the throne room, which should be empty at this time. On the other end of the throne room, through another twisting hall, is supposed to be a single staircase leading down to the dungeons, where Julian should be.

But as I feel along the space of the corridor, something happens. I stop moving toward the stairwell.

My legs are taking me elsewhere.

I turn the corner, moving surprisingly fast despite not being able to see more than what is inches from me. I know where I'm going, though I don't know why.

I hear voices as I walk down the familiar, carpet-lined hall. I hold my breath and press myself against the wall as a Jute walks past, a gold and white goblet in his hand. This part of the palace isn't empty. I turn down an empty hall and stop at the door as it swings open.

A short, dark-haired maid tiptoes out, a satchel clasped in one hand, a candle in the other. She starts when she sees me watching.

"Can I help you, miss?" She asks, running her gaze nervously down my clothes.

"Is the Queen awake?" I ask. The maid nods quickly, and pauses. She raises the candle to see my face and I throw up my hand to shield the light, but it's too late.

"Princess?" She breathes, her voice far too loud. I dart a quick look around.

"Is the Queen awake?" I repeat, my voice hard.

"She mustn't be disturbed. She is ill, Your Highness." The maid bows.

"Tell no one—"

But only the walls hear me. And all they do is stare blankly, absorbing everything, revealing nothing.

I pull open the door and slip inside. I don't have much time—from what I've learned, maids can spread word faster than they can do anything else.

The room is the same as when I last saw it, unadorned except for the dark chaise on one end. I cross the foyer leading to the Queen's rooms and hold my breath. I don't knock before entering.

My eyes fly to the flickering oxygen candle on the bedside table. Beside it, the length of a body glows in the shadows of a large, canopied bed.

I hurry forward, tripping over a thick rug I didn't see and stop. Hold my breath.

She's not ill. She's near-death. The Queen's pale skin is near translucent. Her red, ankle-length nightgown is drenched in sweat. It looks like blood.

"They say a mother's will is stronger than any."

I inhale sharply and raise my eyes to her face. Her moonlight eyes glow an eerie white gold as she stares at me.

"The last word you said to me was 'mother.'" Her voice is soft. I lean closer. "I never saw you again."

She watches me. I know she wants me to fill this void, but words fail to form. I can't even part my lips. She fills the silence herself. "Julian was right, Rowan is mad."

She called him by his name.

"Rowan poisoned you," I say. Rowan said he would avenge the woman who raised him as her own son.

She laughs softly, her eyes straying to the flickering light. It's a real laugh, the first I have heard. I snatch the sound and tuck it away, deep within my heart. The sound of my mother laughing. Because the woman in front of me is my mother. Not the Queen.

Her eyes fall on mine. "Why are you here, daughter?"

"I came—" I stop, my throat suddenly tight. "I came to warn you. Rowan plans to burn down the palace."

Silence follows my words. She's staring, not at me, but *into* me. I swallow and drop my eyes away.

"I'm a murderer," she whispers.

"Why Lissa? Why would you warn me?" I search her face. But her question is pure curiosity.

"I don't know," I say finally. "Come with me." I don't know why I say this. I don't know why I suddenly want my mother to live. Why I care.

"This is where I'll die," she whispers. She reaches for me and I step closer. Her fingers brush my face, stroke my hair. Her touch is cold. "I only wanted to see you one last time. As my daughter."

Tears sting my eyes and my throat tightens. But why? After all she has done, why is it so different now?

"I'm sorry, Lissa," she breathes. I fold her hands across her stomach. I think of all the innocent murders she ordered—Chancellor Kole, Wren, her own sister and so many people I will never know.

She smiles. Her lips curve up, trembling as they go. Tears trickle down her eyes, run over the bridge of her elegant nose and dampen her pillow. She tightens her hand around mine.

"I really am. It wasn't all a game. You weren't meant to be a tool. I did love Slate once, and he, me. Tell him that. I loved you too. Forgive me, Lissa."

"I…" but I can't say the words. How can I?

"Forgive me," she whispers again.

Her hand falls from mine.

Dead. My mother is dead.

I will never be able to forgive her. She will never know that peace.

I've wanted a mother for years, yearned for one. But what is worse? Watching your mother die or not having one at all?

The Jute lying before me now, her heart unbeating, wasn't Queen Rhea. She was sorry. She was my mother.

I bite back the sudden tears wrenching in my chest. The door to the room flies open and I fling myself against the wall, grateful for my dark clothes.

I shudder and wipe my eyes as nobles filter into the room, their voices loud as they follow the short maid. And before they can see me, the lost princess, I slip out of the room, not bothering to close the door behind me.

And I know why my feet carried me to my mother instead of Julian. Because what she said was true.

A mother's will is stronger than any.

Was that really her last wish? To see me? To ask for my forgiveness?

It doesn't matter now. My mother is dead.

The palace is bustling with nobles running back and forth, their faces flushed from exertion.

I run past them, keeping my head low as I dart through the halls. Does Rowan know I'm missing? Is Eli okay? Does Dena have enough blood to distribute? Where's Mia?

My mother is dead.

There's an ache in my chest and I don't understand how I can mourn her when she was so heartless. She was so many people—a queen, a murderer, a Jute, but she was my mother, even if only for a few moments before her last breath.

And when the time came, would she have really taken my blood?

"Princess!" Someone calls when I reach the dungeon stairwell. I hurry down the dark hole.

I don't blink and my eyes sting as punishment. A stench slams into my nostrils, full of decay and waste. I hear a moan followed by a soft cry. My skin crawls.

"Who is it?" A thick voice echoes on the cold, stone walls.

I catch my breath and press myself against the wall as I creep down the staircase. Flames burst to life feet away from me, illuminating a guard, his eyes heavy with drink.

I reach toward my ankle and close my fingers around a dipped dart. He doesn't notice. He's still slouched in his chair but he runs a hand across his face. His black eyes peer out at me from beneath his dust-brown hair.

"Who're you?" He spits. He jerks his head toward the metal bars to his right. "Get out before I throw you in one of them."

"The Queen is dead," I say, watching him closely for a reaction. But his mind is too thick for thinking. "You're needed in her chambers."

He bellows a laugh and I flinch at the sudden noise. "In her chambers, eh? I can imagine. Fo' what?" He struggles to stand and his foot slips, a snarl escaping his thick lips. Anger bursts in his dull eyes when he shoots to his feet and pats around his waist, searching for his weapon.

I throw the dart. It makes its mark, embedding itself into his thick neck. He slumps back in his chair with a wheeze and his eyes droop shut. Asleep.

When his breathing slows, I'm painfully aware of the many eyes burning into me and the labored breathing of every inmate watching me. But somehow, somehow, I know Julian isn't one of them—I would know if his eyes were on me.

I peer into the darkness of the cells. The torchlight sets an eerie blue glow across the rusted metal bars. But I can't see anything aside from the dark gaping pits beyond them.

"Free us," a voice whispers. I swallow before realizing the voice comes from the cell I've been watching. I take one step closer, trying not to think of who—or *what*—might lie inside. With every pounding pulse, I feel the daggers against my bare skin, reassuring me with their cool whispers.

"If I free you, how do I know I'll be safe?" I ask slowly, my voice measured. I catch a flash of brown movement and step back as a boy scuttles forward with wide eyes and matted brown hair.

My throat tightens. He can't be more than ten.

"I did nothing, miss." His voice is barely audible through his thin lips. He presses his small, dirty fingers against the bars and something inside me breaks.

"What's your name?" I ask softly.

He wears nothing but a long shirt with frayed edges. It's too dirty to know what color it once was.

"Bo," he whispers, his breath clouds in the cold.

"Ye'll need them keys," a gruff voice says off to my right. I flinch and meet the green eyes of a large man, his auburn beard a knotted mess beneath his chin. He studies me closely. "I know who ye are."

I inhale sharply and hurry to the dozing guard, my footsteps echoing in the musty darkness. I search his pockets, around his neck, and pry open his fisted hands, but come up empty.

"Above," the man says. I look up. The keys are nailed to the post behind the guard. I yank them down and stop at the boy's cell. He watches me warily, as if the thought of freedom is too good to be true. I slip one of the two largest keys into the slot and turn. It clicks.

I swing open the bars and Bo stands, his back still arched, and I wonder if he will be forever marred that way. He stares at the ground in front of him and I see his body quake, but he doesn't move.

"You're free," I say softly. His eyes snap up to mine.

"Where will I go?" He asks. I open my mouth. I don't know.

I glance at the bearded man, who watches in silence. "Will you take him?"

His eyes flicker in amusement. "I s'pose. If I ever leave here, yeah. I can 'take him.'"

I open his cell too, knowing I could be letting loose a killer, a dangerous man who could do a number of things to me, worse than death. A man who knows who I am just by looking at me.

"You came here for someone else, didn't you?" He asks. He takes the keys from me and hands me the other large one identical to the one I used to open his cell. "I'll free them others."

"Thank you."

He snorts and turns to the other cells. "I've done too much wrong to be thanked."

I leave Bo staring at the ground outside his cell. There's something about the bearded man that makes me trust him, as daunting as he looks. Bo will be safe. I hope.

All thoughts of Bo's safety disappear as I walk past cell after cell. Panic zips up my veins. The dungeons are long, and by the time I've reached the end, Bo is even smaller when I glance back. But Julian isn't here.

The triumphant shouts of the escaping men fill the air. I wonder if I'm making a mistake, letting loose so many men who committed deadly crimes. But what about Bo? He couldn't have done any wrong.

My breath shudders and I rub my arms from the sudden cold. As light begins to filter through the small barred windows, I see it.

The familiar dark hair. The coat he wore that night, draped across his shivering body. A strangled cry escapes my lips.

Julian.

38

MY FINGERS TREMBLE AS I TRY TO SLIP the key in the slot. After several attempts, the lock clicks and falls away.

And a sharp, stinging scent hits me.

Burning. The palace is on fire.

The stone walls will keep us safe from the flames, but it won't be long before the smoke travels down and the palace collapses. There is no such thing as safe on Jutaire.

I don't have enough time. The cell door groans open.

"Julian," I whisper. His shivering form blurs in my vision. I collapse on my knees beside him when he doesn't move. I let loose a deep breath.

Slowly, slowly, he raises his head from between his knees. He looks at me, but his eyes are elsewhere, wavering. He untangles his arms from around his knees. His right eye is bruised and his skin shines with sweat. His face is a mess of cuts and bruises.

But it's Julian. He's alive. And it aches deep inside my heart. Tears swell to my eyes.

How did I ever think Rowan and Julian were alike?

And from the way he stares at me, even half-delirious, there's no mistaking the love Julian has for me. The love I feel for him, deep inside, even if I don't fully know it yet.

"Lissa?" He whispers. I press my lips together because I don't trust my voice. "I didn't-I didn't know if it was you. You're in my blood, Lissa. I've been sensing you for days."

Only it hasn't been days, I don't say.

"I'm sorry," I sputter.

Sorry for everything, I don't say. Sorry for existing, sorry for not coming sooner.

He shakes his head as if he can hear all my unsaid words and he's denying them all. A ghost of a smile flickers across his lips and he reaches for my face with a trembling hand. Brighter light slips through the bars as the day grows.

"When my mother died," he says softly, "all I ever wanted was to join her.

"That night, in the Chamber, that was supposed to be my last. I wanted one night of danger before then." He laughs softly and looks away. Splotches of color seep into his cheeks and my heart warms. "Then you came. You ruined everything, I said, remember?

"But ever since that moment, I've wanted another chance. I wanted to live. I wanted you, even after I knew who you were. Even after I knew I couldn't have you. And look now." His eyes turn back to mine, as intense as they were that first night. In the silence, I can almost hear the flames crackling outside.

But I pretend nothing is wrong in the world. No one is hurt. No one is dying. The palace isn't on fire. I pretend I can't smell the smoke creeping through the bars.

"I made this for you," he says. He pulls a folded sheet of paper from his pocket. I open it, holding his gaze, breaking away only to drop my eyes to the paper.

To a drawing. To me. Exactly how I looked the night of the ceremony.

The sketch is lifelike. He captured everything, from the folds of the cream dress to the jewel around my neck and the curls in my hair. My hands hold up my dress, my lips are parted, my eyes shine—I look alive.

"How did you draw this?" My voice is deathly still. There's a wooden stake, skinnier than a pencil, by his side, stained a dark shade.

He narrows his eyes. "Beet juice. Beets were all Ilen could bring me."

I sigh in relief and he laughs softly.

"What did you think it was?"

"I...never mind," I say, shaking my head. It looks so much like blood.

I fold up the drawing and tuck it into my tunic. I meet his eyes. Intense, strong, so much like the Julian I know. He shivers, pressing himself hopelessly against the stone wall behind him. The way he lies there, helpless and uncaring, shatters something inside me.

"Kiss me, Lissa." His voice is no more than a whisper. My heart beats. Once. Twice. Only two heartbeats to be stunned by his words.

And my lips are on his. I lose my grip and fall into his lap. He cups my cheeks in his burning palms and lowers his face to mine, his lips curved in a small smile. His lips are scorching. And soft, so soft. He is always soft, despite his strength and fearlessness. His heart will always be gentle.

His arm moves to my back, pulling me closer. I can feel his weakness in his touch, in his burning, trembling body. I reach for his hair, wrap my fingers around the silk and pull him closer, closer.

He tastes like sweat and pain and tears. Tears I should have spilled for him, but he spilled for himself. Tears that should have choked my throat, but I was intoxicated with Rowan.

Last night rushes back. Guilt heats my cheeks. How could I do such a thing?

I pull back and his feverous eyes search mine. He trails his trembling finger across my lips. His breath is as hot as his skin. "What is it?"

"Rowan," I say. My eyes flicker to Julian's lips and I swallow to keep myself from leaning forward again. I tremble beneath his touch. His left arm burns into my back, reminding me of how wounded he is.

"Did he... hurt you?" He asks softly.

"No," I whisper. "But the palace is on fire."

His brow furrows and his eyes narrow. "Already?"

"You knew," I say suddenly, sitting up. "You've known all along what Rowan planned to do."

"I've known for days," he says. "I tried to tell the Queen." He pauses. "But she didn't listen to me. I thought by taking you away from the palace, you would be safe."

The metal bars rattle. It doesn't matter now. The palace is already on fire. The Queen is dead. We'll die here too, if we don't move. "We have to go."

He shakes his head. I leap to my feet and he sits still, staring at his hands. "I can't."

"What do you mean?" I crouch down. My heart beats faster.

"I can't, Lissa," he says, defeated. He finally looks up at me. "I'll only slow you down. Go." Like I slowed him down when he broke into the Chamber.

Debris showers down from the ceiling and I glance up as the dungeons rock once more. What has Rowan done?

I wrap my hands around his arm and tug. "No, Julian. I'm not leaving without you. Get up. Please."

His eyes bore into mine when I say his name. For a moment, he is eerily still, and I'm afraid he'll refuse again.

But he clenches his jaw and closes his fist. I see the pain in his eyes and in his quivering muscles as he slowly pushes himself to his feet. He steadies himself with one hand against the wall. He squeezes his eyes shut and exhales as the walls quake again.

"Hurry," I say.

He opens his eyes and nods, reassuring himself. He slowly releases his hold from the wall and takes one step toward me, favoring his right. Lines crease his forehead. His coat slips off his shoulders. He stumbles. I grab him and steady him against me, the burning heat of his body searing into my side. Something is wrong.

"Julian," I whisper. I help him out of the cell as a chunk of the ceiling collapses behind us. "What's wrong?"

"I-I can't hear. My ear it's-it's- I don't know what's wrong." His voice is filled with self-loathing and despair.

He raises one shaky finger and presses it beneath my eye, taking away a single bead of my pain for him. "Don't. Please."

The walls shudder in another warning. We need to move faster.

He leans against me, and we make our way awkwardly through the corridor. He doesn't have to speak for me to know how disgusted he is of himself. I keep my eyes on the ground as we step over rubble and debris.

Every few moments, I raise my head to check our progress. Soon enough, I can see the stairwell at the other end, illuminated with light from above. The ground trembles beneath my feet and a shower of white rains down again. The pieces are small, but soon, they will grow.

"We won't make it," Julian says. I glance at him in surprise because he sounds so much like himself.

"We will," I say, focusing.

"There's something in there," he says softly, carefully reaching for his ear. I gently push his hand away and brush the hair from his ear. He holds his breath. I clench my teeth.

"What did they do?" I ask. He shudders in answer.

Dark, dried blood covers the entire lobe. At my touch, pieces crumble away. He flinches.

"Let's go," he says, not looking at me. "I'll do it while we move."

We run now. I catch Julian before he stumbles, keeping close to his side as we go. A jagged piece of the ceiling sails down and we swerve as another piece drops down.

It slices into my shoulder and I cry out, clutching my arm as white-hot pain ricochets through me.

Julian glances at me with concern, but doesn't stop. "We're almost there."

I grit my teeth against my throbbing arm. Blood coats my fingers. My blood that started this entire mess. That started a race for a planet long thought destroyed.

"Lissa." Julian's voice is warning. I sway and grip his arm. Now I need him to keep me steady. "Stay focused."

I usher him up the stairwell first and follow. His coat trails along the stairs. It's melancholy, in a way, watching his dark form rising into the light.

He stops at the top of the stairs and I nearly run into him. I glance up, squinting against the sudden light as smothering heat rolls down in waves. I carefully step beside him and look out.

The sun is inside the palace.

It shines where the Queen's throne once was. Because where the Queen's throne should be, the palace wall is gone. I can see the sun, the sky, the blue and red and a bright halo of light.

A choked sound escapes my lips. Fallen Jute lie on the bloody ground. Rowan did more than set fire to the palace. Rowan and his men massacred.

As if on cue, Rowan steps from the opening beside the Queen's platform, his hair ruffling in the wind.

"You left," he says to me.

He's too far for me to see his eyes. Julian's hand closes around my arm as Rowan draws closer with my every breath. Something roots me to the ground, stops me from fleeing when I should.

"Lissa," Julian breathes through clenched teeth. "Come on."

I shake my head. He hisses. "Lissa."

I face him. "You go. I have to do this alone."

A mixture of confusion and pain flashes across his face. But he turns and leaves through the door far behind us.

But I can't move. I close my eyes as Rowan's steps grow louder and louder. When I open them, he's near enough for me to see the blue of his eyes. A half-smile flickers across his face when I don't move. His eyes are ablaze when he reaches for my hand. And when I don't move away, his gaze softens.

"Why did you leave?" He asks. His voice is wrought in pain.

"You can't do this," I say. Eli said I could help him. I *want* to help him. "You said you don't kill. You said you only follow orders. You lied."

He glances at my bloody shoulder, then down at a body barely feet away from us. The white tile stretching out before us is smeared in red. Red of Jutaire. Red of the Jute. What's left of the white walls still hold the swirling gold, a remnant of what was once beautiful, however disastrous.

Blue and purple flames lick up from the ground.

How can Rowan ruin something as magnificent as this? Why? This is how Earth ended, they said. The rumors said man ruined Earth.

Earth gave mankind everything—food, water, shelter, a way of life. And they ruined it. Set fire, dropped bombs, went mad.

Just like Rowan.

"You know what it's like to not have a mother. You said so yourself." I know my words are reaching him, for he is silent, deathly still. "What will his children do when their father doesn't come home?"

I point to a body of a young soldier. "And his mother? She'll wallow in grief for the rest of her days when she realizes her son is never coming home." Anger raises my voice. "Did you ever think, Rowan?"

"Sometimes, sacrifices must be made for the greater good." I flinch at his flat tone and he breathes a humorless laugh. "You of all people should know that, Lissa. You're the one who sides with whoever is more beneficial to your treacherous lips."

My face burns and he smirks.

"You're wrong," I say, but my voice lacks the force of my words. His smirk fades and pain flickers in his eyes.

He runs a hand through his hair. Like Julian. I bite my lip. "I thought you"—his voice drops—"loved me."

I flinch at the desperate pain in his voice. When I look at him, I don't see a madman. I don't see a killer. I see a broken boy. A beautiful broken boy so much like his brother.

"You don't. You never did. It was all an act, wasn't it?" He asks. Funny he should think my part was an act when I can only think the same of him.

"It wasn't," I hear myself say. It was *supposed* to be an act. But it wasn't. And now, staring into his eyes, I don't know what to do.

"I'm not a fool, Lissa," he breathes, changing into someone else. "I know why you kissed me. I know everything was for him."

My blood runs hot. Every sliver of sympathy I felt for him fades into blinding fury. I wrench away from Rowan's grip and he laughs, but it chokes at the end, and with it, so does my anger. "Run away, Lissa. Run away. But remember, you'll come back to me. You'll need me. You'll beg for me. And I'll make sure you never leave me again. Not even Julian can help you then."

He turns and leaves. I rush to the door. Julian's there when I slip through.

I look down at my hands and slowly unclench my fists. His fingers brush the side of my arm. I press my lips tight to hold back the tears.

The palace trembles, but he is still, waiting for me to speak. But I'm afraid, I realize. Afraid of his rejection. A voice whispers in my mind, *you only did it because of him*. But it lies. That was what I had planned. But my body was treacherous to my heart.

So I say nothing and he turns away.

"Your ear," I say before I can stop myself.

"It's a bit better," he says tonelessly. Disappointedly.

He leads the way. Every few steps, he pauses, reaches for something and steadies himself. He never touches me. His cheeks are flushed and his breathing is labored. My mind is swimming in worry and gnawing with guilt.

We sidestep bodies as we go. I try not to look down at their mouths parted in silent cries, their eyes staring into the open sky. Where are they now?

"Where are we going?" I ask, my voice small.

"To my house," he says, his eyes forever moving. His lips are turned down in a slight frown. He looks stronger. As if all this pain and destruction has given him strength. Smoke begins to rise from the flames and my eyes sting.

Darkness begins to settle as we move deeper into the palace. The sun shines where my mother's throne once was, but it is far from us, and we get farther still. Smoke hangs like a shadow over everything. We sidestep debris and dodge the occasional collapsing wall. My heart aches at the ruin. My shoulder throbs and blood continues to soak my sleeve.

"We should tie that," Julian says. He pulls a strip of cloth from his pocket and wraps it around my arm. He notices me watching him. He raises his eyes to mine and my pulse quickens when he takes a deep breath and stops, as if he means to say something. But he doesn't.

We move on. I pull the mask over my face and he holds his arm across his nose when the smoke thickens. But Julian says the smoke of Jutaire isn't like the smoke of Earth. It doesn't kill as fast.

The door lies flat on the floor, barged down by escaping Jute. As I step over the fallen plank, I wonder if they made it out in time. I wonder where they are and if they are safe. Julian reaches for my face and brushes my hair away from my eyes. He knows what I think. He always knows.

He takes hold of my hand without a word, envelops me in his soft strength. I wonder if he can forgive me, I wonder if he knows and if he doesn't, if I can ever tell him.

We run, because there isn't much time.

And we don't stop until we reach the place where I kissed Rowan, and never wanted him to stop.

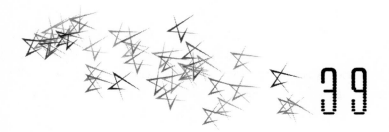

39

I CAN ALMOST FEEL THE STRANDS OF Rowan's hair brushing against my forehead. But I don't feel disgust anymore. I feel guilt. Guilt that I did such a thing.

Hate doesn't well up when I picture Rowan's face. And for that, I hate myself.

"Are you alright?" Julian asks, because I'm frozen, my eyes glued to the spot where I stood in the moonlight. His gaze flickers to the wall and back to me. "Lissa?"

"I'm fine," I say breathlessly. I rush past him and push open the unlocked door. Shame burns my skin.

The house is as dark as it was last night. Even the light of the sun can't penetrate this darkness. Julian doesn't follow and I wonder if he needs a moment to himself. A moment of solitude, without me to interrupt.

The house is eerily empty, and a sudden thought raises my pulse. I walk past the empty living room and throw open the door to the room with the fireplace. It's empty. My heart pounds faster. I run into the other corridor. I check the dining hall. Empty. I rush back and fling open the door to the room that I called mine for a day.

"Eli," I breathe in relief. Why I was afraid I wouldn't see him, I don't know. He raises his head from against the chair beside the bed. When he sees my arm, he shoots to his feet.

"Mission successful?" He asks, checking my arm.

"The palace is in ruins. It's collapsing." An overwhelming sadness chokes my voice.

"There was nothing you could do about that," he says. He tilts his head. "That isn't why you went there though. Why did you go there, Lissa?"

"I…" I trail off and his fingers pause around my arm. "I went there for Julian."

"And were you successful?" He asks again.

"Yes." Julian says behind me. "Did you ever doubt her?"

Eli laughs and I turn back to him, eyes wide. If I had heard his laugh before, I would have known right away that he's Julian's father.

Julian joins him, his laugh softer in comparison. He stops abruptly, his jaw clenched as he steadies himself against the doorframe, one hand pressed against his head.

"We don't have time," Julian says, his voice tinged in pain.

"We don't," Eli agrees. "Let me take a look at that. As soon as his work is done, Rowan will head for the ship." He turns his eyes to mine. "But I suspect he'll come back for you first."

"I don't think so," I say softly, looking away. Eli shakes his head.

"You're in his blood, Lissa." I flinch and Julian inhales sharply. "He listens to you. You're making him see the world through a different lens. You're making him human."

I shake my head. I want to tell him about all the deaths Rowan has caused.

"He needs you. To the extent that it's bordering madness." Eli sighs. Julian watches me intently.

My cheeks burn as my mind replays last night. I leave before my face betrays what words cannot. But even as I ease the door closed behind me, I can hear Julian's quiet question. And for once, I wish he didn't know. I wish he couldn't read me the way he can. But he can.

And he always will.

I splash water on my burning face. My reflection stares back in the rippling water. I am as red as the land around me. I slip out the back door and climb the short wall surrounding Eli's land, easing myself on the six-foot stone ledge.

I pick at the clean fabric Eli wrapped around my arm. The aching pain has faded to a dull throb because of the Jute blood in me.

I raise myself to my feet, balancing myself on the foot-wide wall. Beyond Julian's house, and the clear Louen covered plantation Eli owns, beyond the many houses and buildings, smoke billows from what's left of the palace. My eyes burn as if the flames surround me, not the remains of a magnificent building so far from here.

How can one feel so sorry for a heartless construction?

Somewhere out there, Rowan stands as I do, staring at his work. His masterpiece of destruction.

Soon, nothing will be left but ashes. Charred, darkened bits of a palace that once was. The bodies of the Jute that once lived powerful lives will deteriorate with it. Green eyes flash in my mind, reminding me of Mia. Is she still in that hidden room, nibbling away at her ration of bread? Why couldn't she come with me? Is my mother still inside her chambers? Is she still asleep, her gown draped over her elegant figure?

She's dead.

Soon, nothing will be left. Soon, Rowan will herd together his men and make way for the ship. Soon, he'll land on Earth and take what is not his.

No. Soon he'll come back for me.

I sit down on the ledge, dangling my legs over the edge. My head spins when I glance down.

Somewhere to my left lies human territory, and Dena. I wonder if she made it back safely, and if she has given my blood to every human alive.

"You're hiding from me," Julian teases as he climbs onto the ledge beside me with a small smile. His face is clean, the bruises less prominent. The wind picks up, blowing the strands that have come loose from my braid. It blows his hair too, but his piercing gaze never wavers.

"I'm not," I say. "I was wrong."

"Oh?" He raises one eyebrow.

"I thought I wanted Earth, but I was wrong. I still want Earth but not"—take a deep breath—"not without you by my side."

He stares at me, deep in thought.

"No matter what the cost?" He asks quietly.

"No matter what the cost," I echo.

Pain flickers across his eyes. "Then I'll make sure you get just that. For as long as I can."

"Forever," I say softly, confused. "I want you forever."

He says nothing. I rub at an invisible ache beneath my heart.

"Did Rowan hurt you?" He asks.

I breathe a laugh. It sounds bitter. "No. He would never hurt me." I sound as if I'm defending him.

"I see," he says distantly. His eyes burn into my soul.

"I kissed him," I whisper. The words tumble out. I don't say how much I wanted it. How much I needed it. How I never wanted it to end. But my eyes swell with tears.

He reaches for me. Pulls me against him, so my cheek rests against his chest. I hear the rumble of quiet laughter by his heart. And when he speaks, his voice is tinged in amusement. "You've been through so much, and this is what makes you cry?"

I sputter a laugh and his fingers trail down my hair. So gentle. Like the wind. Only beautiful. Real. It hurts.

I pull back and look at him, our faces inches apart. "You aren't upset."

"Upset?" He tilts his head and touches his nose to mine. His whisper brushes my face. "Because my brother wants what I do? Rowan and I are alike in almost every way. It would be impossible."

He laughs. "So no, I'm not upset."

He said Rowan wants what he does. But didn't I want Rowan last night too?

"Your ear," I say, raising my hand. I brush my fingers over the soft, cool skin and a blush explodes across my face. The touch seems more intimate than it's supposed to.

"Is fine," he finishes.

"You were feverous," I say. He's still warm, but not scorching.

"I'm fine. My dad is pretty good with medicine," he says. He leans against my hand and closes his eyes. I notice everything in those few heartbeats. The way his clean shirt clings to his chest and arms. The stillness of his features. The defining ridge on his nose that Rowan doesn't have. The angle of his jaw. The way the silky strands of his hair fall over his pale bronze skin.

"You're beautiful," I whisper. The moment I say them, the words hit me in the face, slam into my heart. His eyes fly open and my heart skips a beat at the intensity of his gaze.

He exhales a shaky breath and trembles beneath my hand before he leans away. He runs his tongue across his lips and I hear a multitude of words in his silence.

"Then we're a perfect match, aren't we?" He asks finally. His low voice reminds me of Rowan and shivers race through me. He grins at my blush and I quickly pull out his sketch and hold it out to him.

"You keep it," I say, because it means more to me if it's with him. "Do you have more drawings?"

"I used to," he says softly. "But I destroyed them all when my mom died. But in the dungeons, I-I *had* to draw you, to see you. Because I was so sure I wouldn't see you again. And I drew another, a redrawing of one of my favorite old sketches afterwards, to get my mind off you."

He pulls another slip of paper from his pocket and unfolds it with his long fingers. It's a careful sketch of an old clock, blurring into a rippling sea. Now, in the light of the sun, I can tell the lines are more purple than red. "It's supposed to stand for our life. Time we don't have, time we don't know. It was originally meant to resemble the way we lost track of time when humans came to Jutaire. I didn't have colors, or I would have made the sea blue."

"It's beautiful," I say.

"You think so? I looked through some Earth books to find a clock and the sea. They're all old, so it's hard to find anything clear enough."

"All you had to do was look in your eyes," I say softly. "They're like the sea. Your hair is like the night sky. And your smile is like the moon."

He's silent a moment before he folds the sketch, a slow smile spreading across his face. Dena was right. "And you?"

"Me?"

"Mm-hmm." He nods slowly. "Describe yourself."

"I'm plain ol' me," I say with a shrug.

"No, you're not," he says softly. "Your hair is like chocolate, rich and silky. Your skin is like the moon, pale and bright. Your eyes are like a child's, innocent and wide. And your lips are always parted the slightest bit, always begging to be kissed." He pulls me close and whispers the last words against my lips.

The back door flies open and I pull away, my skin ablaze. Smudges of color blossom across Julian's cheeks and an inexplicable happiness takes hold of my heart, pushing away everything else.

Eli steps into the small space between his house and the ledge. He watches his son with so much love in his eyes that it wrenches my heart. When he turns his gaze to me, I hear two simple words in his silence. *Thank you.*

At once, I feel happiness and the urge to cry. This is the meaning of love. It fills you with longing, want, and so much happiness that it hurts. It hurts enough to cry through a smile.

I leap down and wipe away the tears burning at the edge of my eyes, hoping neither of them notices.

"It's time to go," Eli says as Julian drops down beside me.

"You won't like this," Julian says to me.

"Why? What do you mean?"

"You need to get to human territory before Rowan gets to you," Eli says.

"We can't walk, obviously," Julian says.

"And we don't have a carriage." Eli leads us around the house.

"We'll have to ride there," Julian says apologetically.

I stop in my tracks and meet the creature's piercing red eyes. I have to ride there on a mutant. Bile rises in my throat and I cringe as I force it back down.

"You could ride with me," Julian says behind me. "But we need two, just in case."

"I don't even know how to ride."

"I saw how it affected you when the Queen called them horses. I know it wouldn't have mattered to you if you hadn't obsessed over horses. I know, Lissa, that you know how to ride," he says a-matter-of-factly.

I hear the unsaid words. "Just like you. You've pored over the books just like I did."

"Don't get me started on Julian and Earth," Eli laughs. There's a twinkle in his suddenly bright eyes. He has changed since Julian arrived. It's as though Julian and Rowan have two different fathers.

Julian flushes and disappears into the house to get water and supplies. Eli brings rug-like saddles and tosses it over the mutants' backs. I shiver, wishing I had the gloves Slate gave me. Eli notices. "It'll be fine. You don't even have to touch them. Here."

He hands me a pair of brown gloves as dark as my hair. They're supple and rich, made for slender hands like mine. Cross-stitches line the edges in a lighter shade of brown.

They're unlike anything I've seen before. I glance up at him. "They're beautiful."

He nods and quickly looks away. But not before I see his Adam's apple bob. He hurries back into the house before I can ask him what's wrong. I slip on the gloves, and wiggle my fingers. The gloves are as soft as they look.

"Where did you get those?"

I jump and drop my hands by my sides. Julian's gaze follows my movement. A long coat, like the one he wore on the night of the ceremony hangs from his lean frame. The collar is raised to protect his mouth from dust.

"These?" I ask, raising my hands. He nods. "Eli gave them to me."

Surprise flickers across his face, yet his expression still remains dark.

"He did," he says to himself. He moves toward the mutant and climbs it in one swift movement, throwing a glance back at me. "Do you need help mounting?"

"I can manage," I say. What happened?

My feet kick up dust as I move to the mutant waiting for me. It whinnies, the sound low and guttural. My throat constricts as I hook one leg in the loop and swing my leg over the other side.

How many times have I done this in my mind? How many times have I breathed over the words written in ink in those ancient books, wondering if I would ever ride an actual horse?

I splay my hands on the makeshift saddle for a moment, trying to ignore the sick feeling inside my stomach, rising up my throat. I grip the reins and raise my eyes. Julian watches. His eyes flicker from the gloves to my face again.

"They were my mother's," he says finally, turning his back to me. It's as if his quiet voice moves on another frequency. Reaches into my veins instead of my ears.

I glance at the gloves and I imagine the ghost of his mother's fingers in them. Did she look as beautiful as Julian and Rowan? No, she couldn't have looked like either of them – they don't share the same mother.

"She hated the mutants too, and my dad made her those gloves. After she... after she died, he couldn't part with them."

I don't say anything. I don't know what to say when he speaks of things that pain him. I grip the reins as Julian turns back to me, but before he can speak, Eli bursts through the door.

A smear of blood taints his cheek. He's breathless, his eyes wide. Julian curses and stumbles off the mutant, rushing to his father in heartbeats.

Eli sputters, but he isn't physically hurt.

He meets my eyes. "Mia."

The weight of the stone around my neck threatens to pull me to the ground.

"No," I whisper.

I tumble off the mutant, ignoring its panicked squeals. I pull the gloves from my hands and tuck them into the pocket of my tunic. My movements are jerky and slow at the same time, as if I'm moving too fast against heavy winds.

"Lissa, wait." Julian tries to grab me. I duck and push past him and Eli into the dark house. There's a pain in my chest that no amount of time can ever cure.

Mia. Carefree, bubbly, a beacon of light in our dark world.

Dead.

The house is dark and I don't know where she is. Maybe she isn't dead. Darkness edges into the corners of my vision, tightens around my mind, pulls me to the ground. My breathing is rough in the silence of death. Hands grab me from behind.

"Let me go," I plead. My voice is harsh, hushed. Tight with tears.

"No, Lissa," Julian says.

He pulls me harder, turns me to face him. I stare at him, at his eyes wavering in my tears. "She's not dead."

No.

No

no

"What?" I ask, breath held. She isn't dead?

"She's hurt very badly, but not dead. They're not sure she'll make it. They're trying, but there's a high likelihood of..." he trails off.

I feel as though someone has reached into my chest and twisted my heart.

I gasp for air and sink down, down, to the ground. He drops to his knees in front of me.

"How?" I finally choke out.

"Someone found out. The Queen placed an order to kill her years ago, and one of the soldiers must have tried to follow through."

My eyes widen. Someone who's been searching for years just found out. And it can only be because I asked Eli to find her. To help me.

"I want to see her," I say flatly.

"You can't," he says, shaking his head again.

I snort. "Why not? I've seen enough blood. Gage, Chancellor Kole, countless others. You."

He flinches. "She was your servant. You knew her for less than a day. Why does she matter so much?" He asks harshly.

"I killed her." The words spill in a venomous whisper.

"You did not. She's still alive." His jaw is clenched.

My nostrils flare. "She was hope. This world is so messed up and she-she would have turned it around. Have you ever seen her, Julian?"

He softens when I say his name. He's keeping count, I realize. "Yes, I have. Do you know what she told me?"

I don't answer. She can't die. She can't.

"She said she could never be queen. She wanted it this way. She said she wasn't born to lead. Only some are. Like you."

Didn't she tell me as much? But that was before. Before my mother died. I stiffen. Before the *queen* died.

I am queen.

I break free from Julian's grasp. Every vein in my body is numb with grief, cold with this new revelation. Eli paces outside, questioning the guard about medical methods. He held hope over Mia too. Too much hope. But I know he won't sit still and wait, I know he'll go there himself, wherever she is, and try to save her.

I pull the gloves over my hands and rush outside, flinging myself onto the mutant in one swift swing. Julian runs after me. I reach for the reins, ignore his frantic callings and spur the mutant into action.

I am queen. *Queen.*

And I will bleed for my people.

40

THE MUTANT IS VERY MUCH LIKE A HORSE.
I can imagine it to be a horse, so long as I don't look at it. I
can feel the strength of its muscles working beneath my
gloved hands, undulating in a never-ending loop. Bits and
pieces fly beneath its tread on the brittle ground.

On either side of me, houses come and go. A Jute
will peek out from a corner, sometimes, meeting my eyes
for the barest of heartbeats before I rush past.

Sometimes a young girl wandering the streets will
turn and look at me. Her green eyes will threaten to tear
me apart.

I try not to think of Mia. But everywhere I look, I see
her bright green eyes, her lively white skin, and her fiery
red hair.

I lean forward, urging the mutant faster. Soon
enough, the silence behind me is filled with the sounds of
another mutant. I knew Julian would follow. I knew, yet
here I am, trying to flee.

He's my voice of reason.

"Lissa, wait!" Julian calls.

I squeeze my eyes shut, trying to decide if it is better to ignore him. But I can never run away from him. I am not strong enough to leave him.

I stop and turn the mutant around, and his mutant stops too. He doesn't come close enough for me to see the blue of his eyes. It's almost as though he knows I can't bear to have him any closer.

"Where are you going?" The pain in his voice cuts a gash in my heart.

"To the palace," I say.

"But why? We're supposed to go back to the Tower."

I shake my head. Bite my lip. "You are. Not me."

His eyes narrow. "Lissa—"

"I'm queen, Julian. Queen of the Jute. Mia, Ilen, Wren —there's no difference between us and them. They deserve Earth as much as you and me, as much as every human alive. And together, man and Jute will be stronger than ever."

The wind howls in answer to my words.

"You'll bleed for them," he says as slowly as it dawns.

"Yes," I say without hesitance. "The palace is gone because of me. So many are dead because of me. I can't turn away from that."

"It's not your fault, Lissa," he urges quietly.

"It is." I tug on the mutant's reins. "Go back to the Tower, gather everyone, tell them to bring only what they need. Lead them east. The ship is somewhere there."

"There are roughly ten thousand Jute, Lissa. Your blood in all of them will be your death."

"Then that is what it will be," I say, my voice is calm but my blood is roaring.

He stares at me, slowly clenching and unclenching his jaw. "I won't watch you die."

"You won't. You will head east, remember?"

"Stop it," he growls. "Stop acting so calm."

He jumps down from the mutant in one angry leap and stalks toward me. My eyes widen at his anger, at his lack of control when he is the one always in control.

"And Rowan? What would you do if he got in your way? Tell me, Lissa." He is close enough for me to see his eyes ablaze with fury. And barely concealed hurt.

"Rowan would be a fool to get in my way."

He looks away for a moment and I consider leaving before he clears his mind and never lets me go. But his eyes focus on mine again. And he smiles then, a small, sad smile, filled with pride. The gash in my heart deepens.

"Slate was right. You *are* a warrior," he says softly.

I look away.

"A warrior queen."

He reaches for me, his long fingers curling. I stare at his hand one last time. I memorize the beauty of his face, the pain in his eyes.

And before the tips of his fingers can graze my leg, I turn, leaving him in a swirl of dust.

41

THE CARESS OF THE WIND AND THE mutant's galloping hooves form a steady rhythm, easing my fears into one dull throb. Soon enough, I reach the soot-covered hill where my mother's palace once stood, a striking structure of white and gold.

Gone.

I swallow the lump that forms in my throat. There are more Jute here. They turn their grief-stricken faces to me as my mutant climbs the hill. I don't meet anyone's eyes long enough to know if they recognize me. The princess who is now queen.

But the closer I get to the top, the more I am recognized.

"Princess!" They cry. But the ground is a blur beneath me. Their shouts are a blurred cacophony vibrating through my bones. There isn't time to stop.

The stench of burning is strong when I reach the top of the hill. I stop and leap down from the mutant, the charred remains of my mother's palace behind me. There are Jute men and women, soldiers, nobles, others. A soldier steps forward from the frantic group, one I don't recognize. He wears the same outfit every other Jute soldier wears—a uniform of the palest gold, nearly brown, with white adornments on his shoulders, and the white, ten-pointed star on his shirt-pocket.

"Princess," he says in a gravelly voice, bowing low. I meet his light brown eyes when he stands.

"Where's Rowan?" I ask. I sound like my mother. He swallows.

"My men caught sight of him heading west with his group." West from here, east from human territory. Towards the ship. Maybe Eli was wrong and Rowan *won't* come for me.

And if Rowan doesn't come for me, there's less time to do what I have to do. Less time before the ship leaves Jutaire.

But there's still a chance. If Julian gathers the humans and heads east soon, he'll be able to cross paths with Rowan.

"Is the lab still intact?" I ask.

But before he can speak, another man interrupts.

"Your Majesty, if I may," he says, his voice surprisingly calm. I take in his dark skin and dark clothes, warm eyes. He's the man who held the crown on the night of my ceremony. The same man who stood beside the Queen when I called her mother.

"The Queen is dead."

"The Queen never dies," I say.

"You are right," he says, inclining his head in apology. "Queen Rhea has passed and Mia Leen is alive, but incapable. You, princess, are now the rightful queen."

I clasp my hands together.

"The palace is gone, but our first queen was crowned on this hill. If you approve, I will have the crown brought here. We will call forth every Jute to witness."

"Is that what you suggest?" I ask. Strangely, I trust this man with lulling words.

"Yes," he says.

"Then that's what we'll do," I say.

"As you wish, my queen." He bows low. When he stands, a warm smile stretches across his face.

But all I feel is dread.

Not all of the palace is gone. Entire rooms still stand eerily intact, as though their will to stand was stronger than the fire.

The dark-skinned man's name is Reed, the Queen's assistant and advisor when Rowan proved too young to understand. He leads me to one of the rooms and insists that I change into a gown but I refuse. I would rather look like Julian's last words than a girl in a dress.

I wash up, wiping the dust from the scales of my tunic while he makes the announcement. In moments, the entire Jute population will gather at the foot of the hill, their eyes focused on me. I expect to be worried at the thought. But I feel nothing.

Rowan was right—I am not the same girl I once was.

The door to the room opens and Reed slips in. "If you are ready, your Highness."

"I am," I say. He hands me a crown, darker and smaller than my mother's, more fitting for my dark outfit than my mother's would have been. I don't even know what happened to the crown I wore at the ceremony. Rowan must have it.

"There isn't time for a true ceremony, but this will suffice. This way, your Highness," Reed says. He carefully leads me through the rubble. Smoke lingers everywhere, blocking out the sun. He steps to the side when we reach the palace grounds again. My mutant is gone.

A group of soldiers stand in a half-ring behind me. Days ago, they held Chancellor Kole, Julian, and Dena as intruders. All they do is follow orders. They did what my mother commanded them to. And now that she is gone, they will do what I say.

I glance at Reed, who nods encouragingly, and take a deep breath.

I slowly move forward, to the edge, where a worn stone has been set into the ground. Where my mother once stood, and her sister before her, and however many Kings and Queens ruled before them. I don't know anything about Jute history. I reach for the jewel around my neck.

I know what I'll see when I look down. But when I look over the edge of the hill, the sight of hundreds of Jute staring up at me is still a surprise.

They're my people now.

"My mother is dead."

The wind is my friend. It carries my words down, down, down to the ears of the quiet Jute staring up at me.

"The rumor of Mia Leen was true. She was the true heir to the throne, and is now in a position near-death. Which leaves me as Queen.

"Rowan, first in command, has destroyed the palace. He has taken one-tenth of you, loyal to him, out west. There is a ship waiting to take him and his men to Earth."

Earth, I hear them gasp. I was like them once, when Earth was a dream. Now it's a painful reality. I take a deep, shuddering breath.

"The ship is large enough to hold us all. Every single one of us. I have seen it," I say, scanning over their faces. They are young, old, all of them breathtaking. There is nothing that makes them inhuman besides their unmasked faces.

"The air within the ship is oxygen, as is the air of Earth. Each of you will be given an injection containing a substance that will enable you to breathe both oxygen and the air of Jutaire. Once everyone has been given the shot, you will head west. Take whatever you can. You will never return."

"And if Rowan hurts us?" Someone shouts from below. I stare down where I think the voice came from.

"Rowan has one thousand men, we have nine thousand. If you would rather stay here for the rest of your life, so be it. If you want Earth, you will fight for it. This journey is yours alone."

I step back in the silence of my words. One by one, I hear it. Shouts and cheers, soft at first, then echoing, rippling through the crowd. I close my eyes and breathe a sigh of relief.

The soldiers begin descending the hill, ready to organize everyone so they can easily distribute my blood. Of the three Jute who know how to mix the catalyst and prepare the injection, only one still lives. The other two died in the fire.

"Your Majesty," Reed says behind me. His eyes are wet. I look away. "The lab."

I follow him as he leads me back through the rubble again. Three soldiers accompany us through a different route. A jagged piece of rubble, the height of me and double my width blocks the lab entrance. Reed steps back as the soldiers heave and struggle to move it.

I force myself to breathe. In, out, in out. I look up at the sky, at the sun peeking through the remnants of the palace. I will never see it again. Never.

"My Queen." I jerk my face to the soldier in front of the lab. Reed steps inside and I follow. Debris covers everything. One of the soldiers pulls a sheet protecting a table similar to the one Dena was strapped to and gestures for me to lie down.

I rest my head on the flat surface and squeeze my eyes shut. This is it. I will die.

And I feel nothing. My thoughts, memories, and desires that I thought would plague my mind at the time of death—they are all gone.

I see nothing. Feel nothing.

I am nothing.

I force myself to picture Slate's face, his gray eyes. My father. I see Julian too, his blue eyes wavering with love.

Someone swipes a wet swab across my arm, wiping away their faces with the chilly reality. I can hear the Jute's breathing, slow and hushed. I wonder if he feels sympathy for me. Pity even. Or if he can't wait to get my blood in himself, to breathe the oxygen of Earth.

I force air through my lungs. In, out. In, out.

Hope, I hear Gage's voice. I push it away.

Gage was wrong. Hope isn't what keeps us going. Hope will only ever be within us, hope can only help us breathe one extra breath.

Only will can save us. Only will can get us anywhere. Will and work. We must do, not just think.

I feel the sharp tip of the needle cool against my skin. The man releases one slow breath and pushes it inside. I exhale, feeling the pull as my blood fills a vial.

The needle slips out. Unscrew. Re-screw. The needle slips in. More blood.

And before it pierces my flesh a third time, I hear a crash, the rushing of feet, and three words.

"Drop the needle."

42

"ELI?" I WHISPER, LIFTING MY HEAD.

He rushes to my side, pushing away the Jute with the needle. "Are you sure you want to do this?"

I'm silent a moment. I look down at the dot on the inside of my pale arm before meeting his eyes. His question is this: are you sure you want to die for the Jute?

"Yes," I say. "I've learned there is no difference between man and Jute."

"There isn't," he agrees. And by the way he says it, I can tell he is hiding something. He doesn't meet my eyes.

"What is it?" I ask, narrowing my eyes. If I die, I want to know before then. I'm hungry for one more piece of information, even if it is my last.

"Do you know about the Lost Colony?" He asks me. My fingers tremble. I've wanted to know for so long. I shake my head. He takes a deep breath, steeling himself to tell me.

But someone calls for him from another room. And when he looks back at me again, the moment has passed.

He won't tell me. "I have been around for a long time, Lissa. A very long time. There isn't a difference—"

"Eli!" Someone shouts again. I grit my teeth in frustration. Eli's blue eyes are impatient. I'll never know the answer.

"You would die for the Jute?" He asks again.

"Yes." This time, I answer without pause. Because of me, nine thousand of them will live, thrive. One life to save many.

Where did Rowan get enough blood for all his men? Or does he plan on leaving those men who are risking their lives for him?

Eli turns his head to the door. "Ilen!"

Ilen and another soldier shuffle in, toting a container between them. I sit up quickly, shooting a questioning glance at Eli. A shadow of a smile flickers across his face in answer.

"Gage and I were close friends. He once said you can tell a lot from a person's blood. From how their children will look, how their health will be throughout their life, and snippets of their future. Your blood is different. He said you would make a decision one day. For seventeen years, he drew your blood for testing, and stored it in this. It's a pressurized container that kept your blood safe and fresh, for seventeen years," he says, tapping his finger against the canister. "He knew."

I stare at him, my eyes widening as the words slowly click into comprehension. "I-I won't have to—you can use this?"

He nods. "Reed is already lining up the Jute."

I sit up, unable to hold back a triumphant smile.

"But why didn't you give it to my mother?" I ask.

"I know how important your blood is, Lissa. I vowed to use it only for good."

"And this is good?"

He smiles and helps me stand. "This, my queen, is the best."

I almost can't remember the speech I gave the Jute. I thought I was calm and collected but my mind was numb with fear of death.

Dena was able to distribute the vials amongst everyone, Ilen tells me before he rushes out with Eli and a group of trusted soldiers, needles and supplies in tow.

The sun has passed its zenith by the time they are finished. I climb onto the same mutant from earlier—not that there's a way to tell them apart—tightening my dagger sheaths around my arms and securing a set of smaller knives around my waist.

A low whinny breaks the silence behind me, followed by another, and another. A wave of the guttural sound.

I hold my breath and turn.

Hundreds of mutants stand behind me. Atop their backs are women and elders, children and some men. The rest of the men stand beside them, their faces hard and ready. Sacks are thrown over their backs, weapons tight in their hands.

They stare at me in silence, awaiting my orders. A hand touches mine and I turn to Eli atop another mutant.

"Whenever you're ready," he says. I breathe in the silence, the thickness of the air signifying so much life.

Because west from here lies the ship and death.

Some of the Jute run, others ride. We move fast, the wind desperately clawing at us, howling for us to slow down.

The steady rhythm of the mutant's hooves helps me think, though thinking isn't what I should do. I don't know if Julian is safe, if he made it back to the Tower. Ilen said nothing about him and I am worried.

I don't know if I'll be able to defy Rowan's madness when we meet or if my intoxication will pull me under again.

I don't know many things—and that is what scares me the most.

43

I SEE THE HUMANS FIRST.

Far behind them, I can make out the rows and rows of houses, and the rising spire of the Tower beyond them. Julian *did* make it back safely. Pride wells in my chest because he was able to rekindle the hope deep inside everyone.

But Eli points out something else—a dark cloud of red and black zooming towards them, approaching from far ahead where the ship lies.

Rowan and his men.

They'll clash before we get there.

"Veer left!" I cry, my heart beating in my ears. The Jute behind me echo my words as I lean to the left, leading our group towards the back of the human cluster.

The mutant senses the urgent thrum in my pulse and it rides faster. And despite my hatred towards the sickly creatures, I am grateful.

I force my racing heart to calm, and I push the mutant faster, faster.

We're close enough to make out individuals when the first scream pierces the air. I bite my lip when someone falls. The woman's body is lifeless before the ground touches her face. We're heading toward them as fast as we can, and they don't stop moving forward, which is to our right, to where the ship is.

But Rowan is in between.

"Shed blood as a last resort," Reed shouts. I look to my right, where Rowan and his men are riding hard toward us. They are still far, but close enough to shoot. "Riders, protect the humans at all costs. Those of you without mutants, stick to the middle. Be ready."

I slow my mutant to a stop and watch their silent synchrony as they obey Reed's command. I'm the only one away from the group—at least one hundred feet away. I gauge the distance between Rowan's fast-approaching men and the Jute riders, still circling the humans.

I hold my breath when a mutant breaks free from the center, heading towards me at a fast pace. I see his dark uniform, his chocolate brown hair, his lean frame.

I drop my hood and jump down from my mutant as he does the same.

"Lissa," Slate shouts, running to me. He pulls me close and plants a soft kiss on my forehead. It's not the brushing of his mask against my skin. He leans back and grasps my shoulders with warm hands.

Dena gave him my blood. He can breathe the toxic air that isn't toxic anymore.

"Now every time I want to kiss you, I can."

He presses another kiss against my forehead and grins. It fades quickly. "Julian told me what you were going to do."

"But I didn't," I say softly. "I lived, just like I said I would."

He laughs softly. "He says you did more than that. I've heard a lot of things. And seen some too."

"Seen?" I ask.

"I saw the ship when Rowan showed it to you." He looks away.

I blink as his words slowly click.

My throat constricts. He was there. The night I kissed Rowan. He would have seen me move first, because Rowan is a smart idiot. I replay the night over and over in my mind.

His hands tighten on my stiff shoulders. I lift my eyes to his when he speaks. "I don't know what happened that night, but—"

"It was an act," I say, cutting him off. I don't want to hear his words. Shame heats my cheeks.

He exhales and forces a tired smile. "I know."

But that's the thing. He doesn't. He will never know. Because *I* don't even know.

He fingers the crown on my head, swiftly changing the subject. "Queen Lissa."

"Queen Rhea is dead," I say. He closes his eyes for a long moment and offers me a wry smile.

"Everything is for the best," he says. But his voice cracks and I realize: he loved her. The small part of her that was human. The same part I saw before she breathed her last. I open my mouth to tell him, to let him know she spoke of him, even before her death.

But I don't. My lips press closed.

In his heart, he will always have a piece of her that no one else saw. And now, I will too. I lock away my mother's last moments and keep silent.

I am selfish like that.

"Rowan will be here any moment now," Slate says when we've joined the mix of humans and Jute. Reed assembles a group of soldiers at the front of the crowd. They crouch down, arrows nocked and ready.

Slate pulls his mask from his pocket and presses it against his face. "It's the only element of surprise we have on our side."

"I never thought"—he gestures to the Jute, his voice choked—"I never thought we could be together."

"Neither did I," I say.

"But we have you to thank for that. This should have been done years ago." He looks at me and smiles, squeezing my arm. Sweat and fear make the air difficult to breathe. I slip through the panicked crowd, making my way to the front center. My crown makes me stand out, and people move to let me pass. Something rushes through my veins, despite the knowledge of the bloodshed that lies ahead. Something like hope, only stronger.

Someone grabs my hand and I turn.

"Will you look at that. Queen Lissa, huh?" Dena grins and digs into her pocket, pulling out the little replica of Earth. "You left it in the palace. Oh, I got your blood in everyone, as promised."

"Thank you," I say, slipping it into my boot. She shrugs. "And I almost forgot."

I pull out the gun I stole what seems like years ago and hold it out to her, taking in the look of surprise on her face.

"Looks like you didn't need to babysit her after all," Slate jokes. Dena barks a laugh before flipping off the safety on the gun. She aims it somewhere in the distance and fires. A black clothed figure falls.

"You did the right thing, Lissa," she says, glancing at the Jute protecting us. My eyes are wide, but she doesn't even seem fazed by the life she just took. "We were meant to be together, not separated."

More people fall as we hurry forward. Some young, some old. We don't stop for them. Though with every death, a piece of me withers and falls with their unbreathing bodies. Far in the distance, dark plumes of smoke rise from the remains of the palace.

An arrow whizzes past my right, the tip coated in buzzing blue. It sinks into the ground, sparks dying soon after. Up ahead, Reed's men wait for us to catch up.

I push closer to the front to catch a glimpse at them. Each of the ten has an arrow drawn on a slender bow. The tips are solid black.

"Things are going to get ugly," Dena says, half to herself. I open my mouth to ask her what she means. To ask her if she has seen Julian.

But Reed's men release the arrows.

And Jutaire explodes.

44

I CAN'T BREATHE.

Dust chokes my lungs and stings my eyes. The explosion threw me on my back. I can't see the sky. I see red. Above me, around me. Red is everywhere.

Cries. Screams. Wails. Moans. Agony pierces the world.

I clutch my chest with trembling hands, gasp for air and wonder. Is Earth worth so much pain and suffering? Is anything worth so much death?

I close my fists and blink desperately to clear my vision. Dust coats my sweaty palms. But I still see nothing. My ears still pulse with the echo of the explosion. I don't know if it was caused by man or Jute, but it was a bomb, something I never knew existed on Jutaire.

I feel pain in every inch of my body. Because the explosion grew fingers and threw me down like a doll I've seen some young girls carry.

Dena. Slate. Eli. Reed. Julian. I need to know if they are safe. I need to know if they are alive. I open my mouth, but it's dry I can't form a word. I can't see. I can't speak. I can't move.

My eyes drift closed. It's easier this way, I guess. Easier to drift away than to fight. I've done what I could. Earth really *is* impossible.

Someone calls my name.

Lissa.

I turn my head towards the sound of the voice.

Through the haze, far beyond, I see his tall figure. I see the silhouette of his long coat billowing in the wind.

Rowan.

"Lissa!" Another voice cries to my right.

Julian. Alive. Alive.

His voice sets me in motion. I jump to my feet. Each step takes me further from Rowan and closer to Julian.

I collide with a body and the instant I hit the ground, Julian coughs. He pulls me back on my feet and his concerned eyes search my face. A sound between relief and happiness escapes his lips and he pulls me to his chest. "You're okay."

I nod against him, my throat still dry.

"I thought I lost you," he says softly. And right now, in the midst of the impenetrable dust surrounding, there is no one but us. He pulls away.

He slides his hand down the side of my face and tucks my messy hair behind my ear. A smile flits across his face, so soon, I'm not even sure it is real.

"We have to go." His hand closes around mine. He leads me slowly through the haze. I can't see anything but him and this whirlwind of bloody red.

I stop when my leg kicks something with a soft squelch. And when I look down, my insides tumble.

A body. Mutilated. Blood and skin and organs and—

"Don't look, Lissa." Julian tugs on my hand, forcing me to run with him. Something numbs inside me, and I can't force the image of that body from my mind. Dust is sandy on my skin, layered on my hair, gritty in my mouth.

"We lost so many," Julian says over the howl of the wind. I can't see more than ten feet ahead of me. His grip tightens around my hand. "I thought–I thought I lost you too. I tried to come back for you when you left for the palace, but my dad didn't let me."

He stops and looks at me. "Don't leave me again."

"Never," I say softly. But my voice is too soft. The wind picks up my words and swallows them whole.

But this is Julian. He hears me no matter what. His eyes soften. "Everyone's waiting for you. The ship—"he shakes his head—"it looks like it's rising from a grave."

Already.

When the dust clears somewhat, I see the curving, sleek metal of the ship. So much metal I never knew existed. Such beauty, magnificence and strength. The star shines in its center, iridescent white, reminding me of my mother. "It's beautiful."

Julian glances at me. "It is."

"You could draw it," I say. He murmurs a yes and looks away, but not before I see his Adam's apple bob and the pain flash in his eyes.

The last of the haze clears and Jutaire is once again a plain of red, meeting the fading blue sky where the sun is beginning to set. Far to my right, Jute territory spreads like a sprawling mass of white.

I am suddenly filled with an overwhelming giddiness. My head spins and laughter bubbles to my lips. But there is a little part of me that whispers: happiness comes with a price.

I ignore the voice in my mind. *Paranoia*, Gage had said. That is what the voice is named. Paranoia will get a person nowhere.

I catch sight of Dena and Ilen among the crowd, and then Slate too. But everyone is keeping their distance from the ship, as if they are afraid to get too close. Too much distance, I realize with a sliver of panic.

I ignore it.

"Lissa!" Slate shouts. He runs over, Eli following close behind. "You scared me."

"Better late than never, eh, Lissa?" Eli asks when they reach me, but I see the relief on his face too.

"Where's Mia?" I ask him.

"She's with the rest of the wounded. She hasn't gotten any better," he says gravely. He rests a hand on Slate's shoulder. "We need to go."

"It's almost time," Julian says when they disappear into a throng of frantic people.

With every good comes a bad. With every happiness comes a sorrow.

And I want to tell him: no, it isn't almost time.

A metallic clang reverberates in the radius surrounding the ship. At once, silence falls.

The ship has risen completely, and it's almost impossible to look at. Despite the setting sun, it shines fervently in the waning rays.

The metal doors in the ground grate back to life, rumbling and groaning as they race towards one another to seal the gaping hole again. At the same time, a slab of the ship clicks open and slowly begins a descent to the ground. With a puff of air, it settles at an angle, revealing a dark hole—the door.

But something is wrong.

The silence should be filled with the sound of the rumbling metal gates. But they're frozen, their journey to one another halted partway.

I am not the only one who has noticed. Necks crane forward and silent questions quickly raise the tension. I take one step forward in curiosity.

And freeze as Rowan's men climb from the hole.

And chaos breaks loose.

When the first scream shatters the air, I pull two small knives from the sheaths around my arms, blood roaring in my ears. Julian leaves, determination wrought on his face.

Rowan's men are dressed in full black, a yellow band tied around their upper right arms, setting them apart from the rest of the Jute.

My Jute.

Everyone is scattered, caught off guard. Rowan's men waste no time running through the unprepared crowd, slaying without hesitance. I fling one knife at the throat of a burly Jute rushing towards a woman with a child clinging to her slender neck. He falls instantly, a gurgling sound escaping his colorless lips. She turns to me with wild eyes before running blindly and I watch as another Jute slashes a knife across her chest, killing her and the child. All in the blink of an eye. My breath chokes.

I pull the knife out of the fallen Jute's neck and move on. In the fray, I catch glimpses of single battles. A middle-aged man defending his family with a metal rod studded with nails. A young woman ducking under the blows of one of Rowan's men. A Jute girl defending a human girl.

Around me, human and Jute fall. Rowan's men too. But more humans. More Jute who call me queen.

Air compresses behind me. Before I can turn, an arm hooks around my neck and I struggle against the sheer force. I bite down on his fleshy arm, gagging at the sweat and dirt on my tongue. He yelps and I pull away, turning to face him. I drop my knives and unsheathe the long dagger at my waist as he twirls a staff.

I spit. But the salt of his sweat still lingers on my tongue.

He swings the long staff toward my side. I lean back as it swooshes past and raise my leg, kicking it away.

My breath catches when I meet his eyes. How can such a brute possess features so striking? So mesmerizing?

My vision flashes and pain explodes through my side.

He brings the staff down again, aiming for my head. I grab the blade end of my dagger in my other hand and grit my teeth when the staff slams against the metal.

I drop to my knees and roll away. He falls but catches himself and flips to face me. But I am slimmer. Faster.

And his face opens into one of sheer surprise as my knife sinks into his chest.

I jump to my feet as another shadow falls over me. This one has no chance. I run my dagger through his side and keep running. Through another. And another.

Sharp pain slices across my arm. I cry out, tightening my grip around my dagger as another Jute attacks me, a knife in either hand. I swerve from his attacks and swing my leg. One of his knives drop to the ground, already lost in the swirling dust.

He lunges first, knife aimed for my right. I clench my teeth at the pain in my arm and slide away at the last instant. His fingers wrap around my ankle and he pulls me down with him.

I shout out and jab the dagger blindly. Sweat stings my eyes.

I open my mouth as his knife comes sailing down.

But his grip loosens around my ankle and his body goes limp. I'm confused until I meet Julian's eyes from across the fray, a bow still stretched in his hands.

"Freeze." Rowan's voice penetrates the chaos. It travels on the same frequency as Julian's and the silence is instant. My eyes find him through the mass of Jute and man. He's far enough that I can't read his expression, but his face is angled toward me. He can see me.

He holds something in his hands. A dark box.

"Surrender and you'll live. Or every one of you humans will die." He raises the box. "Such a pathetic way to end your lives. And so, very, easy."

The oxygen control. Relief floods through me.

"You heard him!" Someone yells. A man. A human man, with a mask plastered on his fair skin. "Keep fighting. One box can't harm us!"

The moment the words leave his lips, an arrow sinks into his back. He falls to the wretched ground with a muted thud, blood pooling around the arrow. Only cowards murder from behind, Gage had said.

But something happens.

Whether it was his words or his death that sparks it, I'm not sure, but every human and Jute attacks. So many of Rowan's men fall in that unguarded instant. Men, women, and even children, attack in a flurry of movement.

Rowan flicks the switch.

There's a moment of stillness when the suctions release their holds and Jutaire air seeps into every mask.

I lock eyes with Rowan through melee. Surprise flickers across his face when no one falls. I feel a flash of boldness and my lips curve into a sly smile. For once, Rowan isn't hurt or in pain or madly in love.

He's furious.

His anger is an odd source of contentment and encouragement that slowly trickles into me. When I blink again, he's gone. Disappeared. Into the battle of bodies and swirling dust.

I run my blade across an oncoming Jute. The bleeding in my shoulder has stopped, though it still throbs. I wipe my blade across my pants and move on. I slay another Jute. His eyes are imprinted in my mind—wide in horror and pain. Did he only join Rowan's army so he could get to Earth and live a better life? I push away the thoughts.

Less thinking, more doing.

And that's when I see it.

A red light flashing above the ship's entrance.

Then I hear it.

A robotic female voice. "Security breached. Safety mechanism engaged. Preparing for initiation."

The ship's entrance is closing.

Time is a quiet evil. And right now, its silent ticking is louder than ever.

45

AS ONE. OUR GOALS SHIFT. TRIUMPHING over Rowan and his men will do nothing if the ship seals shut. Even now, I can tell not all of us will make it.

But I *will* reach the ship. No matter what the cost. My blood roars in my ears when I realize that nothing will stop me.

I don't detour to attack Rowan's men anymore. When one comes after me, something feral takes over me, and in heartbeats he's an unbreathing body.

I see people clambering on board. And Julian swinging a blade mercilessly amongst a group of Jute. My heart jumps when one of them lands a blow on his face. He stumbles back, stunned, and another Jute kicks him to the ground.

No. My heart twists in my chest. I run toward him.

Wind whistles past my dagger as I raise it over my shoulder. I slash it across one Jute's back, and another turns to me, leaving four to Julian.

Our blades connect with a grounding clang that trembles all the way to my toes. I don't look at his face to see his handsome features, though I know they are there.

I shove him away, kicking him between the legs at the same time. He grunts and loosens his hold. I knock the sword from his hand as a small knife embeds into his chest. I don't have a chance to see who helped me.

Another Jute swings a metal rod toward me, bits of rust flying in the relentless wind whipping around us.

He, too, falls with a knife to his chest.

I turn in the direction of my rescuer. Slate and Chancellor Abel limp toward the ship, shielding Eli between them. There's another knife ready in Slate's hand. Around them, battles rage, arrows fly, swords clash.

I duck and run to them. Slate assesses the damage on my arm before he looks at my face. "Eli's the only one who knows how to set the ship in motion. Can you get him there?"

Eli sways on his feet. Wrinkles line his face and I wonder if they are new, or if I simply never noticed them before. I take Slate's place, draping Eli's arm over my shoulder, the weight suffocating me even more.

"Where will you go?" I ask. But he's already gone.

Eli wheezes. We move dangerously slow.

"I'm Abel," Abel says to me. Has he forgotten that we already met? Dena would have rolled her eyes.

"Lissa," I reply. Sweat trickles down my skin. There's a patch of blood on the side of Eli's torso.

He leans closer to me and whispers something in a hoarse voice.

"I know all about you," Abel says with a wheezing laugh. Will he shut up?

"We've met, Chancellor," I say, respectfully. Eli says something again.

"What is it?" I ask him as we near the ship. Julian slides through a group of Jute and reaches to help Eli. Blood trickles from a gash on his neck.

"He lied," Eli whispers, fixing his eyes on me.

"Who lied?" I ask. I don't care if Abel lied, I don't say. A gasp of air chokes from my right. Abel's grip loosens around Eli's arm and he collapses to the ground, an arrow in his side.

Julian begins pulling Eli up the stairs to the ship. I don't have the mind to marvel at the ship now that I am inches away. I can't even grasp the fact that the man I just spoke to is a corpse beside me.

Eli pulls free from Julian and looks down at me, and for a moment, everything is still.

"Slate lied. He can fly this thing better than I can. Gage designed it. He taught Slate how to man it."

I blink. Once. Twice. I ignore Julian's pleas and run.

My father is a machine.

His glistening red dagger never stops moving. And not a single Jute who crosses his path stands a chance. The way he fights is almost beautiful.

Pain pierces my leg. I turn as a leering Jute man swings a small knife in his hands, readying for another strike. I throw a quick and smash the end of my dagger against his skull and he crumples to the ground. I grab his knife and meet Slate's eyes. Panic freezes his features for a moment, before he shouts.

"Lissa!"

The shaft of an arrow is embedded in his leg.

I throw three knives, one after the other. They find homes in fatal places. And while only three Jute fall, the rest turn their attention away from Slate dropping to his knees in pain. I pull longer knives into either hand and twist them in my hands as they approach.

A rush of adrenaline makes me run. I hold the knives on either side and rush past the oncoming Jute, my blades slicing cleanly through them, ending their lives.

When I'm a foot from Slate, I turn back. Seven Jute have fallen. Three remain. From the ship, Julian calls my name, his voice frantic. I catch a flicker of bright white hair as Dena helps people on board.

Men and women frantically surge toward the ship. The door is closing.

A small dart sails straight for my neck. I swerve at the last moment as another Jute throws a fist at my stomach.

Sudden. Pain. Explodes. My senses.

I gasp for air and double over.

"Lissa, the ship," Slate rasps. Panic distorts my vision. Three Jute. The ship. Slate. My pain. Too much. No time.

The Jute sense my weakness. One of them throws a kick at my right, the side I favor. I fall in the opposite direction, my knives dropping soundlessly to the ground. I turn on to my back. Air swooshes through my nose and dust chokes my throat.

"Lissa," Slate shouts, his voice strained. I feel his hand on my ankle. His touch gives me hope. Gives me a reason. But my limbs are laden with lead.

The shadow of a leering Jute falls over me, blocking my view of the reddish clouds. Menace distorts his face. And I think, I think I could let him do as he wishes. I would.

If I didn't hear my name. Thrice.

Slate.

Julian.

And somewhere, Rowan, his voice faint.

My body is fluid in that moment. In a flash, I wrap my legs around the Jute and pull him down. My hand finds the hilt of my knife and without a thought, I plunge it deep into his chest. His body convulses, blood spews from his wound.

I don't waste time. I aim and throw. The knife skims the stomach of one of the two remaining Jute. I pick up the other knife and jump to my feet, the ground swaying beneath me. The dark-haired one lunges for me as the other launches another dart. I duck from both and slash my knife across the dark-haired one's stomach. The remaining one looks at me, eyes wide, mouth slack. He turns and runs toward the ship, dropping his darts as he goes.

The knife slips from my hand. The ground rushes to my face and I hear, more than feel, the impact of my numb body on the ground. Slate pulls himself to me, his eyes frantic. Blood has pooled around him. Sobs rack my body.

"Shh, Lissa, shh," he says softly, as if I'm a child. The child he never got to raise. "You saved me."

"No, *you* saved *me*," I say, my voice hoarse.

His eyes fill with tears. I slowly push myself to my feet, my knees threatening to give way.

The ship isn't too far. I can limp. Crawl even. I can limp with my father.

I can't even move.

Slate gasps then. The sound shatters my heart. I fall to my knees.

No.

No.

"No," I whisper, running my hands across his chest. My hand snatches on something sharp in the hollow beneath his shoulder. An arrow. From behind.

"No, no" I whisper. Not when I finally have a chance to live with him, my father. He doesn't deserve this. *I* don't deserve this.

He cups my cheek and a trembling smile curves across his face. I don't know if the tears on his face are his or mine. Or both of ours.

"Thank you, Lissa, for giving me a chance," he says in a whisper.

"No," I scream. I grip his shoulders and shake. His eyes flutter. "You're not leaving me. You're my father."

My voice softens. "Live. Please."

He shudders.

The last I see are Julian's eyes before I collapse in his arms.

The last I hear is the ship's voice counting down from ten before the rushing in my ears drowns out all else.

46

LIPS PRESS AGAINST MY TEMPLE, SOFT and trembling. I open my eyes, expecting to see my father's pale gray eyes staring back.

But they're blue and drowning in pain.

I leap to my feet and the ground sways. Clean bandages have been wrapped around my shoulder and leg. My cheeks are tight with dried tears. My voice is strangled and hysteric. "Slate."

Julian's hand closes around mine and he pulls me back down. "Calm down, Lissa."

I fall to the ground and press my hands flat against the cool floor. It trembles beneath my hands. I still myself, trying to make sense of this vibration.

That's when I take in the room. The walls are metal, a soft silver that desperately tries to soothe my heart, like softhearted mothers, protecting in silence.

I breathe in, slowly. The blandness of oxygen rushes into me. It's odd. I've breathed the air of Jutaire for so long that oxygen is ugly compared to it.

"The ship?" I ask in a whisper. My eyes find Julian's and he smiles. A genuine smile, so rare. But it's sad, like his eyes.

"Where you've wanted to be for so long."

So long. So desperately. So much that so many lives were lost. Because of me.

"Slate," I say again. A vise tightens around my heart.

"He's fine. He's recovering," Julian says softly.

Fine. Alive. I squeeze my eyes shut and breathe in relief. He's alive.

"Can I see him?" I ask.

"Not yet." He stands and holds out his hand, leading me to a circular window. I stumble at the rumbling of the ship and he smiles again. "You'll get used to it."

Through it, I see Eli's house, and beyond it, the remains of the palace. And slowly, I see all of White Plains, the land my mother once ruled. I see dead bodies, so many, countless bodies. Jutaire will be a world of red death. No one alive exists there anymore. At least, that is what I hope.

All this destruction. So much ruin. For a ship. For a planet that was said to be destroyed long ago.

I wonder if Rowan is alive. If he's looking at the people he killed, or if he's lying with them. My vision blurs.

"Funny, isn't it?" Julian asks.

"What?" My voice is raw. There's nothing funny about death.

"How much you miss something once it's gone," he says softly. I nod, my throat suddenly choked. Tears stream down my face, there's no use holding them back. I held them back for so long. Not anymore.

Gage. Chancellor Kole, Abel. Wren. Even my mother. They're all gone. And Rowan?

"Hush, Lissa," he whispers, wiping my face. He pulls me against the warmth of his chest. "Don't cry."

"What happened to Mia?" I ask.

"She's in the infirmary."

He puts a finger on my lips before I can ask anymore, and pulls me through a short, dimly lit corridor. It opens to a larger room. The cockpit, I think. The wall ahead of me is covered in glass, stretching from left to right, about twenty feet long. I see the sky, blue and red and white. And Eli, with three soldiers. He flicks switches and orders them to do various things. He monitors the screens lining a part of the wall.

"Dad," Julian says. Eli turns with a start.

When he sees me, he smiles and speaks to the shadows to his right. "She's here."

A limping figure steps forward. His pale gray eyes are creased in pain and his left shoulder is bandaged from the arm to his chest. His right leg is bandaged too. Something slips from my lips, a sound between a cry and a laugh. I rush forward and wrap my arms around him.

"Ow," he laughs softly. I pull back and look into his gray eyes.

"You're alive," I whisper. He smiles.

"I've wanted you for seventeen years. I don't plan on going anywhere anytime soon."

"Don't ever leave me, Father," I say. His eyes brighten. Father. He isn't Slate anymore, no. He's my father.

"I won't," he whispers, touching his nose to mine. "I won't."

Through the corner of my eyes, I catch Julian smiling. And Eli. Even the soldiers watch.

"Gage never thought this would happen," Slate says finally.

"He did. He's the one who taught me to hope," I say, pulling away.

He nods. "He taught you, but he never hoped himself. That was his flaw—he calculated and planned too much to leave anything to hope."

And in the end, it cost him his life. A pang of sadness deepens in the bottom of my heart. There is so much I don't know about him—about his part in everything, from my birth to his friendship with Eli.

But something still bothers me. "Gage knew Earth was real and he was preparing to trade me in exchange for passage to Earth. So why did he break into the Chamber?"

"I never got to ask, but maybe he wanted to set everything in motion. Maybe he wasn't ready to give you up," Slate says. I feel a rush of sorrow again.

"There's no point dwelling on the past," Julian says softly.

"He's right. We have a future to look forward to." Slate says with a wan smile.

An unknown future. It could be good, it could be bad. Is that any better than the future we once knew?

"Let me show you around," Julian says, slipping his hand over mine. The warmth of his touch reaches for my heart. Slate watches me thoughtfully before gesturing for me to leave.

The ship is gigantic. There are more rooms than I can imagine. Three thousand or so humans made it, and a little more than eight thousand Jute, some of them Rowan's men.

There's a greenhouse too, with crops and preserved food. A pool of shimmering water spreads beside it. There are storages stocked with clothes, more food, and other essentials.

My mother was well-prepared. I feel sorry then, guilty even. We nearly stole something from the Jute. Their ship. Their freedom. They aren't much different from us, I've learned.

Which reminds me. I need to ask Eli about what he nearly said before. About the Lost Colony. And the mutants. And about what Slate said—that the Jute took everything the humans brought from Earth.

How did they live before humans arrived?

"There's one more room I want to show you," Julian says, breaking through my thoughts. He opens a door beneath the shadows of the stairwell leading to the next floor, right beside the entrance to the ship.

The smell hits me first, musty and old. I scan the large room. Shelves line the walls. Shelves stocked with books.

"There's so many," I whisper. There are four chairs in the center of the room. Along one shelf is a desk and along another is a long sofa to seat three.

"There are countless books about Earth and its history. You can learn everything before we get there."

I stop short, my finger lingering on a fraying spine. How did the Queen store all of this for so long? "*We can* learn. How long will it take to get there?"

"I don't know," he says warily. "They're still sorting it out."

"Something's wrong," I say softly, crossing the room back to him. He touches my cheek with one blazing hot hand. I jerk away.

That's when I see. His pupils are constricted. His eyes are wild. A fine sheen of sweat layers his skin. His ragged breathing bursts into my ears.

"Julian," I whisper. My voice rises hysterically. "What's wrong?"

A deep laugh answers my question. I freeze, because I never thought I would hear that sound again.

Rowan strolls in through another door.

"All you ever wanted was Earth. And look, now you're getting it. But did you think of the cost? Did you ever think of anyone but yourself?"

What does he know of pain and costs? His words only worsen my confusion.

"Silly girl, Julian's a half-breed. Not a hybrid like you. His lungs need the air of Jutaire more than oxygen. The only difference between him and a Jute is that he'll last longer."

No. It can't be. I couldn't have nearly bled for every human and Jute alive and left Julian to die.

How could I forget him?

"But Eli's a hybrid." I am trying to grasp something, anything.

"He's Jute," Julian says softly. "Gage tested your blood on him years ago."

Words, truths, realizations—a vise tightens around my heart. No. No. No. I can't lose him.

"There has to be a way," I whisper.

"There isn't." Rowan answers. But I don't look at him. I look at Julian and see the same look that flashed in his eyes when I first told him about Earth.

He hasn't given up. There has to be a way. I've only ever had Julian. Ever since the beginning, I've had him.

"My blood—"

Rowan cuts me off. "You need the catalyst."

"What is it?" I ask, desperation tinges my voice. I don't care.

Rowan. Just. Laughs.

"There isn't much different about you and me, Lissa," Rowan says. I meet his bloodshot eyes.

Rowan is right.

I've only thought of myself, not the consequences.

I have lost too much. My eyes blur. But we *are* different. I will fight for those I love and those who deserve to be fought for. Rowan only cares for himself. No, Rowan cared for Julian's mother, for Julian and Eli.

"Please," I beg, searching his eyes for the part of him I saw last night.

He scoffs. "Remember what I told you?"

Run away, Lissa. Run away. But remember you'll come back to me. You'll need me. You'll beg for me. And I'll make sure you never leave me again. Not even Julian can help you then.

"Give me the catalyst," I say, gritting my teeth.

He laughs again. Julian gasps for air and sinks to his knees. Something flickers in Rowan's eyes.

"Help him," I beg. "Show me you have a heart. Rowan, *please.*"

He furrows his brow when I say his name, when he hears my pleading. "And then what? You'll go back to him. If he dies, I'll have you all for myself."

Rowan has a sick, sick mind.

"That's what this is all about? You knew all along that this would happen."

He tilts his head. "Maybe."

I stare at Julian's colorless face. His eyes are glassy and his lips are slowly turning blue. Even the honey-brown floor looks more alive than he does.

You're the one who sides with whichever side is more beneficial for your treacherous lips.

There isn't much different about you and me, Lissa.

But we are different. Oh, we are.

"Give him the dose and I'll leave him." The moment the words leave my lips, Rowan holds his breath. Julian shudders and pushes himself up on his weak hands and stares up at me, slowly shaking his head, a silent *no* slipping from his trembling mouth.

"You would do that so he can live?" Rowan asks. He sounds genuinely curious. A normal boy asking a normal question, trying to understand.

And I realize, I *do* love him. The part of him that is human. "But why? What good would it do if he's alive and you can't be with him?"

That is what he'll never understand.

I squeeze my eyes shut for a moment, knowing my every breath takes Julian closer to his last.

"I was wrong," I say, my voice soft. And as if he knows my words are for him, Julian stops heaving and looks at me with burning eyes. "I thought, if you loved someone, that you could never let them go. But I was wrong. If you truly loved someone, you would leave them if it meant their safety and happiness. Just so they could see another sunrise. Breathe another breath. Smile another smile, even if it's without you."

I face Rowan in the silence of my words.

"Give him the catalyst and I'll be yours forever."

Rowan stares at me and I stare back. At his blue eyes so much like Julian's, the sharpness of his cheekbones, the darkness of his hair, and the bow of his lips. He is Julian on the outside. He must be good inside, too. He *has* to be. Maybe Eli was right and I *can* help him.

Maybe I can get over my pain of leaving Julian.

Rowan reaches into his pocket and pulls out one vial, filled to the brim with my blood mixed with whatever the catalyst is. He tilts the small tube, his eyes following the bubble of air that slides back and forth.

"Forever," he breathes.

"Lissa, no," Julian croaks. I drop to my knees in front of him.

And when I meet his eyes, flickering in pain, it hits me again—Julian and Rowan can never be the same. Never. Fresh pain aches through me, trembling through my veins, my limbs, my heart.

"Don't do this," he whispers.

"Why didn't you tell me, *ask* me?"

"I couldn't. I couldn't ask you to bleed for me." I squeeze my eyes shut and open them.

I cup his freezing cheek in my palm. "I won't watch you die."

"You're all I have, Lissa. I have nothing else to live for," he says.

Rowan clears his throat. I stand as one of his men steps from the shadows. Disgust stirs through my stomach—we were being watched.

The man takes the vial and unscrews the lid. He tightens a needle at the end and stands still as Rowan stretches his hand out to me.

"Lissa," Julian pleads. "Don't."

I reach out. My breath catches when Rowan's hand closes around mine, enveloping me in his warmth. He pulls me close, something like pain flickering in his eyes. There is something human in him. It wants to live. But Rowan's madness, his anger, and the pain of his parents' rejection—they will kill him before then.

The man in black crouches beside Julian as I stare into Rowan's eyes. Any moment now, the needle will pierce Julian's skin. Any moment now, Rowan's lips will touch mine and I'll be his forever.

I will never go back on my promise. Even to someone like him.

"It's done, sir," the man says and Julian collapses. My eyes widen and Rowan's hand tightens around mine.

"Take him to the infirmary," Rowan says. I can feel the vibration of his voice through our clasped hands. The man throws Julian over his shoulder as if he weighs no more than a sack and disappears through the door.

"You'll never love me, will you?" Rowan asks. His soft voice pierces my heart.

"I do," I whisper, because it's true. But not the way I love Julian.

"Not as much as you love him," he says, mirroring my thoughts. He is close, so close, his breath mixes with mine. Minty. Free. He drops my hands, pain creasing the edges of his eyes. I stare at him, for a moment, because I don't understand.

But then I do.

He'll let me go.

His eyes travel the length of my face, memorizing every inch of my expression. I offer him a small smile, the best I can muster and drop my hands by my sides. I take one step back, away from him.

"You were right," he says. "You *can* let someone go."

"There was never a catalyst," he says just as the door opens. Dena slowly looks between Rowan and me, her jet black eyes catching everything.

There was never a catalyst. So it was all a lie. A way to make sure we didn't try it ourselves, just like the metal and glass being scarce.

Rowan raises my hand to his lips, holding my gaze. "Bye, Lissa."

And I watch as he strolls out of the room, his long coat trailing behind him.

47

"WHAT WAS *THAT* ABOUT?" SHE ASKS.

I smile. "Nothing."

"I saw Julian being carried to the infirmary. And then Rowan kisses you? That's not nothing." She raises an eyebrow. For a moment, I expect her to be the same girl who called me pathetic. The same girl who said I needed a babysitter.

"Julian wasn't given a dose." I don't say anything else, hoping she'll understand. She does. "Where's Ilen?"

She laughs. "No way. He was just"—her voice turns soft—"a way to stop thinking of Julian."

"I'm sorry," I say softly.

Dena only sighs in answer. In the silence that follows, we wander through the library, though I'm itching to see if Julian is okay, if Mia is recovering.

Dena pulls her hands out from behind her, my crown in her palms. "You're still queen and your people are waiting."

I stare at her.

But she smiles and fixes the crown on my head and drags me out of the room before I can protest.

I still see Julian's blue lips, I still see the arrow in my father's shoulder, and Chancellor Kole's dead body.

But I see something else too. A future.

We climb a dark, empty stairwell. I listen for the sound of life, but I hear nothing. It feels like the walls are holding their breath in silent anticipation. We cross through an empty, white-walled room and she opens the door on the other end.

I meet Julian's beautiful blue eyes, like the ocean, the sky, and brilliance in one. Relief floods through me, despite the sickly tint of his skin. Because he's okay. He'll be okay.

He says my name as if he's never said it before.

"*Queen* Lissa," Dena interjects.

Julian breathes a laugh, holding my gaze. "No. It's Lissa. Just Lissa." I smile.

"I'm yours now," I say.

"No," he says, touching his forward to mine. "*I* am yours. And forever will be."

He smiles with tired eyes. I grab ahold of his hands and pull him to me. He laughs softly, pressing his soft lips against mine. My body tingles, from the tips of my toes to the point of my nose. I taste freedom on him and I feel something deep inside me, something that can only be described as love, even if I'm not fully ready to feel it.

He pulls away and entwines his fingers in mine before leading me to the winding balcony.

Father limps toward us, his eyes shining.

Julian drops my hand and inclines his head. "Go on."

I walk to the railing, my steps slow.

Beneath me, the ship spreads out in all its glory. But I don't see the ship's floor.

I see men, women, and children. Jute and human. I see the people of Jutaire, standing beside one another, every face differing from the next, every face unmasked. There is no difference.

Dena's voice rings out in the silence. "People of Jutaire, your Queen."

Not the queen of the Jute, like my mother. Not the ruler of the humans, like the leading Chancellors.

The Queen of Jutaire—of every being who lived on our red planet.

As Queen, my first task will be Rowan. He needs to be brought to justice, even if I think I can understand the reason behind all he has done. He will need to account for his deeds.

But for now, the crowd erupts in cheers. And the full realization of something hits me as the ship carries us toward a place we have only dreamed of. To a future we don't know. I slip my hand in my pocket and wrap my fingers around the small replica of Earth.

And think to myself.

I will never, ever, be alone.

ACKNOWLEDGEMENTS

UNBREATHABLE owes its publication to more people than the letters in its name and I know I won't thank everyone here.

First and foremost, my greatest thank you goes to my family—to my mom and dad for encouraging me to publish this book when I didn't want to. To Asma, for pestering me to let Julian and Slate live, for endlessly entertaining me and being the first to love my writing, and to Azraa, for wanting my first signed bookmark. And of course, to my brother, for thinking UNBREATHABLE was UNBREAKABLE. My life would be incomplete without the five of you.

A heaping thank you goes to Ashelynn, for supporting UNBREATHABLE from its first sentence. For loving the story more than I did and being there for me.

To Lisa, for your unbelievable caps-lock reaction when I said UNBREATHABLE would be published. For being my BBF – best blogging friend – and for showering me with your endless gifts.

To Christina at Ensconced with YA, for detailing the science behind Lissa's blood and hosting my amazing Twitter party.

Many thanks to Leigh Ann Kopans, Cait Greer, Darci Cole, and Jessica Brooks for giving me the push I needed to pursue self-publication.

To the oh-so-awesome L.M. Augustine for keeping me sane every step of the way and, along with Rachel O'Laughlin, for patiently answering my countless questions and helping me through the heralds of doing everything on my own. I would be an utter mess without you two.

More thanks go to Amanda Foody, Stephanie Diaz, and John Hansen, the original YAvengers. I miss our group.

To Kennedy Thompson, for wanting to fly over and visit me. For being my cheerleader and being the best supporter a girl could ask for.

To Hannah (InkyReads) for hosting my first blog tour and fangirling when the first UNBREATHABLE proof was in my hands.

To Crystal at Crystal in Bookland, Emz at Icy Cold Reads, and Matt Keenan for being a part of my support group, for pushing UNBREATHABLE in every way, and loving it without a reason other than your own.

To Alex Yuschik, for being the best beta reader a writer can ask for and for making me smile with your lengthy love-filled emails.

A huge shout out to Holly Bryan, Kristie Matheson, Shannon at Twilight Sleep, Meredith Maresco, Momo at Books Over Boys, Britta Gigliotti, Alex and Nova, Jaz at Pixelski, and all my Twitter friends and blog followers.

Another big thank you goes to the Laziaf's Legion, my unbelievably awesome street team. You guys rock.

And last, but never least, you. Thank you for picking this book up. For reading Lissa's story and hopefully enjoying it.

Writers wouldn't exist without you.

ABOUT THE AUTHOR

Hafsah Laziaf was born on the east coast on a hot summer day in 1993, raised on the west coast and is now stuck in the middle – in Texas – with more books than she can read.

She's the designer behind IceyDesigns and the blogger behind IceyBooks. UNBREATHABLE is her debut novel.

Find her online at www.hafsahlaziaf.com
or on Twitter @IceyBooks.

CPSIA information can be obtained at www.ICGtesting.com
Printed in the USA
BVOW01s2219020614

355223BV00001B/16/P